BLOOD
AUTUMN

Also by William Sanders

A Death on 66*

The Next Victim*

Hardball

The Wild Blue and the Gray

Steel Wings

Journey to Fusang

Pockets of Resistance**

The Hell-Bound Train**

*a Taggart Roper mystery
**written as Will Sundown

BLOOD AUTUMN

A Taggart Roper Mystery by
• William Sanders •

St. Martin's Press   New York

BLOOD AUTUMN. Copyright © 1995 by William Sanders. All rights
reserved. Printed in the United States of America. No part of this
book may be used or reproduced in any manner whatsoever without
written permission except in the case of brief quotations embodied
in critical articles or reviews. For information, address St. Martin's
Press, 175 Fifth Avenue, New York, N.Y. 10010.

Design by Basha Zapatka

Library of Congress Cataloging-in-Publication Data

Sanders, William.
    Blood autumn : a Taggart Roper mystery / William
Sanders.
        p.   cm.
    ISBN 0-312-11755-8
    I. Title.
PS3569.A5139B57   1995
813'.54—dc20   94-45768
                                                            CIP

First Edition: April 1995

10 9 8 7 6 5 4 3 2 1

For Martha

Grateful acknowledgment is offered to Cathy Carter-White, Father Donald Jackson, and Greg and Eileen Makoff for various kinds of background information and technical guidance. Also to Wayne Morrow for a gag of the heroic school; to Ann Hamilton for the loan of her dyslexic word processor; to Matt Bialer for assistance with certain details of background research; to Rosanne Cash for inspirational music during final composition; and to Ellen Barkin just for continuing to look so damn hot.

• Author's Note •

As usual, I have engaged in creative geography and history; Sizemore County and the town of Redbud are severely fictitious, as is the Echota Creek nuclear plant and its parent corporation.

This point needs special emphasis; this is in no sense meant as a rural *roman à clef*. There are indeed some superficial similarities between the backdrop of this novel and the controversies surrounding the Sequoyah Fuels plant at Gore, Oklahoma. The similarities are no more than that; absolutely no correspondence should be inferred between Hardesty Industries and Sequoyah Fuels, or between Sizemore County and Sequoyah County. Such situations, after all, have occurred in many other parts of the United States.

Most particularly, no parallel is implied between the law enforcement agencies of Sequoyah and Sizemore counties. In fact, throughout the long series of demonstrations and confrontations at the Sequoyah Fuels plant, the Sequoyah County Sheriff's Department behaved in an exemplary manner, showing great professionalism and restraint in a difficult situation, despite powerful currents of public feeling. It would be very unfortunate if anything in this entertainment should be taken as reflecting in any way on them.

The dance ground in Chapter 17, however, exists as described. I painted the sign.

BLOOD
AUTUMN

1

I SUPPOSE IT'S TRUE what they say about people today living in a global village. After all, I might never have gotten mixed up with that bunch of crazy Indians if it hadn't been for a phone call from a drunk Russian.

Not that Vladimir Alekseev Somov was in any way involved in what happened down in Sizemore County. To the best of my knowledge he'd never been in Oklahoma in his life and I was the only person he knew who lived here. And he only knew me from my published writings, which for reasons beyond my comprehension he was translating into Russian. We'd never met in person, never even heard each other's voices before that night when he called me from New York, skunk-drunk and eager to talk.

"You must forgive me," he said sadly. "I know, this is terrible hour to be calling. Have I waked you?"

It was after two in the morning. He hadn't gotten me out of bed, but his phone call had caught me on the way there. But I said, "No, really, it's all right."

He sighed into the phone, a big wet sigh that had to be at least seventy-five percent alcohol vapor. "Ah, you are too kind, Taggart my friend." He said it *Taah*-gart, honking out the first syllable like the opening chord of an accordion solo. "I am afraid I have been seeing too much of this fantastic city."

"Never been to New York before?" I asked by way of making polite conversation. I didn't really know what the hell to say to this guy. All I knew about my one-man Slavic fan club was that he lived in a town near Moscow—I'd found it on a map in the library, out of curiosity, after he'd started writing to me; I had no idea, though, how you were supposed to pronounce it—and that he was a stone fanatic on the history and literature of the American West. I didn't even know how old he was, or what he looked like.

"My first time in your country," he said, "and already tomorrow I must leave for Toronto, Canada. I am interpreting for Russian trade delegation. They all wished to see the nightlife of this city. Fantastic."

He seemed to say "fantastic" a lot.

"We went to a bar," he added, "where there were beautiful women dancing with their breasts uncovered. Then to another one where the dancers were completely naah-ked. *Bozhe moi!*"

There was a brief pause. I thought I heard a faint gurgling sound, but it might have been my imagination.

"So," he said when he came back on, "listen. It is arranged. Your novel *The Last Bugle* is to be published in St. Petersburg in January. Maybe February. Then later in the year will be published *Steps of the Sun*. I am working on translations of the other books."

"Ah, no offense, Vladimir, but . . . how definite is this deal? You know, is it certain?"

Truth was, I felt a good deal of skepticism about Vladimir's project to get me published in his native country. It had been hard enough to believe last year, when I'd gotten his first letter, that there was even one person in Russia who had any interest in the sort of books I wrote. It was damn near impossible to imagine an actual market for stories about Indians and frontier soldiers and the like amid the ruins of the Union of Soviet Socialist Republics.

Vladimir's response was a melodramatically bitter laugh, like something from *I Pagliacci*. "Certain, you say? My friend, we are talking about Russia, where nothing is certain now. If the publisher is still publishing next year, if there is paper and ink to print books, if entire printing is not left forever in some railroad car at some forgotten station in Siberia—"

"Okay," I said hastily. "Okay, I get the idea."

"No, Mister Roper. Excuse me very much, but you have no idea at all." Part of his voice had gone terribly sober. "Even life itself is not certain. Some very bad things are happening. I think there will be violins."

It took me a second to realize that he wasn't predicting a musical accompaniment to events; he meant "violence." His written English, in the letters I'd gotten, had been as good as my own—arguably better—but he was a little less solid on the spoken language. But then he'd had a few tonight. Quite a few, it would seem.

"Ah, but listen," he said. "Enough of depressing current affairs, eh? I must tell you what a fantastic honor for me is this, to have the privilege to introduce my countrymen to the writings of Mister Taggart Roper—"

Well, he went on for a long time like that, telling me over and over how much he loved my work and what my books had meant to him ever since an American engineer from a technical-assistance team had given him a copy of *The Last Bugle*. It was all very emotional and overstated, grotesquely so at times. I'd always heard Russians were like that, particularly when they got oiled, but I'd assumed this was merely one of those national stereotypes. Vladimir, however, did an outstanding job of living up to the image.

Since he kept pausing to reload—I could hear various clinking and clattering noises suggestive of glass and ice; I never found out what he was drinking but clearly it was something serious—the effect grew more pronounced as the conversation continued. Conversation hell, monologue; I didn't get in a dozen complete sentences the whole time.

"You are modern successor to Zane Grey," he declared at one point. "I think your novels are even better than those of the late Louis L'Amour."

I didn't tell him that I couldn't stand Zane Grey and wasn't all that crazy about Louis L'Amour either. You try to take these things in the spirit in which they're offered. Sure, I'd have preferred a comparison to, oh, Ernest Hemingway or maybe Jack London, but what the hell . . .

I mean, I'm not going to pretend it was excruciating torture for me, being told repeatedly and fulsomely how wonderful my writing was. All writers have cosmic egos and I've never claimed to be the humble exception; and it wasn't as if I heard this sort of thing all that often. For a while I wondered if I shouldn't ask him to call up my American publishers and explain all this to them, since they seemed to have a lot of trouble believing that anybody even read my books in the United States.

All the same, fatigue at last overcame infantile gratification, and I had to pull the plug on Vladimir. He didn't get upset when he finally understood what I was trying to tell him, and he only spent another five or ten minutes on maudlin apologies for keeping me up so late.

"I will write to you soon, my friend," he said. "Perhaps one day I can return to your fantastic country. Maybe I will be able to visit Oklahoma next time. Tell me, are there still Indians?"

"Oh, yes," I told him, thinking about one Indian in particular. One who would have been here tonight with me, in fact, if she hadn't called late in the afternoon with a rather confusing excuse about some family crisis having suddenly come up; which was why I'd wound up spending the evening drinking too much Michelob and watching too much TV and playing a little mouth harp before finally deciding to pack it in, which was where Vladimir had come in.

"Fantastic." He sighed. "I would so love to meet a real Naah-tive American. *Nu, tak, dovolno.* Take care, my friend."

"Take care of yourself," I said. "Sounds like things might be getting rough back home. You be careful."

There was that laugh again. "Taggart," he said seriously, "if I were careful I would not go home at all. *Do svidaniya.*"

When he'd hung up I sprinted for the bathroom, making a mental note of a new Rule to Live By: Never drink a lot of beer if you're going to be on the phone with a drunk Russian. I'd been handed a good deal of advice when I was growing up back in Coffeyville, Kansas, but somehow my parents and teachers had neglected to mention this point.

Standing there letting my body deal with the most immediate pressures, I switched hands and checked my watch. Three-fifteen. What a hell of a phone bill Vladimir must have run up; I wondered how much trouble that was going to make for him at check-out time. And what a monster of a head he was going to have in the morning, if his metabolism was anything like mine. I hoped he didn't have to get up early to catch his plane.

At least I didn't have that problem, I reflected as I headed back toward the bedroom end of my old trailer. There was nothing I had to get up for and nothing I had to do at any particular time. I shoved my dog Harry off the bed, ignoring his snuffling whines of protest, and stretched out and hauled the covers up around my ears, telling myself I was going to sleep till noon. Later if I damn well felt like it.

Except that it didn't work out that way. Around eight or so Harry woke me up barking at some unidentifiable sound outside, and then when he caught me awake he insisted he had to go out right away or he wouldn't be responsible for what he might have to do on the floor. Needless to say, he had to check out every square inch of the area around the trailer, selecting the absolute best spot to do his business, while I stood in the doorway shivering in the cool morning breeze, shouting for him to get the hell on with it. My hollering did no good whatsoever; Harry had rules of his own, one of which was that if a thing is worth doing it's worth doing right. As he finally hunched his shaggy black body into position he gave me a reproachful look that said *some* of us still had standards.

By the time I got the damn dog back inside and myself back in bed, I found that I was too much awake to get back to sleep. I flopped and rolled for some time, fighting the covers and trying without success to find a comfortable position for my middle-aged bones; and then, just as I was starting to drift off at last, the internal warning signal went off and I had to get up and shamble into the bathroom to get rid of some more of the previous evening's Michelob intake.

So in the end I wound up getting up again and staying up, showering and dragging on some clothes and sitting at the table drinking up the reheated remnants of yesterday's coffee, cursing inebriated Russians and brain-dead dogs and wondering what I was going to do with the rest of a Saturday that already appeared to be pretty much shot to hell.

All of which must have been why, when Rita Ninekiller showed up a couple of hours later, I was thick-headed enough to let myself be talked into something I knew I shouldn't touch. That's the only excuse I was ever able to come up with, anyway. You'd think a forty-three-year-old man would have more sense.

Even so, if it had been anybody but Rita . . .

2
◆ ◆ ◆ ◆ ◆ ◆ ◆ ◆ ◆ ◆

S HE GOT OUT OF HER car and came striding across
the yard toward the trailer, hands jammed into the pockets of
her dark blue down vest, cowboy-boot heels crunching softly
in the sparse dry grass. The dusty early-fall wind whipped her
long black hair about her face.

"Tag," she called as I opened the door. "Glad you're home.
I should have phoned ahead, but—"

Harry shoved past me and rushed out to meet her, barking
madly, running around and around her in a manic tongue-
dangling orbit, showing his love and respect by doing his best
to knock her on her ass. Rita paused and patted his big addled
head until he settled down to mild-hysteria level. "Harry,"
she said, "have you ever considered switching to a decaf-
feinated coffee?"

I held the door open as she came up the steps. When she
was inside she unzipped the vest and flapped it open and shut
a couple of times. "Damn," she said, "this time of year, I
never know what to wear."

What she was wearing looked fine and more than fine.
Besides the boots and vest, she had on a red turtleneck top,
which went nicely with her black hair and dark skin, and
blue jeans. Honest jeans, too, no fancy stitching or fake fad-
ing or designer signature, and cut snug in the ass and thighs
the way God meant for jeans to fit—at least on women like
Rita Ninekiller. Silver water-bird ornaments dangled from
her ear lobes and a copper bracelet clasped her left wrist.
That was all, but she could have walked down any runway

in that ensemble and had the fashion photographers burning out their strobes.

The eyes were the only problem area. She'd done a bit with makeup, but I could still see a little red. Evidently I hadn't been the only one to have a rocky night.

All the same, she was the one who said, "What happened to you? Up late?"

I nodded, a trifle jerkily. She put her hands on her hips and gave me a look. "Out drinking with Wiley Harmon?"

Wiley Harmon was a garbage-mouthed, severely bent Tulsa cop with whom I occasionally hung out, mostly when I needed information I wasn't supposed to have. Rita disapproved of our relationship almost as violently as she disapproved of Wiley Harmon himself, even though the guy had saved my life at least once. As it happened, I *had* tried to phone Wiley after Rita had cancelled last night's date, but he hadn't been home.

I said, "No, actually, I had what you might call a quiet evening alone. Watched TV, played harmonica, had a long telephone conversation with a drunk Russian. I would have curled up with a good book, only I haven't written any lately."

She didn't rise to the sarcasm in my voice. "I'm sorry." Her own voice carried tones of stress and fatigue. "I hated to stand you up at the last minute like that, Tag, but—oh, hell, I'll tell you about it later." She was looking in the direction of the trailer's tiny kitchen area. "Knowing you, I don't suppose you've had anything to eat yet."

She moved toward the kitchen without waiting for an answer. "You do at least have some sort of food around the place?" she asked over her shoulder.

"There's nearly half a box of Pop-Tarts," I said, trailing along after her, nearly tripping over Harry, who was trying to sniff her bottom. "Well, actually, they're not real Pop-Tarts, they're sort of a generic-brand imitation. See, they've opened this new discount grocery store—"

"Forget I asked." She opened the refrigerator door and peered in, shaking her head. I could have told her she wouldn't have much luck; the old Hotpoint didn't contain a great deal in the way of nutritional supplies. Although I had put a whole twelve-pack in there only a couple of days ago.

"Sit down," she ordered briskly, and started yanking open drawers and doors. "Obviously we'll have to improvise. Do you want a late breakfast or an early lunch?"

What I wanted at that moment was more along the lines of an untimely death. But I said, "Doesn't matter. Couldn't we just go get a burger, or—"

"Shut up," she said, banging a pan onto the stove with unnecessary violence. "Just shut up. I'll manage."

Manage she did, as usual; she found food I didn't know I had, and did things with it I didn't know you could do. She threw out the rest of the day-old coffee and made a fresh batch, chewing me out a little in passing for drinking too much caffeine. By the time the little light came on at the bottom of the coffee pot, my plate was clean and the hollow feeling was receding from my midsection and I was starting to develop at least a marginal interest in going on living.

She poured me a cup of coffee and then got one for herself and sat down at the little table, facing me through the steam. "What was that about a drunk Russian?" she asked a little warily. "Or was that some kind of half-assed wisecrack?"

I told her about Vladimir and his marathon long-distance call. "I'll be damned," she said at the end. "So you're going to be an international literary figure. I'm genuinely impressed." She leaned back and sipped at her coffee. "Want me to pass on the information to that twit who runs the book-news section? Might even be able to set up a little feature piece with a hook like that—'Former *Courier* Staffer To Be Published In Former Soviet Union,' whatever."

Rita was one of the brighter lights on the staff of the Tulsa *Courier*, a deeply conservative daily whose bosses thought William F. Buckley, Jr., was a dangerous liberal; they'd amazed themselves, not to mention everybody else, by allowing an important desk to go to a woman, and a full-blood Cherokee at that. Or so I suspected, and I knew the *Courier* pretty well; I'd worked there for seven years myself, covering the police beat, before resigning to pursue the glamorous life of a novelist. That was where I'd met Rita, though it had taken us a lot of years to get into our present relationship, whatever the hell it was.

"Better not," I said after thinking it over. "The way Vladimir tells it, there are all sorts of ways this thing might fall through. Wait till it actually goes down, if it does."

She nodded. "Okay. I don't suppose you'll make anything on this," she said. "Money, I mean."

I shrugged. "Best I can hope for is a bunch of rubles, too big for rolling smokes and too small for wiping your ass and worthless for anything else. But it'll look good on my credits. And, you know, there's a certain personal satisfaction. *The Last Bugle* went out of print over two years ago and I haven't been able to interest anybody in this country in reprinting it. At least this way it'll be in print somewhere in the world."

She nodded again, not looking at me, staring down into her coffee cup with dark unreadable eyes. I realized she wasn't all that interested in my career right now; there was something on her mind, and she wanted to tell me about it. Had most likely come over here for that purpose, but she was still old-school Indian enough to feel the need to work her way around to the main subject by an indirect route.

But then the set of her shoulders changed, just a little, and I knew that the polite small talk was over.

"Did you ever meet my cousin Chris Badwater?" she said in a different tone. "Or hear me or Tommy talking about him?"

I shook my head. "I don't think so."

I'd met quite a few of Rita's relatives over the last couple of years; her brother Tommy and I were on pretty good terms. But I knew that I'd barely had a token sampling of her family, which, being a Cherokee family, was far more extended than the classic European-American variety. Indians have their own ideas about blood and how it works. Chances were this "cousin" was somebody who wouldn't even have counted as a relative by white rules. That didn't mean the relationship would be any less real to Rita, or the obligations less binding.

"No reason you should know him," she said. "I don't know him all that well myself, far as that goes. He and Tommy have always been friendly, but otherwise he's never had much to do with our side of the family. He's only a kid," she added, "eighteen, nineteen, something like that. I know he went to Northeastern State for a year but didn't go back this term. He's been living with his grandfather Badwater down in Sizemore County."

She raised her eyes to look at me. "That's where he is now. Sizemore County, I mean. They've got him in the jail in Red-bud."

"What did he do? Or rather what's he supposed to have done?"

I stuck that last bit in hurriedly, before she could come back at me. I didn't know Sizemore County or the town of Redbud, but there are certain things that stay fairly constant throughout the small towns and rural counties of northeastern Oklahoma. That Chris Badwater was in jail there didn't necessarily mean he'd done anything; he was, after all, an Indian, which in such places can be considered enough.

"The charge," Rita said, "is first-degree murder. Murder One, I think your friend Detective Sergeant Harmon would call it. Murder very One indeed," she added. "He's up for killing the sheriff."

"Christ!"

"It's been on the news. I thought you might have seen some of the reports."

"No. I, uh, missed the news, the last few nights."

The truth was that I'd been missing the news as a matter of conscious policy, and not just for the last few nights or even weeks. I'd taken a private pledge, back in the spring, to quit watching or reading the news, which had become almost uniformly depressing. Life was difficult enough at the personal level, without being reminded on a daily basis that the world I lived in was being run by a collection of babbling water-heads.

I'd never been much good at keeping resolutions, but I was pretty damn proud of my record on this one. There had only been a few lapses, mostly involving weather forecasts or sports results. The really difficult part had been giving up Connie Chung.

But I wasn't about to explain all this to Rita, who obviously wasn't interested in my little quirks right now. I drained my coffee cup and got up to pour myself a refill. "You want some more?" I asked, holding up the pot.

"No. Yes. Yes, please. Maybe it'll get my brain working again." She held out her cup with one hand and rubbed her face with the other. "I'm so damn *tired*, Tag. Sorry if I'm whining, but I suspect you got more sleep last night than I did, alcoholic Russian and all."

I refilled both cups and put the pot back on the counter and sat down, looking at her. "Talk to Taggart," I said, putting a hand out and touching her face for a moment. "Only take it slow, all right?"

"Don't worry," she said, giving me a very slight smile. "Right now that's the only way I can take it."

Sizemore County Sheriff Rowland Jordan had expired on the evening of the preceding Saturday at his home in Redbud. The body had been discovered a little after eleven o'clock. He had last been seen alive by his wife Emily Jordan at about nine-thirty, at which time he had also spoken on the phone with the duty deputy at the sheriff's office. Time of death, remarkably enough, had been officially estimated as between nine-thirty and eleven.

"Brilliant scientific mind they've got at the coroner's office, down there," I said. "No, wait, I bet they don't even have a coroner, do they? Most of these little boondock counties don't bother."

"Right. Like most Oklahoma counties, Sizemore County depends on the state medical examiner's office. They use the one in Tulsa, I think."

"And that's what, about a three-hour drive? So the deceased wasn't exactly fresh by the time they got a look at him. Strike the snide crack, then . . . go on."

"The wife says she went to bed early that evening. She woke up to a lot of noise downstairs, her husband shouting, scuffling sounds, that sort of thing. Then everything got quiet and when she called her husband's name there was no response. So she called the sheriff's office and they sent a car over, and when the deputies got there the front door was standing open and Sheriff Jordan was lying on the living room floor, dead."

"For God's sake," I said. "You mean somebody, somewhere in the United States, had sense enough to stay put and call the cops instead of rushing to the scene and becoming the next victim? Or at least disturbing the crime scene, screwing up the evidence—"

Rita was shaking her head. "Emily Jordan is confined to a wheelchair. I think the house has one of those electric wheelchair lifts, but still it would have been impossible for her to rush downstairs or anywhere else. You understand," she added, "this isn't a case of temporary disability. Emily Jordan, according to my information, hasn't had the use of her legs for years. I'd imagine her first instinct in any emergency situation would be to call for help."

"Still sounds like she's got a fair amount of sense."

"Oh, yes. Everything I hear about Emily Jordan suggests above-average intelligence. Although why she—"

Rita broke off the sentence and fell silent for a moment, staring past me. I kept still and let her organize her thoughts. Rita had been a journalist for her entire adult life; she liked to lay out the facts in an orderly manner.

"Ever been in Sizemore County, Tag?" she asked at last.

"Only passing through."

"Well, you know the sort of place it is, anyway. Typical eastern Oklahoma county: hilly terrain, mostly woods and pastures and farms, pretty country but nothing spectacular enough to pull in a big tourist trade. No towns but Redbud, unless you count a couple of little crossroads gas-stop communities. Population almost entirely divided between whites and Cherokees, with a good deal of ambivalence along the dividing line, if you know what I'm talking about."

I did. Racial categories can be very confusing in Oklahoma. One person might be regarded as an Indian, despite a considerable degree of white blood, while another citizen with exactly the same ethnic makeup might be defined as white with some Indian blood. And it's not all that uncommon for the same person to shift back and forth across the line, becoming part-white Indian or part-Indian white, according to the social and legal situation of the moment.

There are even entire families that for various reasons work both sides of the street. Wereskins, Rita's brother Tommy used to call them.

"Needless to say," Rita continued, a Buck-knife edge in her voice, "the people who run things in Sizemore County—such as the late Sheriff Jordan—are invariably and unambiguously Caucasian, while the traditional full-bloods, like old man Badwater, rank in the social order somewhere about even with feral dogs."

"What else is new?"

"Right." She sighed and made a face. "As I say, it's a fairly typical area of its kind. Maybe a bit more corrupt than the average such county. Maybe a lot more corrupt," she said, "if the rumors are to be believed."

That was a considerable statement. For flat-out blatant official crookedness and prehensile greed at all levels, from the state capital down to the most obscure county courthouse, Oklahoma has to be one of the contenders for the national title. In the old Indian Territory days, this was outlaw country, the place where you went when somebody was looking for you with a rope somewhere else; and there's always been some doubt in my mind whether Oklahoma has very much transcended its bully-and-bandit origins. In a sense it is a kind of American Australia.

"The one thing that makes Sizemore County unusual," Rita said, "is the Echota Creek nuclear reactor. Surely you've heard of that. There's been enough controversy."

"Well—" I hesitated. I'd heard of it, all right; I just couldn't recall what I'd heard. I gave my fatigue-riddled memory a kick and a couple of fragments fell out. "Didn't I see something about that last summer? Cops arresting a bunch of demonstrators, looked like they were getting a little rough about it? I'd forgotten that was in Sizemore County. No, hell," I said, "I don't think I ever knew . . . is that still going on? I thought they shut that place down."

"Unfortunately, the reactor is still reacting away. Business as usual, despite all those violations the federal inspectors turned up. True, the company's on a sort of probation, but nothing's really changed. And never mind if half the work force glows in the dark by now."

Rita's lips curled downward. "There I go airing my own attitudes. Most of the population of Sizemore County would disagree strongly with that 'unfortunately.' To people like me, that reactor represents an environmental catastrophe waiting to happen," she said. "But to the people who live in the area, it's an alternative to hardscrabble farming. When Hardesty Industries put up that plant, all of a sudden there were real jobs in Sizemore County. It was the biggest thing to happen there since statehood."

"And then these interfering outsiders show up and want to take all that away."

"Exactly. The friction between the environmentalists and the locals—well, you can probably imagine. And it doesn't help that some of the more visible and vocal of the antinuclear protestors have also been Indian activists. The whole affair has picked up nasty racial overtones. That's ironic," she said, "because most of the Indians in the area tend to side with their white neighbors on this issue. Especially since Hardesty Industries doesn't mind hiring Indians—although the higher-level jobs seem to stay in white hands."

Things were beginning to clunk into place, like the gears of a worn-out transmission. She wasn't telling me all this for the sake of table conversation. I said, "Indian activists? I don't suppose that would include your cousin Chris Badwater."

"You've got it. He and some other young militant types, mostly Indian students from up at NSU, have been showing up at the demonstrations at the Echota Creek site. I think in part it's been a way of getting some publicity and making useful alliances, but I know Chris is dead serious about environmental causes, too. He and Tommy have had arguments over whether some of the radical groups, the tree-spikers and suchlike, were going too far."

She pushed her hair back from her face and looked at me. "And, of course, that's how Chris came to lock horns with Sheriff Jordan. Chris called Jordan and his deputies a good many choice names last year during the arrests, and got roughed up for it as soon as they had him down at the jail and out of sight of the cameras. And it's been like that ever since. Tommy's had to bail Chris out half a dozen times."

"And that's why they picked him for the killing? Sounds pretty thin."

"Although plenty thick enough in a place like Sizemore County, with most of the population halfway ready to string Chris and his friends up long before the murder went down. But as it happens, there's something else. Think, Tag," she said. "There's one question you haven't asked. An old cop-beat man like you, I'm surprised."

I ran my mind back over our conversation. My brain worked even worse on playback this particular morning, but after a few seconds something struggled through the fuzz. "For God's sake. The murder weapon? What have they got, a bullet match to Chris Badwater's gun?"

"I doubt if Chris has ever owned a gun. But Sheriff Jordan wasn't shot. You're not going to believe this," Rita said, "but he was killed with a tomahawk."

"A *tomahawk*? Rita, if this is some kind of put-on, I don't really feel like—"

"It's true, Tag. It was lying on the floor beside the body when they found him. And," she said, "it was Chris's tomahawk."

3

◆ ◆ ◆ ◆ ◆ ◆ ◆ ◆ ◆ ◆

I PUT MY ELBOWS on the table and my face in my hands. This was getting entirely too weird.

"Don't tell me tomahawks have serial numbers," I said through my fingers. "Did the kid have his name carved on the handle or something?"

"Worse than that. Chris took it with him to a demonstration at the Echota Creek plant, back this spring, and started waving it around, showing off for the TV cameras. Jordan and the deputies grabbed him and charged him with carrying a deadly weapon, among other things. The judge dismissed that particular charge, since the tomahawk wasn't concealed, but Sheriff Jordan kept the tomahawk anyway. Seems he even hung it on his wall at home and showed it to his guests, made quite a joke of it."

"So plenty of people can identify it."

"I suppose so, but that's not the worst part. Chris was mad as hell about losing his tomahawk—it was a gift from his grandfather, had been in the Badwater family for generations—and, as usual, he had to shoot off his mouth. Went around saying that he was going to go get his tomahawk back one of these days and Jordan wouldn't like it when he did. Or that he was going to go to Jordan's place and shove the tomahawk up his ass, or similar remarks."

Rita gave a little snort. "Of course nobody who knew him took any of it seriously, but it was plenty for the prosecutor's purposes. God knows how many witnesses will be ready to swear that they heard Chris Badwater threaten to kill the sheriff with that damn tomahawk."

I folded my hands and looked at her over my knuckles, thinking. More than one young fool has stepped into his own big mouth in that same way; I'd imagine the prisons are full of them. On the other hand, more than one youthful blowhard has talked himself into doing something horrible and irrevocable, too.

Rita seemed to be waiting for a response. When I didn't supply one she said very quietly, "Thanks for not saying it, Tag. But no, I don't think he did it. Tommy doesn't think so either, and he knows Chris a lot better than I do. He says Chris isn't capable of any actual violence and never has been. Likes to talk tough and put on a bad-boy act, but behind the bluster he's harmless as a rabbit."

I wondered about that too. Every serial killer or mass murderer you hear about is always described by the people who knew him as the sweetest, kindliest soul alive. But I couldn't very well say any of this to Rita.

Instead I said, "So you want me to go down and check things out. That's why you came, isn't it?"

Her hands came up and covered her face. I hadn't seen Rita cry more than half a dozen times in all the years I'd known her, but I thought for a moment she was going to do it now. Her shoulders gave a little heave.

"Oh, Tag," she said. "I really hate myself for this."

She took her hands from her face and laid them on the table. I reached over and covered them with mine. They weren't actually trembling but I could feel the tension. Her fingers felt cold.

"After all the grief I've given you over exactly this sort of thing," she said. "All the fights we've had about it, all the times I've gotten on your back about getting mixed up in other people's problems, putting yourself in dangerous situations, hanging around scenes where nothing good ever happens—and now here I am, asking you to do it for me. I can't believe myself, Tag."

She turned her hands over and grasped mine. "If you want to tell me to go straight to hell," she said seriously, "it won't be held against you."

There were several things I might have said in reply, all of them sarcastic or worse. Rita was getting into a sensitive area.

In the last few years—if half a decade can be called a "few"; that was how I thought of it, anyway—I'd been supplementing my spotty literary income with occasional odd jobs, mostly of dubious legality, for people who required various services not listed in the yellow pages of the Greater Tulsa phone book. Generally these little tasks had been morally grungy and now and then they'd turned low-rent nasty, but things had rarely gotten physically hazardous.

Rita, however, had grown increasingly unhappy with this aspect of my life, and increasingly ready to let me know it. The whole subject had become a real and serious problem in our relationship, and we'd had several stomp-out-and-slam-the-door scenes about it.

And now, as she herself said, here she was asking me to do one for her. To go poking around in a murder case, for God's sake! That wasn't even on the menu for the cash customers. Well, okay, I'd done it once or twice, but that was in the past and I hadn't seen what was coming until it was too late.

There were special reasons for fighting clear of this one. As a rule, I don't do small towns. Nobody with any sense does, unless the money is irresistibly good or the other reasons are king-hell powerful. For all their peaceful appearance and Norman Rockwell happy-face image, small towns tend to be extremely bad places for inquisitive strangers. The crooked ones—and most of them are crooked, at some level—are tightly run, usually by ruthless people who don't care for the attention of the outside world, so it's hard to get the locals to tell you anything, even though they gossip compulsively among themselves. And this place was already pissed off at outsiders.

Not, on the whole, a dazzlingly attractive proposition. I sat back in my chair and took a deep breath and let it out, a little more noisily than I'd intended.

"Ah, hell," I said. "Why not?"

That night, lying in bed beside me, Rita said, "Tag, I hope you'll be careful down there in Sizemore County."

"If I were careful," I said, thinking of Vladimir and his last remark, "I wouldn't go at all."

She worked her body closer against me. "If people were careful, most of us wouldn't even be here. You know what I mean," she said, settling her head onto my shoulder. "Don't get yourself stuck too far into this business. It's not your family or your problem."

"Tell you the truth," I said sleepily, "I'm not sure what it is you expect me to do."

"Have a look around, that's all. Talk with Chris—if he'll talk to you, that is. Apparently he's decided to go the heroic-silence route—"

"Too bad he didn't think of that sooner. Keeping his mouth shut, I mean."

"You're telling me? But I'm not asking you to do a lot of digging, try and find the real murderer, anything like that. Just see what you make of the situation and let me know what you think. I can't go anywhere right now—I'm in the middle of a couple of God-almighty important stories—and besides, you know how much luck I'd have in a place like that. I'm the wrong race and the wrong sex to get any answers. They'd laugh in my face or worse."

"I don't know that I'll do any better."

"At least you won't have those two strikes against you going in. And," she said, "I'm worried about Tommy. He's been down there since Thursday evening. You know what he's like sometimes, Tag. I'd feel better if you were with him."

From the other end of the trailer came a knocking noise: Harry scratching, shaking the flimsy metal walls with the vigor of his efforts. I'd have to make arrangements with old Mr. Berryhill, my nearest neighbor, to take care of him while I was off investigating tomahawk murders. Better not say anything to Mr. Berryhill about the details. He was Creek and might think I was making fun of him. And he was only now starting to forgive me for letting Harry get loose, a couple of years back, and impregnate his beagle.

"If you can do anything to help Chris," Rita said, "okay, so much the better. Maybe you'll spot something the defense can use, who knows? But I don't seriously expect it of you. Just find out what's going on, and try to keep Tommy out of trouble, so I can sleep nights."

"Starting with this one?"

"Oh, not yet." She gave a dirty little laugh and rolled over and hung a long naked leg across me. "I'm not *that* tired. Are you?"

I thought I was, but now it seemed I wasn't. Fantastic, as Vladimir would have said.

I said, "Well, if you don't mind getting on top—"

"I thought you'd never ask," she said.

When I woke up the sun was coming in the trailer's windows and Rita was gone. A note on the bedside table said that breakfast was in the microwave. I got out of bed and shrugged into my ratty old robe and went to let Harry out. While he was taking care of business I got myself a cup of coffee—she'd made a fresh batch, too—and stood beside the door inhaling the steam and wondering what I'd let myself in for. Sizemore County, good *God*. I was going to have to check the map just to find out how to get there.

Standing there, sniffing the coffee and blinking against the morning sunlight, I realized suddenly that it wasn't this particular job that was bothering me. Right now I didn't want to take on any God-damned job at all, for Rita or anybody else; and, despite last night's fun and games, I felt a trace of anger at her for getting me into this.

Not that I'd lost my nerve, or gotten burned out, or anything like that. Actually I'd been feeling pretty good lately. Things had been going unusually well for me this year. Too well; that was the trouble.

Early in the spring, I'd finally found a publisher for a novel that I'd been trying to sell for over a year. Swallow Street Press had liked *Staked Plain* so well, they'd asked if I had anything else in the works, and I'd wound up selling them a second novel, *Black Water,* even though I was still cleaning up the final draft. Both books were scheduled to come out next year, and Swallow Street was showing signs of getting serious about promo and advertising. There was talk of releasing paperback editions under a subsidiary imprint.

All of which was splendid medicine for my middle-aged ego, but it also meant that for once I was reasonably flush. The combined advance money, even after allowing for the annual IRS ripoff, amounted to enough to let me live decently— by my own less than posh standards—for at least the rest of the year.

And I'd been looking forward to a nice little vacation, a break from working the shady side of the street. I'd already turned down several offers, including a couple of really tempting ones, and I'd been wondering how I could spread the word that Taggart Roper was temporarily out of the odd-jobs business.

Now this. But I told myself it shouldn't take long to wrap things up. From all Rita had told me, Chris Badwater was on a straight-line course to the state pen, and Sizemore County wouldn't waste time on more than minimal due process before sending him there. A good lawyer might be able to help him on appeal, later on, but I couldn't see how my efforts would make any difference.

Out in the yard Harry was finishing up. I yelled at him until he finally came back up the steps, and then I closed the door against the wind and went back to see what sort of breakfast Rita had left me.

"Sizemore County?" Wiley Harmon said when I finally got him on the phone. "The fuck you want to know about Size-more County for? Far as I know there's not a damn thing down there but a bunch of crazy Indians and half-witted red-necks. Even the spooks got better sense than to live there."

I didn't feel up to explaining the situation to Wiley Har-mon. He didn't care anyway; he was merely doing a little re-flexive needling. I said, "I'm doing a favor for a friend."

"Some fucking friend you got, making you go somewhere like that. I'm telling you, Roper, you want to keep your ass clear of those little shitkicker counties. The Indians aren't any worse than any other bunch of Indians, I guess, but those Gomers in the overalls and the John fucking Deere caps, all cross-eyed and wearing extra fingers because their parents were cousins or maybe brother and sister—"

"Wiley," I said, "if you don't mind? Not that I don't enjoy your little dissertations, but it's all going on my phone bill."

"Right. Okay." He let out a big sigh. If his breath was up to its usual toxic standards, I was glad I was calling from the far side of the river. "Let me think," he said.

I let him think. Whatever he thought of would be worth the dimes. Or if he didn't come up with anything, that might mean something too. I'd known Wiley Harmon a long time—we went back to my days as a police-beat reporter for the *Courier,* during which period we'd done each other a few discreet favors—and I'd heard him lie to superiors and judges and my colleagues of the press, slander every known ethnic and racial and religious group including his own, and use the word "fuck" as every possible part of speech, but I'd never known him to blow smoke at me. What Detective Sergeant Harmon told you in confidence, you could take to the bank. Where, to be sure, you might run into him again, depositing what you had paid him for the information, along with gratuities from other private citizens, but never mind that. . . .

"Sorry," he said at last. "I really don't have anything for you this time. This is off my usual turf, you know? I'm a city boy. Out there in heifer-humping country, any John-Boy moron of a county mountie knows more than I do."

I wasn't very disappointed, or surprised. Wiley Harmon had joined the Tulsa PD after leaving the force in St. Louis under murky circumstances. His idea of howling wilderness was Mohawk Park. Still, it had been worth a shot.

"All I can tell you," he went on, "is I've heard things, weird shit with no real handle to grab on to, know what I mean? And I never paid it much attention because, like I say, that's outside my home grounds. But I do have the impression there might be something going on around Sizemore County, beyond the usual shit like dog fights and bootlegging and some fifty-year-old railroad widow turning tricks in the back room of the town pool hall. What the fuck kind of action there could be in a jackoff place like that, I couldn't guess, but you never know. That's not much, and I'm not even sure—"

"No," I said, remembering Rita's remark about corruption in Sizemore County, "that's worth something, Wiley. It sort of backs up . . . something I heard. Thanks."

"Hey, don't mention it. No charge on flimsy crap like that," Harmon said. "Tell you what, though, I'll do some asking around if you want. I know a few people that might have something. Take me a couple of days to run it down."

"Sure. I'll call you around the middle of the week."

"If you're able. Ask me, you need your head examined, fucking around in the boondocks. You better keep your head between your legs so you can watch your ass all the time."

"I'll try to be careful," I said dryly. "Since it means so much to you."

He made a farting noise into the telephone. "Laugh all you want, asshole. You'll find out. Everybody talks about city streets, but those little country towns wrote the book on mean."

"I know."

"Do you? I hope to fuck you do. We're not just talking your normal roust now, chance of maybe getting slapped around a little. Those Bubbas, man, they don't give a shit if they kill you. All those woods and creeks and caves and shit, plenty of places to dump a body. Watch out it ain't yours."

I had another telephone conversation that day; Tommy Ninekiller called me from somewhere in Sizemore County. Come to think of it, I never did find out where he was calling from.

"So what's the story, old pigmentationally challenged bro?" he said. "Rita says you're coming down to take charge of the investigation. Or something like that." He laughed. "What'd she do, walk into your office and give you a flash of stocking top and offer you three hundred a day plus expenses? Real Bogie stuff."

I told him what he could stuff and where he could stuff it. He laughed some more. Tommy and I went back some years; we were pretty good friends, considering that he knew I was screwing his sister.

"Listen," he said, "you don't have to do this, you know. I can take care of myself, whether Rita thinks so or not. Baby brother doesn't need a hand to hold onto."

I said, "Tommy, if my coming is going to be a problem for you, I can still call this off. Say the word."

It wouldn't be easy, telling Rita I was cancelling out on her. But I was damned if I was going to spend the next few days dealing with Tommy Ninekiller's attitudes. I knew, as she had said, what he could be like.

But he said, "No, no, that's okay. Didn't mean to get in your face. Actually, I wouldn't mind having you around. The way things are starting to look, just having somebody like you along for a witness—"

He stopped. After a moment I said, "Things getting rough?"

"Not actually," he admitted. "Not so far. Just a feeling I'm starting to get. Yeah," he said, "come on down. Here, I'll tell you how to get to Grandpa Badwater's place. That's where I'm staying."

There were no phone calls at all that night. I sat on the trailer's steps for a while playing harmonica, making a hopeless boggle of "September Song" but otherwise blowing better than usual. Then it got chilly and I called Harry and we went inside.

Monday morning I fired up my old Camaro and headed for Sizemore County. I stopped at old Mr. Berryhill's place and dropped Harry off. Mr. Berryhill wanted to know how long I'd be gone. I told him I figured I'd have my business wrapped up in a couple of days.

Sometimes I don't seem to know a damn thing.

4

YUCHI PARK, WHERE I live, is on the south side of the Arkansas River, so there was no need for me to involve myself in the horrors of metropolitan Tulsa traffic. I didn't bother getting on the turnpike; it was only about eighty-five miles to Redbud, according to my road map, and I was in no particular hurry.

I took Highway 64 instead, all the way to Muskogee, where I crossed the river on the high, wind-battered bridge and began working my way along a series of blacktop county roads that wound and meandered over the hilly countryside with seemingly aimless abandon. That antique gag, "You can't get there from here," could have originated in eastern Oklahoma; evidently it was impossible to drive from Point A to Point B without using up most of the remaining alphabet.

That was okay; I was enjoying the drive. The old Camaro was running well—back in January I'd done a small and not excessively illegal job for the owner of a shop that specialized in high-performance auto work, and he'd paid me in services—and the wiggling country roads were fine for getting in some pleasantly hairy driving. The day was warm for early October, warm enough to let me keep the windows rolled down, and the fresh country air smelled wonderful; I live about thirty miles from downtown Tulsa, but the wind had been from the northwest all weekend and my sinuses hadn't been enjoying the sustained dose of second-hand pollution.

The woods and fields looked dry, though, and there was a good deal of dust in the air. We'd had a long hot summer with almost no rain—all of Oklahoma's precipitation allotment seemed to have been misrouted northward to help drown the Midwest in catastrophic floods—and the effects were showing; the trees and bushes along the roadside had a tired, wasted look. I figured it wouldn't take much to start some really bad fires. Wonder it hadn't happened already.

Dust almost obscured the small green-and-white sign that told me I was entering SIZEMORE COUNTY. I took my foot off the gas and eased the Camaro down to a legal fifty-five and then a couple of ticks under, remembering the warning Tommy Ninekiller had given me over the phone Sunday afternoon. It didn't make any difference, though. I got pulled over before I'd been in Sizemore County fifteen minutes.

The cop car was waiting at the bottom of a long downhill straight, sitting by the roadside in plain sight, and the red and blue lights started flashing even before I was past. I sighed, said a couple of bad words, and pulled off onto the narrow gravel shoulder. This was about to get expensive. When they don't even bother to find something to hide behind, it usually means they don't particularly care whether or not they actually catch you speeding. They're simply going to ticket you and, if need be, perjure themselves blind in front of a local judge who's liable to double the fine just to punish you for questioning the word of an officer of the law.

The brown patrol car came to a stop behind the Camaro and the door opened and a uniform got out. It was a two-tone brown uniform—dark brown long-sleeved shirt, tan pants tucked into dark-brown goat-roper boots, tan Dudley Do-right hat—and it contained a short, skinny, slightly bandy-legged man with a pasty white face. A pair of large mirror shades hid his eyes.

He walked unhurriedly up alongside the Camaro, putting a certain swagger into his walk: the law in these parts, mister, and don't you forget it. His right hand rested lightly on the butt of his holstered revolver, but as he came up by the window I saw that the safety strap was still snapped down. Somebody was going to kill him one of these days if he didn't learn better technique. The thought cheered me a little.

He said, "Morning. Want to show me your license, please?"

I didn't, but I hauled out my wallet and handed over my license all the same. He examined it carefully for several seconds, peering over the tops of the mirror lenses. I saw his lips moving slightly as he read.

"Yuchi Park?" he said finally.

I nodded. "This address correct?" he wanted to know.

"Yes."

"Mmm hmm." He studied the license a bit longer. "Kind of a long way from home . . . any particular business in Sizemore County, Mr. Roper?"

It was a question I didn't have to answer, of course, and my natural inclination was to tell him to go fuck himself; more citizens ought to make that suggestion, or something similar, to arbitrarily inquisitive cops. You could call it a civic duty. But I was here on special business, and getting into confrontations with the local heat wouldn't help. I took a laminated press card from my wallet and passed it over.

His caterpillar eyebrows went up as he looked at the card. As well they might; it was a damn impressive-looking piece of work. Utterly bogus, to be sure, but first-class bogus all the same; I'd had to do a couple of very solid favors to get it.

He said, "Reporter, are you? What kind of a story do you think you're gonna find in Sizemore County?"

"I believe you've had a pretty unusual homicide lately," I said. "Sheriff murdered with a tomahawk, right?"

He looked at me through the mirror shades. Something funny was happening to what I could see of his face; it was as if he'd been ready for an altogether different answer, and the one I'd given had caught him off balance.

"Yeah," he said, "I guess that would make quite a story at that. Hmm. Thought you might be—"

He chopped the sentence off. He'd decided not to tell me what he'd thought I might be. Instead he said, "Well, Mr. Roper, did you know you were doing sixty-eight miles an hour back there?"

That was a God-damned lie, and his tone and stance said that we both knew it but what was I going to do about it? I made a meaningless grunt in response and he said, "I'm going to have to cite you for exceeding the speed limit," and pulled out his little ticket pad. I didn't try to argue; it would have been a waste of time and energy and might well have pissed him off enough to get me a few more phony violations.

It took him a little time to write the ticket; the wind kept trying to blow the flimsy paper out of his hand and the mirror shades kept slipping down his snubby nose. Finally he got it done and handed my copy in through the window, along with my license and the press card. "You need to be careful on these country roads," he said with a straight face. "Slow down and keep it safe and legal, all right?"

I assured him that I would. I thought I sounded reasonably humble and submissive, but there must have been something in my voice or face; his acne-scarred cheeks flushed and he took a step back. "You watch yourself while you're in Sizemore County," he said sharply. His voice had gone half an octave higher. "Because we'll be watching you."

He turned on his heels and stalked off toward his car, his back very rigid, his hand resting on his pistol again. A chancy job, and it makes a man proud but a little lonely. I might have had myself a good laugh, but I'd already looked at the schedule of fines on the back of that ticket, and my hilarity threshold wasn't as low as it might have been. A few seconds later he was hauling the brown cruiser around in a rubber-squealing U-turn and heading back the way we'd just come, no doubt to resume his vigil by the roadside.

Wishing him a fine morning and a carload of heavily-armed drug-crazed psychopaths in the afternoon, I started the Camaro and headed on up the road toward Redbud. A metal sign, its support post knocked twenty or thirty degrees off vertical by somebody's bumper, informed me that I still had fourteen miles to go.

It was a longer drive than that for me, because I didn't go straight on into Redbud. Grandfather Badwater lived several miles west of town; I couldn't say how far, in a straight line, but it took hell's own lot of driving on some incredibly bad dirt roads before I finally found the place.

For some reason my corny imagination had pictured something on the rustic side: an old weathered log cabin, or at least a tin-roofed Erskine Caldwell shack with rusty screens on the windows and Grandpa in a rocking chair on the porch, calling out a warning about that loose board on the top step. And chickens running around a hard-dirt yard, and an old pickup truck up on blocks . . .

There was a cabin, all right, or rather what was left of one, but it was obvious nobody had occupied it for a long time. There were a couple of chickens, too, but the only vehicles in the yard were an old but clean-looking Oldsmobile 88 and a little light blue Toyota that I recognized as Tommy Nine-killer's car. And the only thing up on blocks was a shiny house trailer, at least as big as mine and considerably newer. So much for the colorful home life of America's aborigines.

Grandfather Badwater was a tiny, white-haired old man with a face like a dried apple and the glittering dark eyes of a gentle ancient turtle. "Got here just in time for dinner," he said in a high soft voice, and wouldn't accept a refusal.

Lunch consisted mostly of fried fish and cornbread; I'm not much on fish, generally, but this was pretty good. "Caught them yesterday afternoon, down on the river," he said. "You do any fishing, *chooch*?"

I admitted I didn't. He said, "Well, if you get to wanting to try, there's a good spot where the river makes that big bend. Deep hole down under the bluffs, must go halfway to China. That blacktop road you came in on goes right past the place, a couple of miles before you come in sight of Redbud. More fish, *chooch*?"

He didn't quite have an accent, only the careful phrasing and slight hesitancy of a man more at home in another language. A couple of times he and Tommy talked briefly in Cherokee, their voices rising and falling in the oddly Asian-sounding tones of the Oklahoma dialect. I wished I could speak Cherokee; Rita had tried to teach me, but it had proved to be a murderously difficult language, harder even than Vietnamese.

When the conversation finally worked its way around to Chris Badwater's case, the old man's expression turned to one of bewildered sadness. "I feel sort of to blame," he said. "It was me gave him that tomahawk. It was real old, been in the family a lot of years. Not a regular war axe, it was one of those pipe tomahawks, you know?"

I nodded. I'd seen pipe tomahawks, mostly modern reproductions on display in Indian-souvenir shops. I'd even toyed with the idea of buying one, back before I gave up smoking altogether. With that long hollow handle to cool the smoke, they looked to be nice pipes, but I'd never seen one that would do for a serious weapon. On the other hand, you can kill a man with almost anything if you can get in the first strike.

"Chris always admired it," he went on. "So I promised it to him if he'd finish high school. Wish now I'd never let him have it."

There is a widely held belief among white people that Indians never show emotion. Whoever dreamed up that piece of bullshit should have been in the kitchen of that trailer that day. The old man's face was carrying more pain than you'd think one human could stand. A couple of tear tracks glistened among the wrinkles below his eyes.

"I don't know exactly who you are, *chooch*," he said to me, "or where you fit into all this business. But if you can do anything to help Chris, I'd be truly grateful."

Later, as we rumbled and rattled back down the dirt road toward the distant blacktop, Tommy Ninekiller said, "The old man took a liking to you, Roper."

"Yeah? What was that *'chooch'* bit?" I asked. "What's it mean, 'white asshole'?"

Tommy laughed. "No, no. Just kind of an affectionate expression an older person uses to a younger guy. Comes from *ajuja*, 'boy.' Like saying 'son' or 'kid' in English."

"Hm. Something of a compliment at my time of life."

"Well, like I said, he likes you. . . . God damn it," Tommy said with sudden anger in his voice, "if Chris ever gets out of jail I'm going to personally kick his ass in."

I took my eyes off the washed-out gravel track long enough to give Tommy a quick glance. He was a nice-looking young guy, somewhere in his middle twenties as best I could recall, lean of face and body, with dark brown skin and thick blue-black hair that he kept in a single long braid down his back. Right now his face was taut with strain, and his eyes, as they stared out through the Camaro's dusty windshield, were a lot older than they'd been the last time I'd seen him.

I said, "You think he did it, then?"

"Did what?" Tommy looked startled. "Whacked the sheriff, you mean? Oh, hell, no. I've known the kid all his life. All that big-badass-Cherokee-warrior routine he's into—it's all a load of shit. He wouldn't even fight to defend himself, all through school, and the sight of even a little blood is enough to make him dump his lunch. What I meant," Tommy said, "he needs to have his ass kicked for setting himself up for something like this. If he hadn't run his big mouth so much, and waved that old pipe-hawk around like a God-damned fool, he wouldn't be in the can right now. And that poor old man wouldn't be sitting alone in that trailer eating his heart out."

Tommy snorted. "Not to mention the trouble this is making for other people. You know I had to cancel out a couple of important shows, so I could come down here and try to help the little bastard?"

Tommy Ninekiller was an artist, something of a rising star among the current generation of Indian painters. Lately his work had begun to attract serious critical attention, and the collectors were starting to notice his pictures and finger their checkbooks. For him to drop out of a major show, at a time like this, was a genuine sacrifice. I wondered if any of my relatives would have done anything like that for me. No, screw that; I didn't have to wonder at all.

He said, "And then here we have the noted author, Mr. Taggart Roper, taking time off from his authing to come all the way down here to the back end of nowhere. Have a pleasant journey?"

I told him about my brush with the county cop. He was laughing before I was half done with the story. "What'd he look like?" Tommy wanted to know. "Little skinny pissant, face like one of those salt maps they make in third grade? Walks like he's got something stuck up his ass?"

"Sounds about right."

"Yeah," Tommy said, "that'll be Deputy Tovin. Not exactly the leading light of the Sizemore County Sheriff's Department, as you might have guessed. Hell, that's why they had him out there on that country road handing out bullshit speeding tickets. It's about all they'd trust him to do by himself. Mostly he works paired off with this big mean gorilla name of Pace."

His face became more serious. "And hey, Roper, don't make any mistake about these bastards. Don't underestimate them because your first encounter happened to be with a useless dipshit. Even then," he added, "I sort of wish you hadn't showed him that press card. He's sure as hell going to report it, and you'll get some attention that I imagine you'd rather avoid."

I shrugged. "I'd have had to show it around, anyway. There's no way I can come into a town like Redbud and start asking questions without being noticed. The press card gives me at least a minimal cover."

"I suppose that's right. Gives you a little protection, too, doesn't it?"

"Some. How much depends on where you are, what's going on, a lot of variables. But yes, nowadays even the rural law tends to be dubious about how they treat people with press cards. A pissed-off journalist can bring down all kinds of unwelcome attention. Especially if the journalist gets a sniff of something beyond the usual boys-will-be-boys cop crap."

"And your nose is twitching now?"

I spread my hands on the steering wheel. "A little. Deputy Dawg was obviously relieved to hear that I was only interested in the murder, which suggests other matters that nobody wants outsiders looking into. Mostly, though, I think I'm reacting to things I've already heard about Sizemore County."

"From Rita?"

"And Wiley Harmon, if you remember him."

"Harmon? Christ, is he still on the force? I'd have thought they'd have kicked his crooked ass out by now—but your nose isn't lying to you, Roper," he said. "There's definitely something rotten in the county of Sizemore."

I looked at him again and jacked my left eyebrow upwards. He said, "Oh, don't get me wrong, I don't really know dick. I'm not from around here, after all. Cherokee County may be only a half-hour drive away, but it might as well be Central Asia for some purposes. And I don't have your background," he added. "Don't guess I'd understand the specifics of a crooked operation if somebody drew me a schematic diagram. All I know, I've been picking up little scent particles here and there, in the short time I've been here, and they're starting to add up to a really rancid stink. If I may push the metaphor to the redline limit."

The dirt road had emerged from a patch of dense second-growth woods, to intersect with a marginally better-looking streak of graded gravel. "Hang a left here," Tommy said, "it's shorter than going all the way back to the blacktop. Understand, I don't personally give even a quarter of a rat's ass what sort of redneck-Mafia games they're running out of that old WPA courthouse. Just as long as it doesn't involve my family."

"Any chance it could? I mean, could Chris have been mixed up in something?"

"You're thinking maybe this is one of those more-than-meets-the-eye cases?" He rubbed his face reflectively. "Interesting idea, but I don't think so. God knows the kid's made enough waves in this county, but it's all been Indian issues or environmental stuff, like that business at the nuclear plant. Far as I know, he's never gotten involved in local politics. Anyway," Tommy said, "in Chris's book, the whole white-dominated system—cops, courts, politicians, business, you name it—is so hopelessly corrupt from top to bottom, the details don't really matter."

"He talks like that?"

"Yeah. Last year or so especially. Doesn't help his present situation a whole hell of a lot." Tommy gave me a look. "Of course I'm not saying he's wrong."

"Of course," I said in no particular tone.

Tommy leaned back in his seat. "Damn, Roper, you're not going to let me bait you at all, are you?"

"Not if I can help it."

"Shit. You're as bad as Rita. Never want me to have any fun."

I didn't say anything. After a minute he said, "Ah, hell, don't mind me. I'm so full of shit sometimes. . . . All I want is to get my cousin out of their jail and my elegantly contoured Native American ass out of their damn county. After that, they can sell the place to the Arabs for all I care."

5

❖ ❖ ❖ ❖ ❖ ❖ ❖ ❖ ❖ ❖

REDBUD WAS EVEN SMALLER than I'd expected. The little sidebar on my Oklahoma road map claimed that there were just shy of 2,500 people living there, but I couldn't figure where they kept them.

The downtown area—the "business district," as the local boosters undoubtedly insisted on calling it—was five or six blocks long, depending on whether you counted gas stations. Old brick buildings, possibly of some historic interest if you knew their stories, housed such enterprises as men's and women's clothing stores, a small café, a hardware store with farm equipment hanging in the windows, and a pool hall. There were two banks, both branches of statewide bank chains, and a post office.

"Redbud's about like any other small town, nowadays," Tommy Ninekiller commented as we rolled slowly down the main street. "Downtown's almost ready to dry up and blow away. You keep going, on past that intersection up ahead, and you'll see where the action is now. Big Wal-Mart, Burger King, that kind of stuff, all strung out along what used to be country road—it all came in after Hardesty Industries built the Echota Creek reactor, and it's sucking the old part of town dry. Come back in a few more years, you'll see empty storefronts and boarded-up windows all along this street."

The courthouse was located midway along Main Street, a big gray New Deal–era structure, larger than a place like this really needed; I guessed somebody had known somebody, back during the Roosevelt years. It sat in the center of a typical small-town square, surrounded by good-sized shade trees and fall-yellow lawn. There were the usual monuments to the local veterans of various wars—no cannon, for once—and the usual uncomfortable-looking benches on which old Indian men sat and watched whatever there was to watch. On this particular afternoon they watched me park the Camaro and then they watched Tommy and me as we walked up the courthouse steps.

"You understand," Tommy said as we entered the building, "there's no guarantee we'll get to see Chris at all. They don't have to let him have any visitors except legal counsel and clergy, which we aren't, and immediate family, which you aren't and I may or may not be. Depends on which asshole we have to deal with."

The Sizemore County Sheriff's Department took up several large rooms—a considerable chunk of the ground floor of the courthouse, in fact—but, at the moment, there was nobody around except a couple of youngish secretaries, busy doing whatever secretaries do, and, back of the main desk, a reddish-faced, overweight man in a deputy's uniform. He wore rimless glasses and a worried expression, but no gun.

"I don't know about this," he said unhappily. "Everybody's out right now except me. Got a big truck turned over out by the high school, they're all out there. Don't think I've got the authority to allow any visitors—"

He dithered on like that for a few minutes, telling us repeatedly that he didn't know about this. I showed him my press card, which clearly impressed him but didn't quite get him off the pot; then I slid another bit of printed matter across the desk, and suddenly he decided that he did know about this after all.

"All right," he said, palming the twenty with a deftness that would have done credit to a professional magician, "but it's only for a little bit, you understand? This could really put my nuts in the wringer around here."

Behind him, over by the window, one of the secretaries said sharply, "Hey, Gerald, I don't have to listen to that kind of language, all right?" She was blond and not bad-looking, despite the effect of what had to be the last authentic beehive hairdo in North America; she had a voice, though, that would have etched glass. "I'm a Christian," she added over her shoulder.

"Sorry," Gerald mumbled.

"Well, watch that shit," she said, and went back to her typing.

"Boy," Gerald said feelingly as we followed him down the badly lit stairs to the basement cell block, "now I got Rayjean pissed off at me on top of everything else. What a day."

Behind me I heard Tommy Ninekiller humming softly in his throat. It took me a minute to recognize the tune: "A Policeman's Lot Is Not A Happy One."

Chris Badwater wasn't at all as I'd pictured him. I'd met quite a few of Rita's relatives over the years, and they'd all been the lean, long-boned type, like Rita and Tommy. I'd assumed Chris would fit the same pattern.

Instead, the word that came to mind and stuck there was *soft*. He wasn't actually fat, particularly; a little pudgy, maybe, with a round cheeky face that accentuated the effect. But the softness was in the eyes as well, and in the loose passive way he sat on the iron-framed bed; and while he seemed to be trying to make his voice very strong and manly, there was softness there too. Going for tough, he succeeded only in sounding petulant, like a sulky child.

He said to Tommy, "So who's the *yoneg*?"

Yonega is Cherokee for "white"; when a modern-day Cherokee says *yoneg*, the meaning isn't inherently derogatory, but it tends to work out that way. Chris Badwater managed to pack the maximum load of hostility into the word, though he wasn't even looking at me.

Tommy said, "This is Taggart Roper, Chris. The writer—you know. You've heard me talk about him."

"Oh, right." He looked at me now, a single quick glance and not a friendly one. "Rita's white boyfriend. How could I forget?" he said with industrial-weight sarcasm.

He switched to Cherokee then, spitting a long string of nasal syllables at Tommy, who came back at him in kind. While they argued back and forth—at least it sounded to me as if they were arguing; they could have been discussing the mutual-funds market for all I knew—I looked around the place.

There were four cells in the basement of the old courthouse, each with an iron-slatted bed bolted to the wall. Each cell also held a toilet with no seat. That was all the furniture. Down at the end of the basement was a large open cage, created by the installation of a row of bars across the basement itself; evidently this was meant to function as a holding pen for larger numbers of prisoners, perhaps on rowdy weekends or holidays or following a major bust. There were no prisoners in the pen now, though. The only prisoner in sight, besides Chris Badwater, was a shabbily dressed little man who was snoring noisily in the cell at the far end of the row.

The light was poor, but I doubted if better light would have made things look any prettier. The gray concrete floor and walls were dingy and damp-looking, and the cell bars were scabby with rust. The air was stale, heavy with mold spores and various human bodily fluids and that peculiar smell of hopelessness that you get in jails. I decided to cut Chris Badwater a little extra slack. A few days and nights in this place would be enough to make anybody impossible.

He was looking at me again, while Tommy continued to talk to him in Cherokee. Tommy sounded angry, but the kid was ignoring him now.

"Well," Chris said, "what's your angle? Going to write a book about Lo the Poor Indian?"

There wasn't any point in trying to reply to a line like that, so I didn't bother. I leaned back against the bars—Tommy and I were both standing, there being nothing in the cell to sit on but the bed and the toilet—and studied the dark round face for a moment. He had his lip curled in what I guessed was supposed to be proud disdain.

I said, "I understand you're not offering any kind of alibi or defense. Are you just stonewalling the cops for now, or are you planning on standing mute at the trial, too?"

He sat up a little straighter. "We do not recognize the jurisdiction of this court," he recited in a flat formal voice, his eyes going slightly out of focus. "We do not recognize the authority of the white colonialist government of the so-called United States, or the effect of its laws, over any Native American. Therefore questions of guilt or innocence in this case are irrelevant."

His face broke open in a smug little grin. "Fucking *yoneg* judge," he added in his normal voice, "he's got nothing to say to me, man. Doesn't matter if I offed that worthless pig or not."

Tommy said something under his breath in Cherokee. I said, "That's it? That's what you're going to say in court?"

"You got that right, whitey. That's *all* we're going to say—"

"What's this 'we' shit?" Tommy asked him. "You got a tapeworm? No, wait, I see it now. You never came up with that little speech all by yourself. Who's gotten to you?"

"You'll see." Chris Badwater folded his arms and looked

away. "Got some brothers on the case. Seems there's still some real Indians around. Not like certain apples I could name."

"Apple" is a serious insult among Indians of a certain age and disposition, an apple being red on the outside but white on the in. Before Tommy could slug him I said quickly, "Tommy, is there any chance of doing anything with a jurisdictional question? Maybe get the case transferred to the Cherokee tribal courts, or at least a federal judge? He might get a fairer trial—"

Tommy was shaking his head. "The crime wasn't committed on Indian land—shut the fuck up, Chris, I *know* it's all Indian land, I'm talking law here—and Chris wasn't on Indian land when they arrested him. And the victim was white, and a cop at that. Even if the Cherokee Nation of Oklahoma had any grounds for claiming jurisdiction, they wouldn't touch a case like this. A murdered white sheriff? No way."

"Fuck the Cherokee Nation of fucking Oklahoma," Chris said. "Gutless bunch of puppets, ready to drop their pants and squat every time Washington says shit. We don't recognize them either."

I took a deep breath and let it out. "Look, Chris, your convictions are all very fine, but if you don't come up with some kind of a defense you're going to prison for a long, long time. Or worse," I said. "You'll recall Oklahoma is a death-penalty state. A very damn enthusiastic death-penalty state."

It was pretty hard, but I figured he needed shaking up. I could have saved myself the effort, though.

"Let them do it," he said, giving me his best heroic-redman look, like a chubby edition of Wes Studi in *Geronimo*. "You think I'm afraid to die?"

I started to say what I thought he was, but then suddenly he threw his head back and began singing, a high-pitched monotonous song that rose and fell over a six-tone scale. The lyrics seemed to consist entirely of "hey ya, hey ya," repeated over and over. It didn't sound like any Cherokee song I'd ever heard; it sounded like one of those things you hear Plains Indians singing at powwows. He had his eyes closed and he was beating a rhythm on the bed with one fist.

Tommy did hit him then, crossing the cell and swinging a fast right hand before I even realized he was moving. Tommy's open palm made a solid cracking impact against one soft brown cheek and the kid's head jerked violently to the right. The singing stopped, leaving a sort of vacuum of sound for a moment. Chris raised his own hand to touch the impact area. His mouth opened and his eyes opened wider, but he didn't speak; he only made a tiny soft wordless sound of pain and shock.

"You worthless little bastard," Tommy said quietly. "You run around blowing off at the mouth and making a spectacle of yourself—waving a God-damned tomahawk, for Christ's sake, like an extra in a John Wayne movie!—till you get yourself busted, and then when people come and try to help you all you can do is hand out a lot of smart-ass insults. Okay, I don't give a shit, nobody's doing this for you anyway. This guy's doing it for Rita and I'm doing it for the family—like that old man you're killing with this stupid shit."

Chris started to say something in Cherokee and Tommy chopped him off. "Speak English, God damn it, your Cherokee is so bad it makes my teeth curl. You don't even speak your own language worth a damn," Tommy said furiously, "but you've picked up that whole Plains routine, haven't you? Well, by God, you're not going to do that fucking howling in *my* face. Shit!" Tommy put his hands on his hips and glared down at the kid, who was shrinking back as if expecting to be hit again. "Some fine fucking excuse for a Cherokee you are. I'm going to check with your grandfather, see if you're really blood. I think maybe we adopted ourselves an Osage."

Calling a Cherokee an Osage generally comes under the category of attempted suicide, but Chris Badwater hardly even seemed to notice. He continued to stare up at Tommy with shocked eyes. His face had gone pale as mine.

"And don't give me that it's-a-good-day-to-die crap, either," Tommy added. "If they give you the big one—and the odds are they will, if you keep this shit up—there won't be any romantic business with a firing squad at dawn, or even a rope in the sunshine. You know how they do it now in this state? They strap you down on a fucking operating table, just like in the hospital, only the patient doesn't get to survive the operation because they stick a fucking needle in your fucking arm—"

Chris Badwater turned suddenly and dived for the toilet. Tommy stopped and stood waiting until the retching and heaving had subsided, but he didn't move from where he stood. Neither did I.

"Of course," Tommy went on impassively, as Chris straightened shakily up, "you might not make that particular honor. Seeing as you're so young and all, maybe you'll just get life at McAlester. Where they've got all these great big ugly white and black guys who just *love* to see nice young Indian boys come in the gate. You know what they do to fresh meat like you?"

He told Chris about it in some detail. I watched the kid's face. There was fear in the eyes now, all right, and it wasn't just Tommy that Chris was afraid of. Well, it was about time for him to get real.

But when Tommy ended the horror story, the kid shook his head and said, "Yeah, but—" and I realized we'd lost him again, if we'd ever had him.

He sank back on the bed, hugging himself. "You don't understand," he said hopelessly. "This is how it's got to be. Don't hit me any more, Tommy. You just don't understand."

"Oh, hell." Tommy turned and put both hands flat against the wall at the back of the cell and pounded his head, none too gently, against the graffiti-covered concrete. "Damn it, Chris—"

He stopped and turned. We all turned, looking back toward the far end of the basement, where two men in uniforms were coming down the stairs. The first one was Gerald, and he didn't look happy.

Behind Gerald was a tall white-haired man who said, in a voice that boomed and echoed through the cell block:

"God damn it, I don't know who the hell you people are or what you're doing here, but I better get some answers fast and they better be good ones. Otherwise you're going to have plenty of time to look at the inside of my jail."

6

GERALD SCUTTLED ACROSS the basement to unlock the cell door. His face wore an expression of utter wretchedness, his body was hunched as if expecting a kick, and his shirt was patched darkly with sweat even though it was chilly in the cell block. He reminded me of the groveling half-wit assistant in one of those old mad-scientist horror movies. Or a dog that's just shit in the house and knows he's about to catch hell for it. I might have laughed, if I hadn't gotten a better look at the man who came down the stairs behind him. That was enough to shut down my humor circuits until further notice.

The new arrival was, I judged, a bit over six feet tall, and he was using every bit of it; he stood bowstring-straight and as upright as a Doric column. An old-fashioned journalist would have said he had a military bearing. There was definitely a military look about him: gleaming shoes and pistol belt, tailored uniform with razor-edge creases, close-cropped white hair.

The hair threw me at first; I thought I was looking at a considerably older man. But then as he strode unhurriedly across the cell-block floor toward us, I saw that the hair was pale-blond white—platinum, they call it on a woman—rather than the dead white of age. The long narrow face was smooth and unlined except for a few little tracks at the corners of the eyes; this was a man younger than myself, I decided. Middle thirties, possibly.

He stood beside the cell door as Tommy and I emerged, and he looked at us without any particular expression. He had large, slightly protruding eyes of a remarkably pale blue, set close together; his nose was long and might have been considered aristocratic if you'd never actually met any aristocrats. He had a strong chin that went well with the rest of the look, as did a set of cheekbones that would have done credit to one of Tommy's people. Only the mouth seemed a trifle wrong; the lips were just a bit too full, almost sensuous, for the Spartan image the rest of him gave off.

"Webb Mizell," he said. He didn't stick out his hand to shake; he had his thumbs hooked into his cartridge belt and he left them there. "Chief Deputy, and at present Acting Sheriff of this county. Now suppose you tell me who you are."

We did, getting out wallets and ID and going through the whole routine. "Ninekiller," he said to Tommy. "All right, I remember, your name's on the list of authorized visitors. Normally a cousin wouldn't be considered immediate family, but I understand the prisoner doesn't have many closer living relatives. No problem with your visiting him, provided you follow the rules and procedures."

His voice was higher and softer than you'd have expected, coming from such a tall macho-looking guy. He spoke with crisp precision; there was no trace of the slurring redneck accent usually associated with rural Oklahoma cops. I thought I heard a faint touch of Tidewater Virginia in there now and then, but it wasn't strong enough for certainty.

He handed Tommy back his ID. "However," he added, "that doesn't give you the right to bring in outside visitors without authorization. The prisoner can receive visits from legal counsel, religious clergy, or persons on the list of immediate family. Anyone else has to be approved by me, or by court order."

He looked at me. "Didn't one of my deputies cite you for speeding a few hours ago? Up on the old Cabin Hill Road, near the county line?"

Deputy Tovin might be a geek, but obviously he hadn't screwed around. I nodded. Mizell said, "Well, it seems you're off to a bad start in this county, Mr. Roper. Too bad."

He looked at my press card. "What newspaper are you working for, Mr. Roper?"

No use bluffing; he'd check out whatever I told him. I said, "I used to be with the Tulsa *Courier,* but I've been independent for some years." "Independent" sounds better than "freelance," which to most cops is practically synonymous with "bum."

"Right now," I went on, "I'm just making a preliminary study of this case. Thought there might be the makings of a book in it."

The pale blue eyes came up to study my face. "Write books, do you? Crime books?"

"Historical fiction." I wished now I'd brought a couple of books along; sometimes a casual display of a dust-jacket photo of the author, and maybe the gift of a signed copy, works wonders on the hostile gendarmerie. "Market's drying up lately," I added casually. "Been thinking of branching out, doing a few of those true-crime books. They seem to sell pretty well."

"Is that a fact?" Mizell's face reflected neither belief nor disbelief; it is an expression only cops and shrinks can pull off. "If you're here to offer the prisoner some kind of payment for the rights to his story, you'll have to—"

"No, no." I held up both hands. "As I say, this is strictly a scouting mission. I'm not at all sure there's even enough story here for a book. And I'd have to talk with my publisher, of course."

Mizell handed me back the press card. "I don't know a

damn thing about the literary business," he said. "What I do know is that you have no legitimate grounds to see the prisoner at this time. If you want to interview him, you can come back tomorrow, or later in the week, and apply through the proper channels. If you try again to see any prisoner without authorization," he added with no change in his tone, "I'll see that you're arrested and charged with interfering in police business."

I put the card back in my wallet and gave him my best shit-eating smile. "Sure, Sheriff. Always glad to cooperate. Tell me," I said, "how do I get an interview with *you?*"

"You don't," he said flatly. "Or rather you've just had one, and I suggest you try not to have another."

He turned—it was very nearly a drill-field about-face—and moved smartly toward the stairs. Halfway there, without turning around, he said, "Gerald, if these two men aren't out of the building in five minutes, you will place them under arrest and then begin cleaning out your own locker. Do I make myself clear?"

"Yes, sir," Gerald said miserably. "I gotcha."

When Mizell was gone Gerald said, "I hope to hell you guys are happy. Got my ass in more shit than I'll ever get out of. What'd I do it for?"

"Twenty bucks," Tommy pointed out. "As I recall."

"Huh," Gerald grunted scornfully. "He took that too. Rayjean told on me."

I started to dig out my wallet again, but Gerald flapped his hands and shook his head. "Just get out of here," he said. "Just go on away and leave me alone. You two ain't nothing but trouble."

Outside, in the car, Tommy said, "Well, so much for the simple approach. I knew it was going to be a waste of time, but sometimes you have to try, don't you?"

I rested my hands on the wheel and looked at Tommy. "Has he been like this all along? Chris, I mean."

Tommy blew out his breath in a very long sigh. "Oh, yeah. He's gotten even worse since the last time I saw him. That little speech he rattled off," Tommy said, "that's something new. I wonder who wrote it for him. I was going to get Gerald to check, find out who's been to see him, but that's all been blown. God damn it."

"You don't know what's going on either? That 'we' business—"

"No, hell, I'm almost as much on the outside as you are. All I know, he got involved with some radical types while he was at NSU—mostly young guys from other parts of the country, Sioux and Chippewa and the like, you don't see all that many Cherokees around these Pan-Indian scenes—"

"American Indian Movement?"

"Could be a few of them belonged to AIM. Mostly I got the impression of a bunch of pissed-off young skins, with enough smarts and education to realize how bad their people were getting fucked over, and no patience for the more approved ways of trying to do something about it . . . but no actual affiliation with any organization that I ever heard of."

Tommy drummed thoughtfully on his knees with his fingertips. "That may have changed, though. If some organizers came around from AIM or one of the other militant outfits, these kids were ripe for the picking and then some."

He stared off down the street, where there was nothing to see but a few slow-moving cars and pickup trucks and a fat young white woman waddling across in the middle of the block, her long dress billowing about her pale thighs in the afternoon wind. I waited for Tommy to speak again, but he seemed to have gone off somewhere inside himself; and at last I said, "Anywhere you need to go?"

"What?" He turned and looked at me for a second as if

trying to remember who I was. "Oh. Sorry . . . I guess I better get back out to the old man's place," he said. "He'll want to hear about our meeting with Chris, although I'm not looking forward to telling him. Besides, I need to get my car."

"Sure." I reached for the key.

"If you don't mind driving me all that way," Tommy added. "Hate to make you play chauffeur."

"It's all right," I said. "I don't know what to do next, anyway."

I started the Camaro and pulled out onto the main street. The old Indian men on the courthouse-lawn benches watched impassively from under the brims of soft black hats and mesh-backed gimme caps. They didn't wave.

On the way out of town Tommy said, "Think I was too rough on him?"

"How do I know?" I shrugged. "I don't know a damn thing about the kid. Or your relationship."

He rubbed his eyes with his knuckles. "Oh, fuck, Roper, I'm so tired. Maybe that's why I blew up like that . . . but somebody needs to wake his silly ass up. And soon, because it's not going to be long before he gets his big chance to throw his whole damn life away."

I knew what Tommy meant. Now and then, for reasons only God knows, it happens that an otherwise healthy and viable young human grows obsessed with the idea of romantic self-destruction. Commonly, in this society, the phenomenon shows up in such forms as drinking and serious doping; my own generation got heavily into the combination of booze and fast driving, so that several members of my high-school class had to be scraped off various bits of Kansas roadway.

In other parts of the world there are revolutions and civil wars to provide opportunities for the young and the brainless to go out in a blaze of glory and high explosive; and, of course, teenage suicide has been popular at least since Romeo and Juliet. I've often wondered how many impressionable Elizabethan kids knocked themselves off after seeing that play, though I don't suppose it ever occurred to their parents to sue the Globe Theater.

Chris Badwater had at least found a relatively fresh approach; but I couldn't shake the feeling that there was something else, a private reason, beyond the militant rhetoric and kamikaze heroics, for the stonewall act.

"He lost his parents when he was little," Tommy said. "His mother took off one day and never came back. His father blew his own head off with a shotgun not long after that. Chris was the one who found the body. Maybe that's why he can't stand the sight of blood.

"Anyway, Chris got raised by uncles, aunts, and cousins, and then finally by his Grandfather Badwater. Some of the people who brought him up were traditional Cherokee, like the old man. Some, though, were assimilated types, trying to be as near white as they could. They felt they were doing Chris a favor by keeping him away from all that Indian nonsense. So his head got pulled this way and that all the time he was growing up, and it's no wonder he's the way he is."

We rode a while longer in silence. Finally I said, "Is there a motel in Redbud? I need to get a room."

"At last a question with a simple answer. Sure," Tommy said. "Out on the north edge of town, on the road that goes to Tahlequah. You can't miss it."

The Moonlight Courts Motel—I swear—was an old, gone-to-
¹ place, the kind with separate little cabins rather than continuous blocks of rooms. A sign beside the office said WEEKLY AND MONTHLY RATES AVAILABLE. The leaf-strewn parking area held no more than half a dozen vehicles.

The office was empty and the door locked, but I leaned on

a cracked plastic button and heard a buzzer go off somewhere inside. After the third buzz a small, skinny woman with an astonishing henna-red hairdo came out of the back and opened the door. "Help you?" she asked irritably.

My desire for a room seemed to strike her as unreasonable; she muttered to herself a good deal while she filled out the registration form, and she shoved the key at me with the put-upon manner of a New Yorker giving money to a panhandler. My cabin was Number 12, which proved to be down at the far end of the row of cabins. I parked the Camaro in front of the little concrete-block cube and got my suitcase out of the trunk and went in, wondering if this was going to be as bad as I expected.

It was. The interior walls were a dull more-or-less beige, with chipped spots along the baseboard and around the door, showing several strata of cheap latex paint in other colors, relics of bygone efforts to refurbish. There was a low, hard-looking bed—when I tossed my suitcase on it there was no bounce—and a dresser in peeling blond Formica, with a rickety wooden chair. An uncurtained alcove held a length of iron pipe for a clothes rack. Hanging from a bracket on the ceiling was a no-brand television set. When I went into the bathroom the prospect didn't get any better.

Ah, well, I wasn't here on vacation. I opened the suitcase and dug out the liter of Jim Beam I'd brought along—if Redbud was at all a typical small Oklahoma town, the liquor prices would be lethal—and had myself a drink straight out of the bottle. While the bourbon spread its soothing warmth through my body, I went back out and got my number-two suit from the back seat of the Camaro and hung it on the iron pipe. It dangled there all alone in its plastic cover, looking rather pathetic; even a struggling salesman would have had at least a couple more.

And that, for the moment, seemed to be that. In a proper

novel or movie, this was the point at which the detective would get out his Smith and Wesson and check the loads, maybe even take it apart and clean it, before strapping on the old shoulder holster and going out to find exciting clues and meet horny women in dark bars.

As it happened, however, the only pistol I owned—an old and unfashionably low-tech .380 Colt—was back at my trailer in Yuchi Park, and so far I'd seen no reason to regret having left it there. The part about the women might be fun, perhaps, but I didn't imagine there would be all that much first-string talent in a town like Redbud; and as for clues, I wasn't sure I'd know one if it buggered me.

That was the other thing: I wasn't a detective, either.

I sat there a little while, thinking and having a few more sips, and finally I got up and went looking for a place to eat. There was a brown patrol car parked across the road when I pulled out of the parking lot, and I expected it to follow me as I headed back toward town, but it didn't. I couldn't see the driver's face.

Donna's Café, down on the main drag near the courthouse, was as unpromising in appearance as everything else in Redbud; but the food, to my amazement, was first-rate, and the prices were more than reasonable. The cook actually knew what "rare" meant, and the mashed potatoes were made from real potatoes, not powder; there was even genuine fresh-baked peach cobbler for dessert. Mark up one plus for this town, then.

When I got back to the motel the patrol car was gone. I went into my cabin and switched on the television and stretched out on the bed. The picture was poor and the colors were off, but there wasn't anything on the tube that I particularly cared about anyway. I watched a lurid account of Michael Jackson's current difficulties, and an interview with a mother and her two adult daughters who had all posed naked together for *Playboy*. I was engrossed in the confessions of a man who was going to get a sex-change operation because he had fallen in love with a lesbian—talk about giving your all for love—when the phone rang.

It was Tommy Ninekiller. " *'Siyo,* Roper. Care to take in a bit of the local nightlife?"

"What did you have in mind?"

"Little place," he said. "Might be a chance of picking up information. If you've got no other plans for the evening . . . ?"

"Okay with me," I said. "Want me to come get you?"

"No, hell, you've had your share of dirt-road driving for the day. I'll be there in an hour or so," he said. "Dress casual, bro. This isn't the Ritz where we're going."

7

CHARLIE'S FOXHOLE WAS A smallish concrete-block structure with the general outlines and proportions of an inverted shoebox. It sat in the middle of a rough gravel lot on the southern outskirts of Redbud, a little way from the railroad tracks, on a dark narrow street that was only technically paved.

"Local skin hangout," Tommy said as I eased the Camaro into the parking lot. "I figured we could do a little hanging out ourselves, might learn something."

I parked the Camaro and we got out. The lot was poorly lit and I stumbled a few times on the hard uneven ground. Only a few pickups and heavy, old-fashioned cars were parked in front of the ugly little building. Charlie's Foxhole didn't appear to be doing a brisk trade, but then it was Monday night.

"Guy named Charlie Redfox owns this place," Tommy said as we neared the front door. "His mother was my Aunt Minnie's—ah, hell, you don't want to hear about all that. I don't really know him that well, anyway."

The door opened and an Indian couple emerged, hanging on to each other. The woman was chubby and very unsteady on her feet. The man was considerably thinner but just as drunk. As they lurched past he gave me an unfriendly stare and said, *"Gado haduhne, yoneg?"*

"This may not have been such a great idea," Tommy mused. "Maybe I should have come alone."

The thought had already occurred to me. There are Indian

bars where the occasional white visitor is regarded as no big deal. There are others, however, where non-Indians are distinctly unwelcome, and the white man who disregards the early warning signals—or, God help the fool, gets pushy—can find himself in serious trouble. I didn't know what kind of scene this was, and evidently Tommy didn't know either.

"Wonderful," I said under my breath, and hunched my shoulders and followed Tommy through the entrance, hoping there would be a free table close to the door. Or at least a weak spot in the wall.

Inside, Charlie's Foxhole was a cleaner, better-lit place than I'd expected. The air smelled of cigarette smoke and beer, but nothing worse. A country-and-western record was playing on the juke box; the high whining steel-guitar melody line punctuated by the click of balls from the pool tables at the end of the room.

The crowd was definitely on the thin side. A quartet of young Indian men sat on one side of the U-shaped bar, watching a football game on the bar TV and exchanging comments in Cherokee. On the other side of the bar a middle-aged woman, a trifle overdressed for a place like this, looked up expectantly as we came in and then glanced down at her watch, registering disappointment. She stood up and called out something to the short, homely man behind the bar, who nodded and reached under the bar and handed her the telephone.

A couple of heavyset guys sat at a table in the back, laughing and talking with a pair of attractive women who didn't quite appear to be buying their act. A leathery-faced old man in a fancy cowboy shirt and a black hat sat in a booth with a considerably younger woman with mammoth breasts and a bad perm. Three men and a pretty ponytailed girl were gathered around one of the pool tables. That was the house, as far as I could see.

None of them looked at me with any particular expression, except for the old man, who raised a hand in greeting and gave me a pleasant grin as I walked past. So much for my Caucasian paranoia. I followed Tommy to the bar, where the middle-aged woman was holding the phone to her ear and looking more and more unhappy. "Son of a bitch," she said at last, and hung up the phone with unnecessary force. *"Wado, Jali,"* she said, handing the phone back to the barkeep, and scooped up her purse and headed toward the door, her heels stabbing viciously at the concrete floor.

"Howa," the little man called after her. Then, to Tommy, " *'Siyo, Tami, dohiju?"*

" *'Siyo, Jali."* Tommy reached across the bar and they shook hands. "Beer okay?" he said to me.

I nodded. "Whatever's on tap, Charlie," Tommy said, and a few minutes later we had a couple of foaming mugs in front of us. I sampled mine while Tommy spoke to the barman in Cherokee. It wasn't great beer, but it was okay; at least it was cold, and didn't have that flat metallic taste you sometimes get with cheap-bar draft.

The barman grinned at me as Tommy finished whatever he was saying. "Nice to meet you," he said, sticking out a hand. Evidently I'd just been introduced. "You're the writer, huh?"

I always like it when people say it that way, since it implies that there are no others. I admitted my guilt, shook Charlie's hand, and went back to my beer while he and Tommy resumed their conversation in Cherokee. Down at the pool table the three guys were talking to the ponytailed girl, evidently insisting she take the break. Watching her bend over that table in her tight jeans, I didn't have to wonder why.

Charlie wound up his dialogue with Tommy and moved away to take care of the football fans. Tommy said, "Charlie says he hasn't even seen Chris since a couple of months ago, when he kicked him out of here for trying to get beer on a fake ID. Says Chris and his friends wouldn't have been too popular in here anyway. About half the regular customers work at the Echota Creek plant."

The girl with the ponytail made her shot. It wasn't a very good break, but the three guys all applauded anyway.

"The suggestion was made," Tommy added, "that we should be careful about bringing up any of that shit in here. If these dudes get the idea we're involved with the people who want to shut down the place where they work—"

The ponytailed girl sank a ball. I couldn't see which one. Hell, I wasn't watching the balls. Tommy turned his head to see what I was looking at. "Hey, all *right*," he murmured approvingly.

The door swung open and half a dozen Indians trooped in. They stopped and bunched up in the middle of the room, looking around and talking in low tones among themselves; then, without asking leave of Charlie or anybody else, they proceeded to shove a couple of tables together. I heard Charlie say, "Shit," and then, louder, "Louise! *Nula!*"

The ponytailed girl laid her cue across the table, made an apologetic face at the three guys, and hustled back to the bar to pick up an order pad and a pencil. Charlie came over and looked at Tommy and me and shook his head. "Kind of hoped they wouldn't be back," he said. "Bunch of loudmouths."

The newcomers were dragging up chairs and seating themselves. There were four men and two women. They all looked to be somewhere in the same age bracket, middle twenties to early thirties, though the range and the light made that no more than a guess.

Beside me Tommy said softly, "Oh, Christ. How long have *they* been around here?"

Charlie shrugged. "First I ever saw them was last Friday night. They might have been in town before that, though."

"Christ," Tommy said again. He gulped his beer and stared at the group in the middle of the room. His eyes had taken on a dark flat look that I didn't like at all. "Now it's all starting to add up," he said. "I should have known those bastards were in the picture, somehow."

Clearly something important had just been established; and, even more clearly, I didn't know what the hell it was. All I knew was that my bad-scene warning systems were starting to blink and beep like mad.

I studied the new arrivals over the rim of my beer mug. Only one of the six looked familiar, and after a second I decided even that was merely the effect of the attitude he projected; he had the air of somebody who expects to be recognized.

There wasn't anything particularly remarkable about his appearance; he was just an average-height, average-build Indian man, dressed in jeans and a denim jacket. He had a long face and a big tomahawk nose, and he wore his hair in two long braids; in fact he looked like a younger version of the guy on the buffalo nickel.

He had something else, though, that had nothing to do with looks or clothing. Call it charisma or presence or maybe just the aura generated by a powerful ego; whatever he had, he knew he had it, and so did his companions. There was no question at all who the Alpha male was in this particular group. You could see the deference in the way the others looked at him and spoke to him, and listened when he spoke to them.

On his left sat a tall, broad-shouldered fellow in a dark gray three-piece suit, with a bone-hairpipe choker in place of a tie, and a single braid like Tommy's. On the other side of the Main Man was a short, lumpy-faced young guy who wore a black leather jacket and, for God's sake, dark glasses—I thought at first he must be blind, but then I saw him watching the waitress's ass—and loose, straight, shoulder-length hair.

A big, hefty-hipped young woman in jeans and a red sweatshirt sat beside the guy in the suit, one hand resting possessively on his shoulder. The remaining chairs were occupied by a nice-looking couple, lighter-skinned than the others but still clearly Indian. The man wore short hair and an OSU jacket, the woman wore a blue dress and heels, and both wore slightly nervous expressions, as if they weren't sure what they were doing here.

Beside me Tommy Ninekiller said, "War Party."

I turned to look at him, and my face must have registered a good deal of confusion. He gave a short laugh with very little amusement in it. "War Party," he repeated. "That's who they are, Roper. I assume you were wondering."

He drained his mug and held it out to Charlie for a refill. "Radical splinter group," he said as Charlie scuttled away. "Broke off from the American Indian Movement—or got kicked out, depending on whose story you believe—a couple of years back. Supposedly the dispute was over tactics, with these bastards advocating head-on confrontation and even a certain amount of violence. Or violent rhetoric, anyway," Tommy added. "Of course you can hear other stories, too. Including persistent rumors about the War Party leadership siphoning off funds into certain non-political sidelines, such as dope dealing."

Charlie came back with a pair of full mugs, even though I hadn't quite finished my first. That was easily remedied. I set the empty down and looked at the sextet in the middle of the room. War Party? It was a new one on me, but then my knowledge of minority-group politics approached zero. "Local outfit?" I asked Tommy.

"Huh uh. In fact I've never before heard of them operating

in Oklahoma. Usually they work the reservations, especially up north and out in the Southwest. Or in cities with big Indian populations, like Albuquerque and Minneapolis and Los Angeles."

The man with the braids was speaking—holding forth, really—while the others listened respectfully. His voice wasn't particularly loud, but it carried like the middle range of a pipe organ.

"The white people," he said, "have never truly regarded Indians as human beings. Deep down, they still think of us as wild animals. Even the whites who think they love us." An ironic tone came into his voice. "Have you noticed that the ones who romanticize Indians are also the ones who romanticize animals? To them we are merely another endangered species to be preserved for their enjoyment."

"Marvin Painted Horse," Tommy said to me. "Santee Sioux—Lakota, they like to be called. Founding father and boss dog of War Party."

The guy in the Fonzie jacket laughed and said something I didn't catch, banging his hand on the table for emphasis. He was obviously pretty drunk. The fat woman gave him a nasty look.

"The Ramones reject is Vince Lacolle," Tommy said. "Chippewa, and one mean son of a bitch. Did some time in the Wisconsin state pen for assault. Nothing political, even though he pretends it was. Way I heard it, he got drunk and put a guy in the hospital in a fight over a Canadian whore."

Marvin Painted Horse was saying, "Oh, yes, they all loved that movie, didn't they? Dances with wolves, hangs out with Indians—it's all the same to the white mentality."

"The big-assed woman is Linda Blacksnake," Tommy continued. "Another Santee, I think she's some kind of relative of Marvin's. Very popular on the college lecture circuit these days, does this Indian-feminist number that you have to hear to believe. Remember that woman who cut her old man's crank off? Linda was running around saying that 'the sister' obviously had Indian blood."

"I believe it," Charlie Redfox said seriously.

"Who's the suit?" I asked.

"Ah. There, now, we've got an authentic homeboy. From Muskogee, in fact," Tommy said. "Nehemiah Harjo, half Creek and half Seminole and all asshole. I didn't know he'd gotten involved with War Party."

"Another ex-convict?"

"Worse," Tommy said. "He's a lawyer."

"The other two live here in town," Charlie said. "That's Jimmy Cottonwood, I don't know his wife's name. Has his own surveying business."

"Cherokees?" Tommy asked.

Charlie nodded. "Damn," Tommy said, "two more middle-class mixed-bloods trying to get in touch with their roots by hanging out with the crazies. All we need."

Marvin Painted Horse was still holding the floor. "You might have noticed," he said, "every public discussion of 'racial problems' in this country always turns out to be about whites and blacks, and nobody else." He gestured dismissively with one hand. "Oh, now and then they'll throw in a token reference to Hispanics and even Asians—but have you ever heard anyone mention Indians?"

He shook his head. "The highest unemployment and suicide rates of any group in the so-called United States, but we don't count. Because, of course, we aren't really human."

"Fucking niggers get everything," Vince Lacolle said suddenly. His voice was loud and harsh. "We don't get shit."

The others looked embarrassed. But Marvin Painted Horse said, "Don't talk against the African brothers. They've learned the big secret—that the whites respond only to fear and intimidation. We could learn a great deal from them."

" 'Power grows out of the barrels of guns,' " Nehemiah Harjo quoted solemnly.

"Yes," Marvin Painted Horse said approvingly. "Of course it's no longer fashionable to quote Mao, but he still makes a lot of sense in some respects."

Tommy Ninekiller said something ugly-sounding in Cherokee. He was staring at Marvin Painted Horse and his face was a bad thing to see. His knuckles were white around the handle of his beer mug.

"But for now," Marvin Painted Horse went on, "there are other weapons we have to use, other kinds of battles to be fought. Take the present situation, here in Redbud—"

"All right," Tommy said, and stood up. "*All* fucking right."

He was halfway across the room before I even realized he was in motion. "You son of a bitch," he said, putting his hands on the table and glaring down at Marvin Painted Horse. "What the fuck are you trying to pull?"

The place got very quiet. Even the pool players stopped moving.

Marvin Painted Horse looked up at Tommy for a second and then broke into a smile. "Tommy Ninekiller," he said, and put out a hand. "We met at one of your shows, didn't we? Chicago, was it? This brother is a truly great artist," he said to the others. "You should see—"

"Don't give me that brother shit, you Sioux prick," Tommy said. "And get that fucking hand out of my face if you want to keep it."

"Hey," Vince Lacolle said indignantly.

"How'd you get to Chris?" Tommy said, ignoring Lacolle. "I don't know what kind of game you're running—"

"Oh, yes." Marvin Painted Horse lowered the hand, but he continued to smile. "Chris is your cousin, right? He mentioned you."

"We're here to help Chris," Nehemiah Harjo assured Tommy. "In fact, I'm his defense attorney."

"Great." Tommy crossed his arms and stared at Harjo. "Wonderful defense strategy, counselor. Refuse to offer any evidence, refuse to plead, defy the court's authority, and program your client with a line of bullshit guaranteed to destroy any sympathy he might have going for him—did I miss something?"

"You don't understand," the lawyer began.

"The fuck I don't." Tommy swung back to Marvin Painted Horse. "Christ, now I see the whole thing. Going to have the kid take a dive, aren't you? Make absolutely damn sure he goes down, so then you'll have your very own martyr. Then you can go all over the country holding rallies and making speeches and oh, yes, raising funds. I bet you're already having 'Free Chris Badwater' buttons made up."

"What do you know about it, you Cherokee dipshit?" Vince Lacolle shouted furiously. "You better watch your mouth—"

Reluctantly, with deep misgivings, I detached myself from the bar and moved over to stand near Tommy. I thought I was being very quiet and discreet, but all the seated Indians turned and looked at me.

"Who's this, your faithful white companion?" Marvin Painted Horse said to Tommy. And then to me, "I'd suggest you go back to the bar and stay out of this. It's not your affair."

Linda Blacksnake gave Tommy an evil little grin. "What's the matter," she said, "are you queer for white guys? I've heard about you artists."

"Nobody was talking to you, Princess Buffalo Butt," Tommy said without looking at her. "Listen, Marvin—"

That was when it all came apart.

Nehemiah Harjo stood up, knocking his chair over backwards. "You can't talk to her like that," he said, and took a swing at Tommy.

Tommy turned almost lazily, deflecting the wild swing with his left forearm. "Sure I can," he said, and hit Nehemiah Harjo in the stomach with one of the fastest rights I'd ever seen.

Vince Lacolle was coming up out of his own chair, his face flushed almost black. He started toward Tommy and I swung the pool cue I'd borrowed from the nearest table. The big end caught him smartly on the side of his left knee joint, right where I'd aimed. His eyes went wide and his mouth opened, and then he fell noisily to the floor as the knee buckled under him. I turned, raising the cue, but Marvin Painted Horse already had both hands up, palms outward. His face was calm, but a little paler than it had been.

Nehemiah Harjo was bent over the table, clutching his midsection and making little gagging noises. Linda Blacksnake was holding him by the shoulders and looking death and torture at Tommy Ninekiller. The Cottonwoods hadn't moved from their seats. They looked paralyzed.

Linda Blacksnake said something angry-sounding in a language I didn't recognize. In another second, I realized, she was going to let go of her lawyer and attack Tommy, probably with some sort of ad hoc weaponry. And Vince Lacolle was pushing himself up off the floor with blood in his eye. I took a step backward, shifting my grip on the cue, and then the door boomed open and the cops came in.

The first one through the door was my pal Deputy Tovin, minus the mirror shades but otherwise much as I remembered him from that morning. Mizell must have his lads working strange shifts, or maybe Tovin was trying to rack up some overtime; it had been almost twelve hours since he'd written me that ticket. But then I got a look at the man behind him, and I forgot all about Tovin and his work schedule.

Tovin's partner wasn't freakishly huge, like some jock types I'd met, but he was big enough. He stood at least six feet tall and he had the massive build of a pro wrestler, or a bouncer in a biker bar. He had heavy black eyebrows and a black mustache, and a mouth that seemed permanently turned down at the corners. His hair was slicked back in an Elvis Presley pompadour, complete with sideburns. One large hand held a nightstick. With him holding it, it looked like something out of a Tinkertoy set.

It was Tovin, though, who spoke first. "What the hell goes on here?" He put his hands on his lips and surveyed the room. "Little disturbance?"

Over at the bar, Charley Redfox said nervously, "No trouble, Deppity Tovin. Nothing happening at all."

"Shut up, chief. We'll decide if there's any trouble or not." Tovin looked at the big man. "What do you think, Pace? Should we haul the lot of them in for drunk and disorderly?"

A low mutter ran through the room. The big man looked around and grinned. "Any of you redskin bastards want to add a little resisting-arrest charge?" He slapped the nightstick against his palm. "Speak up."

"Right," Tovin agreed. "We'll do our best to accommodate you."

I said, "Excuse me."

The deputies' heads snapped around. Before they could speak I said, "This gentleman accidentally tripped over a chair and fell. His friend happened to be in the way. That's all."

The two cops were staring at me with identical expressions of disbelief. So, apparently, was everybody else in the place. Well, even I didn't believe myself just now.

The big bastard walked slowly toward me. The room was so quiet that you could hear the creaking of his leather gun-belt under the meaty slap, slap, slap of the truncheon against his palm.

He stopped close in front of me and turned his head and deliberately spat on the floor. "And who the fuck are you?" he wanted to know.

"Pace." Tovin appeared beside him, wearing a strange expression. "Pace, wait a minute."

Pace continued to stare at me, like a bull trying to decide which horn to use on an inept matador. Tovin tugged at his arm. "Hey, listen, Pace, come here—"

Somehow he managed to lead Pace aside. They talked for a few minutes, their voices too low for me to pick up more than an occasional word or phrase. I did hear Tovin say, "Of *course* I'm sure, I was writing him up before Webb Mizell even met him—" And, a moment later, something that ended, "—have our asses if we fuck up."

Whatever point Tovin was making, Pace wasn't buying it at first; he kept looking over his shoulder in my direction, and it was plain he was in a mood for some serious head-busting. But finally he nodded, very reluctantly, and grunted something to Tovin; then they both turned and came back toward our little group.

"Okay," Tovin said. "If you're certain that's how it was—"

"I'd swear to it."

Pace pointed toward the door with his club. "All right, clear out. I see any of you blanket-asses again tonight, you're busted."

Everybody began moving out. Pushing past me, Vince Lacolle hissed, "This ain't over between us, whitey."

Pace stationed himself by the door. When I started to leave he raised his nightstick and touched me, not hard, on the arm. "You need to stay away from these Indians," he said. "This ain't no place for a white man. We don't want you getting hurt, do we?"

* * *

On the way back to the motel Tommy said, "Hey, Roper, you need to understand—most of that shit Marvin was laying out back there, I *agree* with him. Even if the son of a bitch is trying to get my cousin railroaded for his own purposes, he's right more than he's wrong."

"I've heard you say most of those same things, over the years."

"Yeah, well, it all needs saying. In fact it's too important to leave the job of saying it to manipulative fuckheads like Marvin Painted Horse. No offense, Roper, but you don't know what it's like."

"I was a cop-beat reporter in Tulsa for seven years," I pointed out. "I've seen a few things."

"Huh. You've seen a little, maybe, of what goes on in Oklahoma. Which is bad enough, but you wouldn't believe how bad it gets in some parts of the country. Vince Lacolle is a punk, okay, he'd have been a punk if he'd been born white or black or green—but up there in Wisconsin, where he grew up, they call us 'woods niggers' and display bumper stickers that say 'Save a Fish—Spear an Indian' and the governor himself came out and said publicly, a few years back, that even if Indians do have certain rights they better not insist on exercising them or they'll get hurt. Can you imagine any public official in this country saying something like that about any other group?"

He fell silent for a minute or so. Then he said, "Feel up to a little drive tomorrow? Guy I know up in Tahlequah, there's a good chance he'll have some information for us."

"Why not? Right now I'm up for anything that gets me out of this town."

Tommy chuckled. "Place does have that effect on you, doesn't it? Okay," he said. "In the morning, then? It's only a half-hour drive."

8

BUT WHAT TOMMY SAID next morning was, "Half an hour? Did I say half an hour? Man, was I full of it or what?"

We were inching along Highway 82, a little way north of Tenkiller Dam, behind a column of backed-up local traffic. It was already well over half an hour since we'd left Redbud, and we were barely halfway to Tahlequah; we hadn't even hit the Cherokee County line yet.

Up at the front of the procession, oblivious to the creeping hell he was creating for everyone behind him, an old man piloted a small green pickup truck at speeds any healthy armadillo could have bettered. There are very few places on that tortuous hilly road where a driver lacking a death wish can pull out to pass. . . . When I finally did get past, I caught a glimpse of a wrinkled face and huge glasses and a braid-decorated naval officer's cap. Maybe he thought he was at the helm of an aircraft carrier.

Tommy rolled down a window and screamed curses as we passed, and got a cheerful smile and a friendly wave in return. "Old turd," he grumbled. "They ought to put a bounty on them."

I'd known there was a good chance of getting held up like this. Some years ago a national magazine named the Tahlequah area as one of the best retirement places in the country, and life on the local roads hasn't been the same since. It takes some doing to drive worse than a native Oklahoman, but the

Golden Years Brigade proved more than equal to the challenge.

"Try driving this stretch in summer," Tommy said, "when you get the tourists in the Winnebagos too. Enough to make you wonder why there's never a crazed highway sniper around when you need one."

"Which we can't say about the cops down in Sizemore County," I remarked. "You did see that cruiser shadowing us out of town?"

"Yeah. Kept thinking he was going to pull us over, but he never did. Looks like there's some kind of hands-off order out on us," Tommy mused. "Now why does that make me more nervous than ever?"

I hadn't been to Tahlequah in a couple of years, but it looked about the same: a quiet, rather sad-looking little town, attractively situated on a series of hillsides and along the valley of a small creek. Following another silver-haired crawler along the main drag at walking speeds, stopping at every light, I got a better look at the downtown area than I'd wanted. Half the storefronts wore FOR RENT or GOING OUT OF BUSINESS signs. There were quite a few arts and antiques shops, though, and galleries featuring bad paintings and bogus Indian crafts. "Jesus," Tommy said, "this town's getting to be as embarrassing as Taos. Now I remember why I left."

While we sat waiting for a light to change, I studied a display of big charcoal drawings in a gallery window. Nudes, all of them, and ugly enough to put a man off naked women for life. "Christ," I said, "do the models around here really look that awful, or are the local artists simply incompetent?"

"Both of the above," Tommy said, and laughed. "And they show that kind of schlock around here all the time, yet you can't buy so much as a copy of *Playboy* in this town. Schizoid place, man, Bible Belt rednecks rubbing shoulders with art phonies whose big creative breakthrough was learning to draw pubic hair."

The light changed and we crept forward again, past the old red-brick structure that had once been the capitol of an independent Cherokee Nation. It was still an impressive building, but the grounds had been rendered hideous with various signs and monuments of modern origin. Tommy groaned. I said, "Well, hell, this still looks pretty good after Redbud."

"Yeah," Tommy agreed, "there *are* worse things than geeky nudes. Hang a left up here."

Following Tommy's directions, I turned down a side street and, a few blocks up a hillside, stopped the Camaro in front of a large two-story frame house in serious need of paint. A big sign over the porch read ROADKILL PUBLICATIONS.

Tommy led the way up the cracked concrete walk. There was an old-fashioned front porch running the width of the house, its sagging roof supported by decrepit wooden columns. A big gray cat lay sleeping on a derelict chair beside the door, its feet and tail tucked up under it in that soft, self-contained way cats have. If it was aware of our arrival it gave no sign.

Tommy began pounding on the door. "Lester! Lester, you half-breed asshole, are you in there?"

Almost instantly the door banged open and a large bearlike man burst out onto the porch and began pounding Tommy about the head and shoulders and yelling in a mixture of English and Cherokee. Tommy pounded and yelled back, while the cat leaped off the couch and sprinted for the yard. I didn't blame it a bit.

After the whacking and hollering subsided, Tommy said, "Roper, this twisted son of a bitch is Lester Bucktail—"

"Or, as my people call me, Dances With Your Wife." The

big man reached up and pushed a pair of heavy-rimmed Elvis Costello glasses up on his nose. "Roper? As in Taggart? Hell, I know who you are. This degenerate and his fine sister told me so much about you, I finally went down to the library and checked out a couple of your books. Damn good stuff."

He shoved out a sizable hand and I took it. His grip was soft and loose; Indians traditionally regard a crusher grip as the mark of an aggressive prick.

Lester Bucktail was taller than me, and nearly as big as Deputy Pace, though a good deal of his body mass was concentrated in an impressive beer gut. His skin was lighter than Tommy's, and his eyes, as best I could tell through the thick and none-too-clean glasses, were hazel rather than brown. His shoulder-length hair was dark brown, but heavily streaked with gray; I figured him for fifty or better. The skin of his face was deeply lined, his features classic big-bone Indian. He wore a black Meat Loaf T-shirt and faded jeans, with a red bandanna headband holding his hair more or less in place. A large rattlesnake rattle dangled from his left ear lobe.

"Come on in," he said. "Watch your step, it's kind of messy in here right now. Just getting out the latest issue."

"Lester is a member of your profession," Tommy explained as we went inside. "Your former profession, I should say."

"I put out a little rag, is all," Lester Bucktail said diffidently.

A large, low-ceilinged room took up much of the front part of the house. Virtually every square foot of floor space was taken up by cardboard boxes and string-bound bundles of newsprint. Tommy whistled. "You mean there's this many people in the world who read your crazy-ass ravings? I wonder how many murdered trees this load of drivel represents. Jesus H. Christ."

"What's the *H.* stand for?" Lester Bucktail said. "I always wondered."

"Harjo," Tommy declared. "He was Creek. Speaking of Creeks, you'll never believe who was down in Redbud last night—"

I picked up a loose paper from a nearby stack. It was a standard-size tabloid, about the thickness of a typical supermarket loony sheet. The logo on the front page read EAGLE FEATHER NEWS.

"Take it," Lester Bucktail said to me, "on the house and worth it. Come on, we'll go back to my office."

He moved off between the stacked tabloids, stopping before a heavily curtained doorway. "Billy," he called, "okay to come through?"

A voice from the other side of the curtains said, "Sure," and Lester Bucktail held the curtain aside while Tommy and I stepped through. The next room had been turned into a makeshift photo studio, with floodlights and a 35mm. camera on a tripod. The back wall was covered with a big sheet of white paper, and a skinny Indian kid was busy arranging a lot of sports-team pennants on it. They weren't real pennants, I saw now, only dummies made from construction paper, but then these team logos would never be seen at any ball park or football field in the world: DETROIT NIGGERS. NEW YORK HEBES. LOS ANGELES WETBACKS. SAN FRANCISCO QUEERS. BOSTON PADDIES. CHICAGO GUINEAS.

And, hanging vertically so as to flank the phony pennants on either side, were a couple of genuine pennants from real teams: the Washington Redskins and the Atlanta Braves.

The skinny kid said, "Hey, Lester, where's the caption going to go?" He had bad acne and a serious overbite. His hair had been braided, Plains style, but he didn't have enough material to make it work; in effect he was wearing pigtails, kind of cute but probably not the look he was after.

"I don't know yet. Shoot it loose, we'll crop it." Lester looked at Tommy. "What do you think? I can't decide between 'Now You Know How It Feels' and 'How Would You Like It?' "

"Leave it alone," Tommy advised. "They get it or they don't."

"You're right. Only, you know, we've got a lot of college-library subscriptions. I can just see the political-correctness vigilantes sharpening their wooden stakes."

Tommy shrugged. "As Geronimo said, fuck 'em if they can't take a joke."

"*Howa.* Come on," Lester Bucktail said. "Better leave the genius to his work."

Lester Bucktail's office was as big as the living room of my trailer. A heavy wooden desk held piles of papers, stacks of books, and a fancy computer setup. The walls were lined with board-and-block bookshelves. A cow skull, horns and all, hung above the window, through which I could see a weed-grown back yard and a white dog licking itself.

A huge painting covered most of the far wall. It was basically a reproduction of the U.S. flag, but all the stars had been replaced by human skulls, and each skull wore a feathered Indian headdress. Across the striped section ran the legend: OH, SAY, CAN *YOU* SEE?

"Yours?" I asked Tommy.

"Afraid so. From my early or obvious period. Lester, if you'll burn that fucker I'll paint you a new one. Something nice, big shaggy buffalo, some powwow dancers maybe—"

"No way in hell, *chooch.* I like this one. In fact I think I'm going to use it for a cover, if Billy can get it to photograph right."

"Who's the kid?" Tommy wanted to know. "Family?"

"Billy Greenstick, and I'm not even sure he has a family. Think he fell off a UFO or something," Lester said. "He really is a fucking genius, you know, even if he does look like an extra from *Revenge of the Nerds*. For one thing, he actually knows how to make this thing work." He waved a hand at the computer on his desk. "I can just barely turn it on and off, if I've got the manual handy."

"White man's medicine," Tommy said. "Like VCRs and garter belts."

"Yeah." Lester sat down behind his desk, while Tommy and I dragged up metal folding chairs marked PROPERTY OF FIRST INDIAN BAPTIST CHURCH. "So," Lester Bucktail said, "what's this about Redbud?"

Tommy gave him a quick rundown on the situation, and an account of our adventures last night. "Uh huh," Lester said at the end, "I heard about Jordan getting his. Forgot Chris was a relative of yours, though. Son of a bitch." He leaned back and put his hands behind his head. "And War Party is on the scene. Well, well. That explains the story I heard about Nehemiah Harjo meeting with that bunch of college kids Chris used to run with."

He looked at Tommy. "And you really think they're planning to throw the case, so they can use Chris for some kind of martyr hero?"

"I'd bet my left nut on it."

"Hmm. Well, I'm sorry to hear Chris is in the can, anyway. Especially that one. I've been there myself." His mouth twisted briefly. "But I won't pretend I'm sorry somebody finally aced Rowland Jordan. If you say Chris didn't do it, okay, but whoever did ought to get a medal. My only regret," Lester said, "is that he wasn't pushed out a window. And that's only because I always wanted to use 'defenestration' in a headline."

"The best defenestration is a good offenestration," Tommy observed.

I said, "Tell me about Jordan."

It had suddenly come to me that I was nosing around in a

murder case without knowing a damn thing about the victim. I didn't even know what he looked like.

"He was an evil son of a bitch," Tommy said flatly. "Then the term 'vicious bastard' comes to mind—"

"Wait, wait." Lester Bucktail held up a hand. "Ease off, Tommy. Satisfying as it might be to sit here and run the dozens on the departed, that's not what this guy's after." He looked at me. "You want to know who might have wanted to snuff his reprehensible ass, right?"

"Actually," I said, "I'm not that far along in my thinking. I'd just like to have a clearer picture of the dead guy."

"Basically Rowland Jordan was your classic small-town bully-with-a-badge figure," Lester said. "Ran Sizemore County with a pretty heavy hand, and no more than a grudging token nod toward such trivia as civil rights and due process. How much of this was under orders from higher powers and how much reflected Jordan's own agenda, I can't say."

"Machine man?"

"Oh, sure. Jordan liked to pose as a maverick, beholden to nobody, but that was merely an act for the rednecks—they love a loose cannon, you know, Ross Perot got quite a few votes in eastern Oklahoma. No, Rowland Jordan was very much a trusty servitor for the people who own and run Sizemore County."

"And who are they?"

"Same kind of people who wind up running any place like that—big property owners, bankers, the guy whose construction company gets all the county contracts. It's less important who you are than who you're related to. Half a dozen families, maybe, with plenty of little medieval alliances and connections . . . nowadays, of course, you've got Hardesty Industries in the picture as well. People like Rowland Jordan, or that drunken old fool Judge Ryson, have to know who's on first and what's on second or they don't last long."

"Did Jordan have any political opponents?"

"Get serious. Sizemore County is solid Democrat at the local level. The Republicans put up a token slate at election time, but everybody knows the Democratic nominees are as good as elected. And the machine always makes sure the right people, like Jordan, get the nomination. Ain't representative democracy wonderful?"

Lester Bucktail looked off out the window. The dog was still licking away.

"Understand, I don't have any reason to believe that the county bosses involved themselves in the day-to-day operations of the sheriff's office, legit or otherwise. As long as Jordan maintained a reasonably clean public image and kept the lower orders in line, they let him have a free hand. I'd imagine they made a point of not knowing about certain things. What the CIA calls deniability."

"I bet that's why Jordan and his goons got so weird over the demonstrations at Echota Creek," Tommy remarked. "All these outsiders, news people hanging around, plenty of shitstorm potential—the big kahunas had to get down and *deal* with it, man, couldn't just sit back and trust the local constabulary to handle something that hot. Jordan must have been under a hell of a load of pressure, all those hard-eyed old bastards looking over his shoulder, ready to cut him off at the crotch if he fucked up. No wonder he got so nasty." Tommy snorted. "And then here came Chris Badwater waving a rusty tomahawk and calling Jordan a fascist pig to his face in front of the TV cameras. Christ, I can't believe the kid's still alive."

Lester Bucktail was nodding. "But don't misunderstand," he said to me. "Jordan was a bad son of a bitch and there were people who would have been glad to see him dead, but he was popular with most of the voters. His deputies might beat the shit out of some Indian who'd had a few, or plant a bag of grass on some Harley-riding drifter, but they knew when to back off. Some old boy with lots of family in the area could walk away from a drunk-driving stop with no more than a warning, even if he was pissing on his shoes."

"What about Webb Mizell?"

"Interesting," Lester said. "He—"

A deep rumbling groan from the street interrupted him. The office door opened and Billy Greenstick stuck his head in and said, "Truck's here, Lester."

"Shit. To coin an original term." Lester Bucktail stood up. "Listen, guys, I've got to get that stuff loaded up—"

"Want us to give you a hand?" Tommy asked. "Senile old fart like you, might throw your back out or something."

"No, that's okay. Got a couple of big husky Indian boys on the truck, they'll do the grunt work. I just have to sort of supervise . . . what I was going to say," he went on, "I've got a big fat file on Jordan, if you don't mind waiting till I get a chance to dig it out."

Tommy got to his feet and stretched theatrically. "Hell, Roper, why don't we go get lunch? Getting about that time."

"No need for that," Lester Bucktail protested. "Stay around till I'm free, I can fix us all something."

"Death threats will get you nowhere," Tommy told him. "Come on, Roper. Let's see if we can find an edible burger for sale in this dismal-ass town."

"Thing to remember about Lester," Tommy said a little later, over lunch, "he's trying hard to make up for lost Indian time. Jesus, is this stuff supposed to be pepperoni or what?"

We hadn't found a credible burger place; we were having pizza instead. Tahlequah seemed to have as many pizza houses as Fundamentalist churches.

"See, Lester's mother was white," Tommy went on, "and she left Lester's daddy after five or six years and went home to her folks, taking the kid with her. She was from this small town out in western Oklahoma, and the people there found it in their hearts to forgive her for the sin of marrying an Indian—since she'd finally repented—but they never forgave Lester for being half Cherokee. He was in his late teens before he finally got to come back and live with his father's family. So he doesn't speak Cherokee very well, and he's kind of self-conscious about not looking Indian enough—I guess he's into compensation, you know?"

Tommy stopped talking and chewed pizza for a little while. I hadn't been able to work up any interest in eating; I drank my Coke and looked through the tabloid Lester Bucktail had given me. It was a professional production, very clean layout and graphics, but I didn't know enough to judge the contents. Most of the stories were on various Indian issues, naturally, but there were quite a few on environmental matters too. Evidently there was a connection; according to the lead editorial, various public and private outfits had a long history of using reservations and other Indian lands as dumping grounds for toxic, radioactive, or merely nasty materials.

"It's all bogus, of course," Tommy said at last.

I looked up, startled, and he waved a hand. "No, no, I don't mean the stuff you're reading. I mean all that who's-really-Indian crap that people like Lester get hung up on. Hell, over half of the enrolled Cherokees in Oklahoma are less than half Indian. We've just about fucked ourselves white, tell you the truth."

He wiped his mouth. "Nobody else seems to worry about that sort of thing," he said. "Plenty of your alleged African Americans have ancestors that didn't come from Africa, and it doesn't seem to bother them. I see these people on TV claiming to be 'black' and they're lighter than me. For that matter, how many Jews are full-blood descendants of Abraham and Moses?"

I said, "What was that about having been in the Sizemore County jail?"

"Oh, yeah." Tommy grinned. "Old Lester has had his problems with Sheriff Jordan and the boys. Back a couple of years ago, when the environmental activists started making serious trouble over the Echota Creek plant, Lester was one of the major local voices in the movement. Printed so much heavy stuff in his paper, in fact, that the big guys got worried. Or maybe just pissed off . . . Anyway, one day last fall, Lester was driving along this country road in Sizemore County when these two deputies pulled him over. Guess what they quote found unquote in his car?"

"Dope?"

"A couple of ounces of the green, green grass of home. Lester got hauled in, spent a couple of nights in a cell—said they only roughed him up a little, whatever that means. Then they let him go." Tommy shrugged. "Very strange, that. He did have this white woman lawyer, one of his environmentalist friends, and she went down and raised a lot of probable-cause hell, but that wouldn't have been enough to get him out that fast. Not in Judge Ryson's court."

Tommy picked up the rest of his pizza and regarded it without warmth. "Do I really—no." He put the pizza back down and shuddered. "Talk about toxic waste . . . Anyway, Sheriff Jordan gave Lester a little private talking-to before letting him go. Explained that next time things would go a lot harder on him," Tommy said. "And ever since then, Lester Bucktail has stayed out of Sizemore County. He may be weird but he's not stupid."

Something came into his eyes. "Hey," he said, "you suppose they might be doing something like that to Chris?"

I thought about it. "It seems far-fetched."

"Shit. This is Oklahoma, man, everything's farfetched. Especially when you're dealing with people like that. Don't forget what happened to Karen Silkwood." He sighed. "But you're right, all the same. For one thing, I can't see any way Chris would have been worth the trouble. He wasn't any threat to Hardesty Industries or anybody else. All he contributed to the movement was a lot of embarrassment."

Tommy pushed himself away from the table and stood up. "Let's go see if Lester's done loading his damn truck."

9

❖ ❖ ❖ ❖ ❖ ❖ ❖ ❖ ❖ ❖

W HEN WE GOT BACK TO the Roadkill Publications offices Lester Bucktail was nowhere in sight. The piled-up tabloids were gone from the front room. Billy Greenstick was sitting in a folding chair, drinking Bubba Cola and reading a comic book. "Lester's upstairs," he said without looking up.

I followed Tommy up a somewhat rickety outside stairway. The upper floor, apparently, was Lester Bucktail's living quarters. He sat on a buttsprung couch, surrounded by the remains of a box of fried chicken. "Be right with you," he said, nibbling on an undersized drumstick.

His living room was an even worse shambles than mine. Empty beer cans and ragged copies of the *Eagle Feather News* littered the floor. An old television set stood against the wall facing the couch, under a tacked-up picture of Sitting Bull. The screen had been smashed in. Broken glass glittered within the dark interior of the wrecked tube.

"Oh, hell, Lester," Tommy said, looking at the demolished TV. "You went and watched Rush Limbaugh again, didn't you?"

Lester Bucktail said something indistinct around a mouthful of chicken. Tommy said, "This is, what, twice you've done this in a year. People are going to quit giving you their old television sets."

Lester raised his hands. "What can I say? Something just comes over me," he said, and gestured with the chicken bone. "It's not so much him, it's the damn studio audiences. What a bunch of dorks."

He tossed the bone at an overflowing wastebasket, missing by a foot or so. "Doesn't matter," he added. "I'd have done it pretty soon anyway. I can't get through Columbus Day without kicking in a TV screen."

"That's right," Tommy said, "it *is* getting on toward the big day, isn't it? I've lost all track of time lately."

"It's next Monday, in fact." Lester Bucktail pushed himself up off the couch. "They're having a big demonstration that day, down at the Echota Creek reactor site. Wonder if Marvin Painted Horse and his disciples plan to cut in on that action."

He looked at me. "I've got the stuff you want," he said. "Happens I brought it up here a few days ago, never did take it back down to the office. I was thinking about running a piece on Jordan and the whole situation in Sizemore County, but then I decided to wait and see what happened to Chris. Didn't want to do anything to hurt his chances. Just a second."

He went into the next room and came out holding a thick manila storage envelope. "Here you go."

It was a hefty package. I thumbed back the flap and had a quick look inside. The contents consisted mostly of newspaper clippings, but there were also some clipped-together sheets of typescript and copies of what appeared to be official documents. In the back of the file, protected by sheets of cardboard, were several large glossy black-and-white photographs.

"Look at this," Lester Bucktail said, reaching in and pulling out the photos. "Here's the late Sheriff Jordan himself, plain as life and almost as ugly."

He passed me a shiny eight-by-ten. It was a head-and-shoulders portrait, obviously professionally done; it showed a heavyset, middle-aged white man, bareheaded but wearing a dress uniform blouse. He had a big knob-ended nose like Karl Malden's, his hair was almost gone in front, and his face was a little on the jowly side; all in all he was no Paul Newman, but I wouldn't have called him ugly. On the other hand, Lester Bucktail did have cause to be prejudiced. I studied the photo and Sheriff Jordan looked back at me without any particular expression.

"Oh, hey, here we are," Lester said, waving another photograph. "This is a shot of the Jordans at home, taken in June on their silver anniversary. This kid Billy knows, works part-time at the local photo studio, he swiped this copy for us."

The picture had been taken in a living room rather than a studio, and the photographer had used a bit too much flash. Rowland Jordan, wearing a civvy suit this time, stood next to a big, expensive-looking armchair, which was occupied by a small, thin-faced woman with curly white hair. At least it looked white, though I couldn't be sure with a black-and-white photo. It was hard to guess her age; her face wore the lines of long-term pain. She stared into the camera with large serious eyes, making no attempt to match the sheriff's folksy smile.

"What's she like?" I asked.

"Emily Jordan? I've never met her," Lester Bucktail said. "People who have, though, tell me she's quite the impressive lady. I believe she was teaching English at the high school in Redbud when she met Jordan, but I may have that wrong. Very highly thought of in the community, anyway."

"Must be a hell of a fine human being," Tommy remarked, "to spend twenty-five years with that son of a bitch without killing him."

"Unless she did," I said, half to myself.

They both stared and then Lester laughed. "Appealing as the idea is, I'm afraid it's not very likely. Emily Jordan's been in a wheelchair for years, paralyzed from the waist down. And she was upstairs when the cops arrived."

Tommy nodded. "Even the local newspaper, which can't

find a pole long enough to touch the story with, mentioned that the wheelchair lift was at the bottom when the deputies came."

"Look here," Lester said, poking a finger at the picture. "See that thing on the wall, right behind the happy couple? That's the murder weapon."

I could see something dark on the wall, but it took some study to identify the shape. I said, "I'll be damned."

"Yeah. Ten gets you one Jordan made a point of having it in the picture. It was a big personal joke with him."

"What you literary types refer to as irony, I believe." Tommy made a whirling motion with his forefinger. "In the immortal words of Mickey Rooney: 'The world turns, and so does the weenie.'"

"No children?" I asked Lester Bucktail.

"Oh, sure. Two daughters, as I recall. One in her teens, still living at home. I heard something about her having to be put in an institution after her father's death, but I don't really know anything. The other one—" Lester shrugged and spread his hands. "Grown up and moved out, that's all I know, couldn't even tell you where she lives now. In fact I don't recall either of the daughters' names."

He tapped the file envelope. "If the information isn't in there, I can do some checking around. No big deal."

"Thanks." I didn't know what good it would do me to learn about the Jordan offspring, but right now I wasn't going to pass up any possible bits of information.

"Take that file with you," Lester urged. "Bring it back when you're done with it, that's all I ask. I've got other copies of all the important stuff, anyway."

I thanked him again and tucked the big envelope under my arm. "What about Webb Mizell?" I asked.

"That's right, you were asking about him earlier. Can't tell you much," Lester said. "Mizell's been Chief Deputy for maybe half a dozen years, and he's built up a reputation as a bad man to fuck with, but otherwise nobody seems to know much about him. Plays his cards very close to his chest, never has gone in for a lot of strutting and posturing like his late boss. Unmarried, no local relatives—I believe he used to be with the Virginia State Police, don't know how he wound up in Oklahoma—"

"Got caught fucking the wrong dog," Tommy offered. "In a manner of speaking."

"Probably. At any rate, he's something of a mystery figure."

"Crooked?"

"All cops are corrupt," Tommy declared. "They enforce the will of the government, and governments are inherently corrupt. Christ, just listen to me," he said in a different voice. "I sound like Marvin Painted Horse."

"I assume he's bent to some degree," Lester told me, ignoring Tommy. "He's been number-two man in a notoriously corrupt county police force for years, and Rowland Jordan wouldn't have tolerated a straight-arrow type in that position. Of course that's all extrapolation. I don't actually know any more than you do."

"And the stories about serious corruption in the Sizemore County Sheriff's Department?"

"Oh, boy. Going for the heavy stuff, are you? Rita told me you were a crazy son of a bitch." Lester Bucktail scratched his shaggy head reflectively. "Where to begin? Again, all I can tell you is what I've heard—"

Feet banged and rattled on the outside stairway. Somebody knocked on the door. A woman's voice called, "Lester?"

"Right there," Lester Bucktail shouted back, and started toward the door. "Sorry," he added over his shoulder.

Out on the landing stood a short, reasonably attractive white woman with short-bobbed dishwater-blond hair. She wore a down jacket and jeans and lug-sole hiking boots. Under one arm she carried a thick manila file envelope like the one I was holding. "Hi," she said to Lester, and then, seeing Tommy and me, "Oh, hey, bad time?"

Lester shook his head. "Come on in, Bianca. The stuff I print, I'm always glad to have a lawyer on the premises."

"Hello, Tommy," she said, entering. "Been down at Redbud? How's Chris?"

"Still out of his tiny mind. I found out who's behind his latest craziness, though."

She listened in fascination as Tommy told her about the encounter with the War Party leaders. "Wow," she said. "That answers several questions, doesn't it? You did know that I offered to defend Chris, free of charge, and he turned me down?"

She smiled suddenly. "And you really hit Nehemiah Harjo? I shouldn't say it, but congratulations."

"This guy here took out Vince Lacolle with a pool cue," Tommy told her. "Roper, say hello or something to Bianca Ford."

She came over and shook hands. "Hi," she said. "Aren't you a writer? I think Tommy mentioned you. What do you write?"

"Historical novels. Which the publishers insist on marketing as Westerns."

"Oh? I never read fiction," she said brightly. "Have you ever considered writing nonfiction?" Her eyes had taken on a certain gleam. "Because somebody ought to write a book about the Echota Creek reactor, and the things that have happened there—"

"Bianca, for God's sake," Tommy said. "Don't you ever lighten up? Bianca's an environmental lawyer," he told me, not exactly surprising the hell out of me. "One of the leading lights in the efforts to shut down the Echota Creek plant, among other worthy causes."

"I don't really know anything about the subject," I confessed. "About the nuclear-energy issue in general, or about the specific problems at the Echota Creek site. Whatever they are."

It was meant as no more than a polite way of getting loose from an unwanted trend in the conversation. I'd failed to allow, however, for the activist compulsion to pick up any available ball and run with it. Her face lit up with a look of holy joy, like a voyeur spotting an open window.

"The issues are really very simple, in this particular case," she said. "The Echota Creek plant has an incredible record of safety violations—even if you only count the ones actually documented by government inspectors, a matter of public record—and yet they keep on operating, and the authorities keep on letting them get away with no more than an occasional slap on the wrist. It's not even a question of how you feel about atomic energy and the environmental dangers associated with reactors of this type. The clear fact is that the people running this one either don't know what they're doing or don't give a damn."

"Probably some of both," Lester Bucktail said. "Hardesty Industries is basically an oil and gas outfit, has operations all over the world—Alaska, the Arab countries, even doing some exploratory work in Kazakhstan. They went into this with no real background in nuclear energy. It was like they figured, hey, fuels are fuels."

"On the other hand," Bianca Ford said, "they also have a horrible record when it comes to environmental responsibility at their other installations—oil refineries and the like—so I suppose it's not surprising that they're running this one so sloppily. Anyway . . ." She sighed. "Here," she said, handing

Lester Bucktail the envelope she was carrying. "Hope there's something in there you can use."

She looked at me again. "We're having a special Columbus Day demonstration at the Echota Creek plant entrance. That's Monday, you know," she said. "Why don't you come and join us?"

"I never try to solve the world's problems. Unless you count overpopulation," I said, "and that was only a couple of times."

Tommy made a choking sound and turned away, his shoulders shaking in what I guessed was a suppressed guffaw. Bianca Ford blinked and said, "Well, of course population *is* a major problem, but . . ." She gave me a warm, slightly gummy smile. "Come anyway. You might learn something."

Later, on the way back to Redbud, Tommy said, "So, Roper, you going to join the ranks of the Earth-savers?"

I grunted, or maybe groaned. Tommy laughed. "Yeah, Bianca's a piss-cutter, all right. I nearly shit when she said that about never reading fiction."

"It's no big deal," I said. "One of the first things you learn is that otherwise nice people will say the God-damnedest things to a writer. At least she didn't ask me if I'd ever had anything published, or tell me she always felt she could write if she only had the time. Do people say things like that to painters?"

"I don't know about other painters. Me, they always just say, 'But why are you so *angry*?' But don't think too hard of Bianca," Tommy said. "She's basically good people. Got Chris out of jail a couple of times and didn't charge a nickel. She's just trying to save the planet."

"This one or the one she's from?"

"Hey, man, I'm not denying she's a dingbat. All I'm saying,

she's okay." Tommy gave me a sly look. "Think she sort of likes you, bro."

"I had the impression she and Lester were, um, an item."

"No way. Actually Bianca's married to this professor at NSU, though I don't know how much that means. But Lester's not in circulation these days," Tommy said. "His wife left him, back last year after he got busted by Jordan's boys. Said she couldn't stand the strain any more, and moved back to New Mexico and her fine white family. Lester's still cut up bad about her."

The road swung around a gentle curve and crossed the Sizemore County line. I was expecting to be stopped or at least followed, but I didn't see any cop cars at all, all the way to Redbud.

That night I called Rita from the Moonlight Courts Motel. After a few basic pleasantries and expressions of mutual horniness, we got down to the case at hand. She listened while I gave her a short but fairly detailed account of everything that had happened since my arrival in Sizemore County. Or almost everything; I didn't tell her about the ticket, since she would certainly have insisted on paying it herself.

Hearing myself telling the story, it didn't sound like much, but at the end she said, "Thanks, Tag. I know this has been a big pain in the ass for you, but I'm glad you went."

"I haven't accomplished a damn thing so far. In fact I don't even know what I'm supposed to be *trying* to accomplish."

"Don't sell yourself short. For one thing, you've kept Tommy out of trouble—or been there beside him when you couldn't. I've seen Vince Lacolle a couple of times at demonstrations that got rough. Tommy could have been hurt."

"Actually your brother throws a pretty solid punch. I was impressed."

"He did some boxing in college." Rita chuckled suddenly. "That isn't all he throws. I imagine it's been pretty wearing for you, hanging out with him this much."

"Oh, Tommy's all right." I passed a hand across my eyes. "Sometimes his sense of humor is kind of, well, relentless."

Rita laughed out loud at that. "Tell me about it. Are you going to spend tomorrow with him, too?"

"No." Please God, I added silently. "We figured we'd split up. He's going to see what he can find out among the local Indians, thinks some of them might talk more freely without me around. Meanwhile I'll be doing some digging and poking on the white side of the street."

I hesitated. "Rita—I don't know if I'm going to stay around this place much longer. I don't see much chance of doing any good, the way it's going. This thing with Chris and these War Party people—it's not for me to involve myself in, you know that. I hate to agree with Marvin Painted Horse, but this really is an Indian thing."

She started to protest. I said, "Look, the rights and wrongs don't really matter now. The fact is that nobody is going to be able to do anything for Chris as long as he's locked into this stonewall business. And there's no way he's going to accept advice on the subject from any white man."

Rita was silent for a moment. "Are you coming home, then?" she said at last.

"I'll stick around a little while longer. Who knows, maybe Chris will come to his senses."

I looked at myself in the flyspecked mirror above the dresser. I hoped I sounded more optimistic than I looked. I sure as hell hoped I sounded more optimistic than I felt.

"I'll give it a couple more days," I told Rita. "If something hasn't happened by the end of the week, though, I've got to get back home. I hate to run out—"

"No, it's all right. You've already gone above and beyond

the call of Significant Otherhood." She cleared her throat. "I hope you're keeping track of expenses, because of course I'll pay—"

"Like *hell* you will," I said, and we argued about that for a little while. Then we did some apologizing, and made some more affectionate noises, and finally said good-bye. I told her I'd call again in a day or so.

After I'd hung up the old dial-face phone I sat down on the bed and got out the file Lester Bucktail had lent me. Most of the material seemed to be related to the late sheriff's handling of the Echota Creek demonstrations. If I'd actually been working on a book, it might have been very valuable. As it was, I couldn't see how any of it was likely to do me much good. I closed the file and laid it aside, resolving to give the contents a closer look tomorrow evening.

I got out the Hohner and played a few bars of "Almost Blue," but for some reason I couldn't get in the mood. Finally I put the mouth harp away and stretched out on the bed with Jim Beam. Jim didn't have much to say that I hadn't heard before, but as always he was a lot better company than none.

10

♦ ♦ ♦ ♦ ♦ ♦ ♦ ♦ ♦ ♦

I SPENT MOST OF THE next day basically making a God-damned fool of myself. That may be a harsh way to characterize my efforts, but I can't think of a kinder way to put it.

I mean, it was *humiliating*. All right, I'd never claimed to be a real investigator; genuine detective work is a highly specialized job, requiring serious training, and the "amateur sleuth" of popular fiction is a severely improbable figure. Still, I used to be a professional journalist, and I'd done my share of probing and questioning, often in search of facts that people didn't want me to have. And had once considered myself pretty good at it; but this time I couldn't even find a place to start prying. The entire town of Redbud simply closed a collective door in my face. I felt like the Avon rep in an Amish community.

First stop was the courthouse. That didn't take long; Gerald disposed of me with remarkable efficiency.

"You can't see the prisoner," he said before I could even speak. "And that don't come from me or the boss, either. We got a request in writing from the boy. He don't want to have no visitors except that Indian lawyer of his. He come up with that on his own, after you and your buddy left here."

I told Gerald I wasn't there to see Chris Badwater. When I asked to see Acting Sheriff Mizell, however, he was just as definite. "Webb ain't here," he said, "but he already said to tell you he wasn't available for no interview. And all the deppities got our orders, so don't go asking *me* no questions."

He glanced nervously over his shoulder. "And don't try

shoving no money at me," he added in a near whisper. "You got me in trouble already. However much you figured on offering, it ain't enough."

The prosecutor's office wasn't any friendlier. I never got past the blue-haired secretary, who returned very quickly from the inner office and told me that Mr. Stinson couldn't possibly discuss an ongoing criminal case, especially with a member of the press. I could leave a number where I could be reached, and if any sort of public statement should be issued, or if Mr. Stinson should hold a press conference, I would certainly be notified.

I told her where I was staying and she asked me, a bit snippily, if I knew the number there. Maybe she thought I was suggesting that she might be personally familiar with the Moonlight Courts Motel. I could have told her that it had never occurred to me that anyone might ever have taken her to a motel, but somehow I didn't think she'd appreciate the thought. People like that can be unreasonably touchy sometimes.

The Sizemore County *Democrat* was published only a block from the courthouse, in a small glass-fronted brick building that it shared with a realtor's office. The editor was delighted to talk with the distinguished writer from the big city, although I got the feeling he was even more impressed by my having worked for the *Courier*. He wanted to know how long I'd be in town and whether I'd be making any public appearances. Perhaps I had a copy of my latest book? The *Democrat* would certainly love to run a review, perhaps accompanied by an interview with the author. . . .

When I tried to get the conversation off me and onto the recent murder, however, he became much less enthusiastic. "We're not a big newspaper, like you're used to, Mr. Roper," he said a little wistfully. "Merely a small country weekly, with most of our stories pretty tame—farm and church news, weddings, local election results, that sort of thing. A murder case is way over our heads."

He gave me a copy of the latest edition. "Everything we know about the murder of Sheriff Jordan," he said, "is in these pages. I'm sorry we can't be more helpful, Mr. Roper."

I'd finally realized that he was employing the editorial "we"; if the Sizemore County *Democrat* had any full-time reporters, let alone lower-ranking editorial staff, they weren't in evidence in the tiny office.

I tried to suggest that sometimes there were things a journalist knew but couldn't print; we both knew that. My implication of professional brotherhood went down well, but he shook his head decisively. "It's all there," he said, tapping the folded newspaper with a fingertip. "Of course, if anything should develop—"

He was a small, balding, harassed-looking man, about my age and not wearing it well. When I told him I was staying at the Moonlight Courts Motel, though, a strange reflective smile spread across his face, as if I'd triggered some warm memory. I left him sitting there at his desk, staring out the window at the sunlit street, smiling at his own inner visions.

I stopped at Donna's Café and drank a cup of coffee while I read the *Democrat*'s account of the case. As I'd expected, it was a skimpy and superficial piece, giving only the bare outline of events and quoting heavily from official sources. No mention was made of any political or racial angle; even the fact that Sheriff Jordan had confiscated the tomahawk from Chris Badwater at a demonstration, presumably a key element in the prosecution's case, was skimmed over in a hurried way. The whole story had an embarrassed air about it, as if nobody wanted to think about such events happening here. It was like a very proper middle-class family discussing Uncle Talbot who likes to take his thing out and show it to people on the street.

The waitress saw what I was reading. "Poor Sheriff Jordan," she said as I refilled my cup. "And that poor wife of his, too, all crippled up and in a wheelchair, and now she's all alone besides. I could just cry, thinking about it."

I hadn't asked for the refill or the commentary either, but I wasn't turning anything down today. She was incredibly fat, with small delicate features and a little rosebud mouth in the middle of a face like a custard pie. Her voice resembled the sound of a chainsaw hitting a nail, but her expression was friendly enough.

"Sheriff Jordan used to come in here every day for lunch," she said proudly, "and he wouldn't let anybody but me wait on him. I don't care what anybody says, that was one fine man. He sure made that worthless ex-husband of mine leave me alone."

She glanced down at the paper I was holding. "I hope they give that Indian the electric chair or whatever they do to them. Now don't take that the wrong way," she added quickly. "I've got some Cherokee blood myself. But that boy ought to have to pay for what he did. I'd say the same if he was white."

She nodded, as if agreeing with herself, and turned and waddled away, emphasizing the strength of her feelings with each swing of her mighty haunches. I drank my coffee and left a bigger tip than the tab justified. She was, after all, the first person in Redbud who'd shown any willingness to talk to me about the murder.

From there on the day went downhill.

The middle-aged woman at the little regional library said, "You won't find many local people willing to discuss this subject, Mr. Roper. It's all very unfortunate for the image this community is trying to maintain." She shuffled a stack of due-date cards, not looking at me. She had a tight closed-up face and a jerky, forceful way of moving that suggested she would best be reincarnated as a stapler. "Some of us would like to put this town on the map," she added, "but not this way." She turned and walked away between the stacks without waiting for any further questions from me. On the way out I sneaked a look at the card catalog to see if they had any of my books. They didn't.

Other responses were less elegant. There was the cowboy-shirted young man, sitting at a bar where I stopped for a beer, who somehow got it into his jug-eared head that I was "one of those environ-meddlers," and was obviously working up to taking a punch at me when the bartender made him leave. The bartender wouldn't talk to me, though. "I mind my own business," he said. "Be a good idea for you to do the same. That'll be a dollar twenty-five, and I'd appreciate it if you wouldn't come in here any more."

Small-town barbershops are supposed to be centers of gossip, and the barbers repositories of all sorts of information; I went into the little barbershop across from the courthouse square and sat down to wait, willing to accept an unnecessary trim if it would get me anywhere. There was only one barber on duty, and a tall bony-faced man was occupying the chair. When I dropped a couple of casual remarks about the murder the bony-faced man said, "Hit was up to me, they'da hung that Indin a long time ago. Come down here trying to make trouble, close up the place where people work and take food outa their children's mouths, I say that's jist as bad as murder." He glared at me as if defying me to disagree. "Commanists," he added. "Oughta all be shot."

The barber said, "Well, it's going to get worse, with this administration." He began talking about why he'd voted for

Ross Perot and I couldn't get him back onto the Jordan killing. When I left the shop untrimmed, having suddenly remembered an urgent appointment elsewhere, he was going on about how he couldn't stand Hillary Clinton.

That afternoon I drove out to the Jordan home.

As Tommy had said, the eastern end of Redbud had experienced rapid and unsightly growth; the original business district had been eclipsed by a half-mile stretch of big slick operations with multistate affiliations. There was a Wal-Mart, a Food-4-Less supermarket, and a block of smaller businesses such as Radio Shack and Sooner State Optical, as well as a selection of fast-food franchises.

It was all raw-looking and new. You didn't have to be a trained economic analyst to figure out the implications: something had suddenly pumped a lot of money into this community, and the obvious something was the Echota Creek plant. No wonder the locals were so pissed off at people like Bianca Ford and Chris Badwater; in their place I imagined I'd have felt the same.

Out beyond the shopping-and-eating area, on the north side of the highway as it headed off toward Sallisaw, was a tract of newish, surprisingly attractive homes. This was no jammed-up ticky-tacky housing development; the houses were fairly large, some with two stories, and spaced well apart along winding lanes with the best pavement I'd seen in Sizemore County.

Sheriff Jordan's place was located at the tip of a meandering dead end named Lynn Lane. Every town between Amarillo and the Mississippi has a Lynn Lane; only God knows why, or cares. The house was a big two-story frame structure, painted a pleasant shade of grayish blue, with a two-car garage and a black iron fence around a front yard big enough for a putt-putt golf course. The fancy wooden sign beside the gate had a large gilt star, presumably meant to represent a badge, above the name JORDAN.

I sat in the Camaro for a few minutes, looking at the house, and finally got out and walked toward the gate. The yard appeared to be empty of anything more aggressive than rosebushes, but I stopped and listened with my hand on the gate, and all the way up the front walk I kept my peripheral vision and hearing tuned up to maximum sensitivity. People like the late Sheriff Jordan, in my experience, often have a fondness for large, socially hostile dogs, of the kind associated with riot police and concentration camps. This had been a bad enough day without an encounter with a couple of charging Rottweilers.

But nothing barked or moved, and I stepped up on the small porch and took a deep breath and pushed the doorbell button. There was a sound of three-tone chimes inside. I leaned against the door frame with one hand, wishing I'd worn a better-looking tie, and half-hoping nobody was home.

The door opened, though, after only a few seconds' wait. A dark-skinned, black-haired, plump-faced young woman gazed out at me. I took her for an Indian, but then she said, "Jes?"

I told her I was there to see Emily Jordan. I handed her my press card and she studied it with fascinated incomprehension. "Joo wait, pleass," she said carefully, and disappeared into the interior of the house. After a few minutes she was back in the doorway, looking even more dubious than before. "Joo come, pleass," she said, and stepped back and held the door open for me.

I followed her down a spacious high-ceilinged hallway. The floor was polished hardwood and the walls were hung with too many framed pictures, mostly Frederick Remington reproductions. At the end of the hall was a long single-rise stairway of dark wood. Alongside the regular staircase ran a shiny metal arrangement that I guessed must be Emily Jordan's wheelchair lift.

The maid, or whatever she was, stopped and turned and made a gesture toward an open double doorway. I went where she pointed and found myself in a big, well-lit, attractively furnished living room. It had to be the room in the photograph Lester Bucktail had shown me, though I couldn't really tell at first.

I wasn't looking at the room anyway. I was more interested in the white-haired woman who sat facing the doorway, studying me with large, faintly disturbing blue eyes. She looked even smaller and frailer than she had in the picture, and her thin pale face bore the marks of recent stress on top of the long-term pain lines. She sat in a high-tech motorized wheelchair that made her look even smaller. She wore a dark blue sweater, buttoned clear up to the throat. A multicolored knitted afghan covered her lap and legs.

"Mr. Roper?" Her voice was steady and clear; you could almost have called it musical. She held my press card between thumb and forefinger with an air of distaste, as if somebody had handed her a ticket to a porn movie. "May I ask what newspaper you represent?"

I stepped forward and assumed a respectful posture. It wasn't difficult; she gave off a certain aura that would have had me clutching my hat in both hands, if I'd had one. Somehow I found myself thinking of her as an old and saintly figure, even though I knew she couldn't possibly be more than five or ten years older than me.

I said, "I'm not working for any publication now, Mrs. Jordan." A minor judgment call, there, but that "Ms." business hasn't yet caught on in places like Redbud, especially with people like Emily Jordan. "I write books, ma'am. Right now I'm studying the possibilities of writing one about . . . your husband's unfortunate death." I made an apologetic gesture. "I realize it's very hard for you, so soon—"

"No." She said the word without raising her voice, but with flat and absolute finality. "No," she said again.

I said, "Ah, pardon me—"

"No, I won't discuss my husband's murder with you," Emily Jordan said. "I don't want to talk with you at all. Please go away."

She held out my press card. As I took it from the pale thin fingers she said in a slightly softer voice, "Please don't take this as a personal affront, Mr. Roper. I've already given the same response to other members of the press, as well as a television crew from Tulsa. I simply do not want to share this dreadful experience with the curious public. As for helping you or anyone else make money from some lurid book—" She made a face that showed what she thought of that.

I said, "I'm sorry to have intruded."

She waved a hand impatiently. "I assume there will be a trial," she said, "and I suppose I will be called upon to give testimony. You and your colleagues will be able to get whatever you need from the trial transcript. Until then—" She tapped a small, surprisingly loud bell on the armrest of her wheelchair, and the maid reappeared in the doorway. "Inez, please show Mr. Roper out."

It was only about three-thirty when I drove away from the Jordan home and headed back toward downtown Redbud. All the same, I hung a left at the first light and pointed the Camaro toward the Moonlight Courts Motel without pausing to think about it. The whole day had been a waste, as far as I could see; but that last bit, that terrible and humbling encounter with Emily Jordan, had finished me off. At the moment I couldn't have asked anyone the time of day.

Back at the motel, I took a long shower and stretched out bare-assed on the bed for a little while, staring at the ceiling and thinking as little as possible. It was one of those times that made me wish I knew some sort of meditative discipline, yoga or something, that would let me take a wet sponge to the scrawled-up blackboard of my mind.

At last I sat up and got out the file envelope again and spent a couple of hours going over the material Lester Bucktail had assembled. As I'd expected, most of the newspaper clippings dealt with the demonstrations at the Echota Creek nuclear plant, and the behavior of the Sizemore County Sheriff's Department, and Jordan in particular, toward the demonstrators. It was interesting enough, and seemed to confirm what Lester and Tommy had said about the departed sheriff's personal and professional shortcomings, but I'd been right in the first place: it wasn't of any value to me now. I did spend some time looking at that photo of the Jordans, matching the pictorial background to the room I'd seen that afternoon—it was the same place, all right—and matching the calm sad face in the photo to the one that had looked at me with so little warmth.

I put everything back in the envelope, got into my other suit, and drove into town. Donna's Café was still open, though the fat waitress wasn't around. I ordered the special—chicken-fried steak, not as bad as it sounds, with green peas and mashed potatoes and a slice of apple pie—and ate at a table by the window, watching the daylight die along Redbud's main street.

It was dark by the time I left the café. I sat in the parked Camaro for a few minutes, wondering what to do next. For want of a more useful agenda, I decided to go pick up some beer. There was plenty of Jim Beam left, but I like a chaser.

Oklahoma has many strange and irrational laws concerning the sale of alcoholic drinks, one of which is that you can't buy cold beer at a liquor store, only at a grocery or convenience store. I found a little one-stop and bought a six-pack of Michelob, and put a few gallons of dubious gas in the tank while I was there.

Driving away, turning up the road toward the motel, I noticed a pair of headlights in my mirror, but I didn't pay much attention until the blue and red flashers came on above them. There was a short piercing *wheeoop* from a siren and I said, "Shit," and pulled off the road, onto the concrete apron of a darkened Kerr-McGee station.

An amplified voice said, "STEP OUT OF THE CAR, PLEASE."

I opened the door and got out, keeping my hands in plain sight. The headlights of the cop car were blinding; I could barely make out the outlines of the two men who climbed out and came walking toward me. From their relative sizes, though, I was pretty sure I knew who they were.

The shorter one said, "Want to get out your license and show it to us?" Tovin's voice, all right; no mistaking that tight-assed monotone.

I pulled out my wallet and handed over my license. From back by the rear of the Camaro, Pace's deep voice said, "You know you got a broken taillight?"

"Oh?" I tried to keep my own voice steady, but it wasn't easy. "Which one?"

There was a sudden small crashing sound. Things tinkled and rattled to the ground and the left taillight went out. "That one," Pace said. "Violation of the vehicle code there, buddy. Have to write you up."

A flashlight snapped on in his left hand. He aimed the beam at my face and I shut my eyes against the painful light. "Looking at you," he said, "I'd say you appear to be under the influence of alcohol or possibly drugs. Better have a look inside this vehicle."

He pointed the light into the Camaro's open door, while I blinked and resisted an impulse to rub my eyes. "Well, well," he said, and reached in and dragged out the six-pack. "Looks like you got an open container of liquor in your car."

"It's not open," I said.

Pace laughed. "Why, yes it is," he said. "See, you're so drunk you don't even know."

He yanked a bottle of Michelob from the six-pack and smashed the neck against the Camaro's door. Beer and glass flew everywhere. Deliberately, Pace turned and swung the bottle up and down in a quick arc, splattering me with beer. "You smell like a God-damned brewery, in fact," he said. "Don't he, Tovin?"

"No doubt about it," Tovin agreed.

Pace dropped the broken bottle and set the rest of the six-pack carefully on the Camaro's fender. "Let's see," he said, "we got a vehicle code violation, we got an open container, we got driving under the influence. What else?"

He switched the flashlight off and hung it on his belt. Then he took a step forward and hit me in the stomach with his fist.

Half-blinded, I didn't see the punch coming, but I don't suppose that would have made any difference. My midsection exploded in red pain and I doubled up and fell against the car, fighting for air.

"Resisting arrest," Pace said dreamily. "That's what I was forgetting. You see this man resist arrest, Tovin?"

"Sure did," Tovin said. "Looks like he's still doing it, too."

"By God, you're right." Pace's big left hand grabbed me by the throat and jerked me semi-upright. "Thanks for the warning," he said, and hit me again in the gut with his right.

He let me go and I fell across the Camaro's fender, knocking the six-pack to the ground with a crash of splintering glass. "Son of a bitch," Pace said. By now his voice was coming to me through a haze of pain, sounding oddly distorted, very loud and yet far away. "You see him attack me with that weapon, Tovin?"

Tovin said something I couldn't understand. Pace clubbed me across the small of my back with the back of his fist. I jerked upward in agony and he laughed and kicked my feet out from under me. When I was on the ground they both stood over me and kicked me a little, and then they handcuffed me and dragged me to the patrol car and dumped me in the back seat. "Watch your head," Pace said mockingly. "We don't want you to get hurt, do we?"

I spent the next little while in a state of semiconsciousness, mind and senses temporarily swamped by the waves of pain and nausea that racked my body. My next clear awareness was of being half-dragged, half-carried down the steps of the Sizemore County jail, while Tovin called out, "Hey, chief, we got some company for you."

They threw me into a cell, making sure I hit the concrete floor hard, and I heard the door clang shut behind me. When they were gone I climbed up onto the iron bed, which seemed to have been mounted several hundred feet above the floor, and lay there clutching my throbbing stomach. There were other parts of me that hurt just as bad, but that was the easiest to reach.

From down at the other end of the cell block Chris Badwater called, "Hey, whitey, they got you too, huh?"

I tried to speak but nothing would come out.

"Man," he said, "so you're the hotshot big-city *yoneg* who was going to help get me out of here? Looks like you can't even help yourself."

He chuckled. "You better get out of this town, man. You

fuck with these bastards, sooner or later they find a way to fuck back. Take it from me."

He fell silent. Later that night, when I got my wind back, I tried to talk with him, but he wouldn't even speak to me. Well, I wasn't in much of a conversational mood anyway.

11

THE LIGHTS BURNED ALL night in the cell block. I took off my jacket and put it over my face but it didn't make any real difference. I hurt too bad in too many places to do much sleeping.

In the morning Gerald brought a foam cup of bitter black coffee and a plastic bowl of gray mucouslike stuff that must have been oatmeal. He wouldn't talk to me either. I drank the coffee, flushed the mush down the toilet, and handed the bowl and the plastic spoon back to Gerald when he returned.

Then there was nothing to do but lie there on the bed, wishing I still smoked, until at last Acting Sheriff Webb Mizell appeared on the stairs and said, "Roper. I need to have a word with you."

He came down and unlocked the cell door, while I got stiffly to my feet and picked up my rumpled suit jacket. I tried to tell myself that if there was any more rough stuff I was going to do some hitting of my own, but the pain of every movement mocked my heroic illusions. I couldn't have thumb-wrestled Pee Wee Herman.

But Mizell merely held the door open and said, "Let's go up to my office," and followed me up the stairs without making any threatening moves.

In his office—Jordan's, actually; the name was still on the door—he waved me to a chair and seated himself behind the desk. "Well, Roper," he said, "we just keep on having problems, don't we?"

"Problems," I said. My voice came out sounding funny; my

stomach hurt when I talked. "That's what you call getting beaten up by that oversized sociopath? Did he and his piss-ant partner work me over on their own, or was that your idea?"

He raised his eyebrows. "According to the report I have," he said, "you were stopped for a broken taillight, turned out to be driving under the influence of alcohol, and attacked the deputies with a broken beer bottle when they tried to arrest you. Under those circumstances, the force used doesn't seem excessive."

He leaned forward and folded his hands and rested his elbows on the desk. "Having said that," he went on, "I'm willing to concede that my two officers may not have handled the matter in the best possible way. Tovin was probably tired and edgy—he's been working a lot of extra hours, trying to pay for an expensive four-wheel-drive pickup truck with a lot of accessories—" Mizell's full lips twitched. "I'll never understand what people like Tovin see in those vehicles. To me, a pickup truck is a piece of farm equipment, but Tovin is as obsessed by the damn thing as a nigger pimp with a new Cadillac. As for Pace—"

"Pace likes to hurt people," I said.

"Perhaps." He shrugged. "Not necessarily an undesirable quality in a law enforcement officer. Men like Pace have their uses, Roper. As I'm sure you know."

He stared at me with those strange, flat, pale eyes. "I've been doing a little checking, Roper. Some people I know in the Tulsa area tell me you're a genuine pro writer, not just some hack freelancing for the scandal sheets. They also say that you worked the police beat for the *Courier* for years, and that you're a man of sense and—um—discretion."

I wondered which cops he'd talked to. Nice to know I was still remembered so kindly by Wiley Harmon's colleagues. For long-term gratitude, give me a crooked cop every time; they'll remember a favor forever. The straight-arrow crimefighter types, the ones with the Elliot Ness complexes, will dump you five seconds after they've gotten what they wanted out of you.

Mizell said, "I'm afraid I may bear some of the responsibility for last night's misunderstanding. There were reports that you had been asking questions around town, making a nuisance of yourself. When Sheriff Jordan's widow called and said you'd been to see her, well—"

He grimaced. "I suppose I made a few careless remarks, in a moment of annoyance. And Pace and Tovin may have overheard, and overreacted."

I said, "You realize I can sue your department cross-eyed for this."

"You have that right," Mizell said, nodding. "Of course, I'd be forced to back my men all the way. It would be your word against theirs—I don't know if there were any witnesses, but I don't think you'd have much luck finding any local people willing to testify against Pace. And the court here tends to be most supportive of the officers of this department."

It didn't matter; I'd just been rattling his cage. When the time came to square accounts with Pace and Tovin, I wouldn't be doing it in a courtroom.

"On the other hand," Mizell continued smoothly, "if you're prepared to be reasonable, so am I. There's no reason these charges against you can't be dropped. In fact they needn't go on record at all."

He gave me that microscopic smile again. "Tell you what. If you're so interested in the Jordan murder case, I can let you see a little of the material in our file. Of course there are things we can't show to anyone, since the case still hasn't gone to trial, but I think this department can stretch a point and make some basic information available to a recognized author like yourself."

What the hell? I said, "Why the turnaround, Mizell? Monday you ran me out of here, yesterday you wouldn't talk to me, last night your tame ape beat me up and busted me on phony charges—which he wouldn't have done if he hadn't had reason to think it was what you wanted. Now all of a sudden you're Mr. Sunshine. What goes on?"

"Just trying to do a little fence mending, Roper," Mizell said blandly. "Wouldn't want you forming the wrong opinion of our county, after all. No telling what you might go off and write about us . . . and we certainly don't want you getting the idea we've got things to hide."

"Perish the thought," I said dryly.

"Look," he said, "I'm making a legitimate offer here. If you want to see that material, I'll tell Gerald to give you all necessary cooperation. If not—" He shrugged. "It's up to you, Roper."

I stood up, not very briskly. "I'll need to go clean up and change clothes first."

"Your car's parked in back of the courthouse. Gerald will give you your keys and other personal effects. You'll find there's nothing missing," he said. "If you do find any—ah—discrepancies, let me know."

As I started for the door he said, "Oh, and Roper? You need to get that taillight fixed."

At the desk Gerald gave me back my possessions, such as they were. Mizell had been telling the truth about one thing, anyway; the cash was still in my wallet, and everything else was there, even the small change from my pockets. My watch had been smashed, presumably in the course of the beating, but Gerald handed me the remains anyway.

I drove back to the motel and stood under a hot shower for a long time, trying to soak some of the soreness away. Looking at my nude self in the mirror, I couldn't see a great deal of obvious damage; Pace had been careful not to touch my face or leave any marks except a few dark bruises on my body.

I got into my other suit, wincing every time I had to bend over, and ran a comb through my damp hair. The bottle of Jim Beam sat on the tottering nightstand, and I picked it up and thought about having a drink on general principles, but after a minute I set the bottle back down, unopened, and headed for the door. Whatever was waiting for me at the Sizemore County Courthouse, I needed a clear head. Of course, I reflected as I fired up the Camaro, if I'd had a clear head to begin with I wouldn't *be* here, but. . . .

In any event, and to my considerable surprise, Webb Mizell proved as good as his word. I wound up spending the rest of the morning at a desk in the Sheriff's Department offices, reading various bits of official paperwork that Gerald dutifully brought in and laid before me.

Most of the information I already had; some of the details were new to me but not particularly surprising or revelatory. But then I'd never expected to be shown any serious prosecution hole cards. I hadn't expected to get to see even this much. And some of the material would have been difficult and expensive to get a look at even back when I'd been a legit journalist working my own territory.

Sheriff Rowland P. Jordan—I never did find out what the "P" stood for—had, as Rita had already told me, made his exit from the world's stage on the evening of September Twenty-fifth, probably between nine-thirty and eleven. Cause of death had been massive blood loss from a severed carotid artery. From an examination of the fatal wound, and other evidence, the medical examiner had concluded that the primary cause of death had been a blow to the side of the neck with the sharp blade of a tomahawk (described for some reason as a "Native American–style war axe"), specifically the one that had been lying beside the deceased at the time the investigating officer first observed the crime scene.

The medical examiner gave as his opinion, but was unwilling to state with certainty, that the blow had been delivered from in front. The body had been lying on the floor close to a couch, but the dispersal of blood suggested that there had been a certain amount of movement, some of it quite vigorous, by the victim following the blow. Since death must have been very rapid, though not instantaneous, the medical examiner believed that the movement had resulted chiefly from involuntary muscle spasms, possibly continuing for several seconds after clinical death. For these reasons it was impossible to determine exactly where the victim had been, or whether he had been standing or seated, at the time the blow was delivered.

I closed my eyes for a second, trying to get rid of a sudden unbidden memory from a boyhood visit to my grandfather's Kansas farm: an axed chicken flopping headless about the yard, blood gouting and splattering, leaving red trails in the grass, while my grandfather stood patiently waiting for the poor damn thing to stop moving. . . .

I skimmed over the rest of the medical examiner's report, swallowing hard several times and wishing I'd eaten something besides jailhouse gruel. There had been no other marks on the body, which seemed a little odd; usually, with a chopping or slashing attack from in front, you get at least a few nicks on the hands and arms where the victim tried to fend off the weapon.

Deceased had ingested a quantity of alcohol not long before death, estimated to have been enough to qualify Jordan as legally intoxicated for driving purposes but not sufficient to cause unconsciousness or stupor. Tests showed no sign of drugs or of sexually transmitted diseases. Victim had hemorrhoids. So it goes: work hard all your life getting ahead in your chosen field, master the skills of political survival and build yourself up a little boondock empire, and then at the end you wind up on a table with a stranger peering up your ass.

I wasn't shown any pictures of the murder scene, but Gerald did bring me an eight-by-ten of the weapon itself. Sheriff Jordan hadn't been killed by any souvenir-shop wall-hanger; this was a serious piece of social hardware. The head was massive, with a wide blade opposite the small pipe bowl, and the handle—or stem, if you thought of it as a pipe—was a thick piece of dark wood that a man could get a solid grip on. The gray iron bore the clear marks of some long-dead smith's hammer, though much of the blade was covered with black dried blood. The handle had been ornamented with brass tacks, and a heart-shaped brass inlay had been set into the flat of the blade.

I wondered if this was the first time it had killed a man.

There were also several news photos showing Chris Badwater brandishing a similar tomahawk—the damn fool had actually posed for a close-up with it, looking very pleased with himself—and one showing Sheriff Jordan displaying the weapon after he'd confiscated it from Chris. There was even a print of the same anniversary photo Lester Bucktail had shown me; the shape of the tomahawk on the wall had been circled with a felt-tipped marker. And there was a notarized statement from some authoritative-sounding character, on letterhead stationery from the Gilcrease Museum, stating that this was a unique design, clearly handmade rather than a piece of mass-produced trade goods, and that the chances of there being two identical pipe tomahawks of this pattern would be virtually zero. I wondered who'd taken the trouble to obtain that particular bit of evidentiary overkill.

I pushed the pictures away and sat back and yawned. The clock above the door said it was twelve-thirty. Time for a break. I called Gerald and told him I was through with this batch and that I'd be back in a little while. "Sure," he said. He'd started speaking to me again, now that it was okay with his boss. "Going to Donna's? They got some good chicken today."

I thanked him and left. Going down the back steps of the courthouse, I saw Deputy Tovin in the parking area, dismounting from an eye-hurting new red pickup with oversized all-terrain tires and lots of add-on accessories. He looked my way as I walked to the Camaro, but he didn't say anything.

When I got back to the courthouse Webb Mizell had another surprise for me. He said, "Roper, you still want to talk with the widow Jordan?"

I stared at him, wondering if this was the lead-in to another of his head games, but he stood there in his office doorway and folded his arms and chuckled in an almost friendly way. "I understand she wasn't very forthcoming yesterday afternoon. If you'd like to try again, however, she's prepared to give you a short interview. I just got through talking to her on the phone."

"You set this up?" I didn't bother to try to mask the suspicion in my voice or face. "Why?"

"What I told you before, Roper. We'd hate for you to go away with the impression that people around here are hiding something. God knows what you might write, or how many of your more persistent colleagues might show up here and drive us all crazy."

He unfolded his arms and hooked his right thumb in his pistol belt. "Of course there'll be certain restrictions," he added. "Mrs. Jordan already understands which items aren't to be discussed prior to the trial. And I imagine there are areas she won't want to get into for personal reasons. I assume you've got sense enough to know when to back off."

I said, "When does this meeting take place?"

"This afternoon," he said. "Unless you've got other plans."

I thanked him and he gave me an ironic little forefinger salute. "Just part of the job, Roper. Press and community relations, and all. You and Emily have a nice visit, now."

Emily Jordan said, "I owe you an apology for yesterday, Mr. Roper."

We were in her living room again: she in her wheelchair, I on the big black couch. The couch looked and felt store-new, as did the thick white carpet under my feet. It wasn't hard to figure why, not with that medical examiner's report fresh in my memory.

"It's difficult for me to talk with a stranger about this," she went on. "My family were Arkansas mountain people. I was brought up to believe that personal pain and tragedy should be discussed, if at all, only with blood kin."

She did have a distinct Ozark accent, with the tight intonation and odd trochaic rhythm of the hill country. Her speech was that of an educated person, though, and she chose her words and framed her statements with deliberate care. Yesterday I'd thought she was being stiffly formal as a way of putting me in my place. Now, though, I realized this was simply her style. It gave her speech a pleasantly old-fashioned flavor; maybe it was one reason I kept thinking of her as older than she was.

"I watch television and read magazines, Mr. Roper. I'm very aware of the modern compulsion to expose all the details of people's lives. When you came here yesterday, my instinctive reaction was to have nothing to do with you." She sighed, a small wispy sound in the big quiet room. "However, Deputy Mizell was most persuasive. . . ."

She lifted a bone-china hand from her afghan-covered lap and touched the armrest of her wheelchair. "I've been restricted to this . . . device, Mr. Roper, for the last decade of my life. A spinal injury, if you're curious, caused by a fall on the stairway." Her lips tightened. "And it's not merely a question of paralysis. There is also persistent pain, sometimes very intense."

She turned her head a few degrees and looked past me, her eyes going out of focus. "On the night of September twenty-fifth, the pain was so severe that I reluctantly took one of the tablets my doctor prescribes for me. I don't like to take them, because they almost always make me sleepy, and that was what happened that evening. At about nine-thirty I decided to go to bed. My husband carried me upstairs."

"Carried?"

"Literally. And yes, I do have an electric lift for getting from floor to floor, but it was something he occasionally liked to do. He was a physically powerful man, even though he was fifty-seven years old. Perhaps picking me up like that made him feel younger."

She stopped. She seemed to be having a little difficulty keeping her voice steady. After a moment she said, "The drug took effect quickly and I fell asleep. Some time later I was awakened by a great deal of noise downstairs. I could hear my husband shouting, sounding angry. There was also a second man's voice, not as loud. I couldn't recognize any words. You understand," she added, "I was still disoriented from the effects of the medication. Before I had quite come to myself, so to speak, the scuffling and shouting stopped. A moment later I heard the front door open and close."

Her face was calm; she might have been describing a meeting of the church bake-sale committee.

"I called out several times," she said, "and when there was no answer I used the bedside telephone to call the sheriff's office. I believe you know what the deputies found when they arrived."

"Do you recall who came?"

"Pace and Tovin. But they immediately called Chief Deputy Mizell, who came and took personal charge of the investigation."

"You were alone in the house? You and your husband, I mean."

"Yes. Inez only comes in during t`.e day. We had no live-in help, if that's what you're asking."

"I understood there was a daughter living at home."

"Oh, yes, of course. Our daughter Felicia was on an overnight trip to Oklahoma City with a church youth group. Thank God," she said. "If you were about to ask to see her, Mr. Roper, she is staying with relatives in Arkansas. The shock of her father's death was very severe. I thought it best to get her out of this house for a time."

"And I believe you have an older daughter?"

"My daughter Paula has not lived here for several years," Emily Jordan said crisply, "and was not here on the night in question, and will not be a topic of our conversation."

She let that settle into place and then she said, "Certain other questions may have occurred to you, so I will save you the social awkwardness of asking them. The wheelchair lift was at the bottom position when the deputies arrived. My wheelchair was still in this room. I made sure all this went into the initial report, even though Chief Deputy Mizell assured me that I was in no way under suspicion, so these facts are a matter of record."

So much for that; and she was right, I *had* been wondering. I said, "Were you personally acquainted with Chris Badwater?"

She gave me a quick fierce look. "Mr. Roper, I agreed to tell you about the events of that night from my own perspective. I think I've done so. I don't intend to let myself be drawn into discussions of such matters as the guilt or innocence of the accused. If you have questions along those lines, you might take them up with the prosecutor." Her face told me what she thought of my chances.

"And I believe this concludes our interview," she said, and hit the bell on her armrest. "Inez will show you out. Good day, Mr. Roper."

Inez appeared in the doorway and I got up and started toward her, while Emily Jordan pivoted her wheelchair smartly about and rolled over to the long windows at the far end of the room, where she stopped and sat staring out at the sunlit yard. Her shoulders were very straight.

Heading for the doorway, I noticed a couple of brass hooks set in the wall, a little above eye level. They weren't supporting anything that I could see. It occurred to me that they might have been employed, up until quite recently, in holding a certain pipe tomahawk. The spacing seemed about right, anyway.

I didn't ask Emily Jordan about that, though. As she'd said, the conversation was clearly over. I followed Inez back up the hallway to the front door. *"Adiós, mi corazón,"* I told her, and walked out into the afternoon sun.

12

••••••••••

TOMMY NINEKILLER SAID, "He *carried* her up the stairs?"

We were sitting at a table in Charlie's Foxhole. It was about eight, by my best guess; I still hadn't replaced my broken watch, and the beer-promo clock above the bar wasn't working. The place was almost deserted. At the end of the room Louise the waitress was shooting rotation pool with a large dark fellow in a checkered shirt and a Marine fatigue cap. I couldn't tell who was winning.

I said, "Could he have done it, you think?"

"Carried her? Oh, hell, yes. Son of a bitch was strong as a bull, man. Played football in school, made a big publicity thing out of staying fit—pictures in the paper of him lifting weights and so on. And she couldn't weigh much."

Tommy shook his head bemusedly and drank off part of his beer. "But damn, it's hard to imagine that evil bastard Rowland Jordan in a tender moment. I guess you never know, though. They say even Hitler liked to play with children and dogs."

He set his beer on the table and looked off across the room, watching Louise bending over the pool table. "My, my, doesn't she own any pants with any room in them? Not that I'm complaining. Well," he said, "at least we've got an answer to one question. About the chances of the wife having done it."

I made a vague sound and Tommy turned back and looked at me. "We *do* have that settled, don't we? I mean, she was upstairs, the chair was downstairs, no way she could have done it and gotten back up there—"

"Right." I had a sip of my own beer. "And after you've seen her in person it's difficult to imagine her doing it, anyway. She's so small and frail, and from what everyone tells me he was big and tough, not an easy kind of man to kill. That's the other thing, though," I said. "I don't see Emily Jordan as a credible suspect, but she's holding back on something."

Tommy looked interested. "How do you know?"

"According to the medical examiner's report, Jordan was killed by a single tomahawk blow to the side of the neck—cut the carotid artery, it must have taken him just under the ear." I touched the spot on my own neck with a fingertip. "Just about the perfect place to chop a man, if you wanted him dead fast. But there were no other cuts on the body, and you'd expect—"

"Oh, right. Guy sees somebody coming at him with a toma-hawk, he's going to throw up his arms, or maybe try to grab it. Either way he gets a few extra nicks." Tommy's forehead went wrinkly. "So the attack must have taken Jordan completely by surprise. But that doesn't make sense if it was Chris, does it? I still can't imagine Jordan letting Chris into the house to begin with, let alone giving him a clear shot like that. But how's that prove Emily's lying?"

"I'm not sure she's actually lying, but her story doesn't square with the facts. According to her," I said, "there was a lot of racket downstairs—the sheriff and some guy shouting at each other, scuffling noises—and it must have gone on for some time, to wake her out of a drugged sleep. Which adds up to Jordan having an angry confrontation with somebody, and you'd think an experienced cop would be on his guard in a situation like that."

"Damn right." Tommy's eyes were all but dancing. "By God, Roper, that's real detective shit. I'm impressed." He frowned again. "What's it all mean, though? You think Emily was in on the hit, or she's covering up for somebody else? Or maybe Mizell or somebody is leaning on her to doctor her story—"

I put my hands up. "Easy, easy. Don't go riding off in all directions yet. There might be any number of possible explanations. None of this would do Chris a bit of good in court. I doubt if the judge would even allow any of it to be introduced."

Tommy sighed heavily. "Sure . . . She's lying about one thing, anyway," he said. "Little daughter Felicia isn't off visiting any relatives in Arkansas. She's in a fancy private cackle factory somewhere in the Tulsa area. Of course it's easy to see why her mama would want to lie about that."

"Felicia's been committed?"

"I don't know what her exact legal status may be, but she's definitely vacationing on the funny farm. That Greenstick kid who works for Lester—you remember him?—he knows some high-school girls from around here. God knows how they found out, but you know they always know everything about each other. Lester's got the kid working on trying to find out the name of the place."

"It's not likely any of us would be able to get in and see her," I pointed out. "They're very tight about visitors in those places. Especially when the patient's a minor."

"Ah, well, so what if it doesn't do any good? Nothing else seems to be doing any good either. You do what you can. Shit." Tommy scowled into his beer. "At least you got out and did some legwork. Sorry you got your ass kicked in the process. I didn't even accomplish that much."

He glanced around the room and lowered his voice. "Nobody in the local Indian community knows anything, or if they do they're not telling. Very few of them would talk to me at all. Most of the Indian people around here are pretty badly intimidated, Roper."

"Scared of Mizell's goons?"

"Not necessarily. Quite a few families have one or more people working at the Echota Creek plant, and there are others that work for the county—road crews and so on. They're more worried about losing their jobs than about getting a visit from Pace. And then a lot of people are in debt, and there are ways they can be gotten at."

He drained his beer. His eyes were very dark.

"That's how it is with Cherokees," he said morosely. "Creeks too, Choctaws, Shawnees, all us eastern people who got herded off to Oklahoma back before the Civil War. These Plains types like Marvin Painted Horse, they look down on us, tell each other that we're not real Indians, because we don't live on reservations and a lot of us have white blood and our ancestors took up some of the white man's ways back in the last century. They don't realize—or don't want to admit— that we were fighting the whites for a couple of centuries before they even found out what a white man looked like. Guys like Dragging Canoe were kicking white ass back when Marvin Painted Horse's ancestors were still living in a Minnesota swamp and shitting their breechclouts every time an Iroquois war party showed up."

He made a sound in his throat, half laugh, half grunt. "You know the biggest single beating the U.S. Army ever took from Indians? Everybody thinks it was the Custer fight, but that's a lot of bullshit. Back in 1791, this general named St. Clair got his ass kicked up in Indiana by a bunch of Miamis and lost over twice as many men as Custer. Only he didn't get himself killed heroically, and the Indians involved weren't riding pretty horsies, so nobody made any movies about it."

He stopped for a minute. I kept quiet and let him gather

himself. I already knew most of what he was telling me; hell, I'd written about it. But Tommy Ninekiller had to make his points in his own way.

"What I mean," he said at last, "eastern Indians go back a long way with you guys, been getting jerked around for a lot of centuries, and it's gotten so everybody's fucking *tired*, man. Burned out. A people with combat fatigue. Rita and me, we had some marketable talents and we managed to break out, but your average east-Oklahoma skin doesn't have our advantages. Give him a chance to make a few bucks to buy his kids some clothes and put a little food on the table besides those damn government-surplus commodities, he's not eager to risk blowing it by talking to outsiders. And I'm an outsider around here, blood or not."

He leaned back and put his hands on the table. "So where do we go from here?"

"In the words of another noted Native American, 'We?' " I drained my glass and stood up. "*I* intend to go back to the motel and take a couple of ibuprofens and try to sleep off some of the aches and pains. Then tomorrow I'm going home."

His face flushed and I added quickly, "Tommy, I've gone over this already with Rita. I'm not doing any good down here, and I've got things to take care of at home."

"Yeah? Had all you can take?" His voice was low and his speech slow, almost thick. "Getting too rough for your fine white ass?"

"Not so much that I can't haul your fine red ass outside and stomp a mudhole in it," I told him. "I mean, if you feel like trying me on."

We looked at each other for a long minute and then Tommy let out his breath. "Ah, hell, Roper, I'm just being a prick because I'm pissed off and you're handy. Go home, for

God's sake. It's what I'd do if I had any sense. . . . Think you might be coming back?"

"Maybe," I said. "I don't know."

"Well, I'll see you when I see you," Tommy said. "Give my regards to Harry."

Next morning I loaded my stuff into the Camaro and checked out of the Moonlight Courts Motel. The frizzy-haired manageress showed easily as much enthusiasm for my departure as she had for my arrival.

I didn't go home the way I'd come. Instead I drove back through downtown Redbud and hung a right. Deputy Tovin might or might not be waiting in the same spot today, but that wasn't the reason for the change of route.

The old state highway ran westward out of town, cutting through a patch of second-growth woods and then straight across overgrazed pastureland, parallel to the nearby railroad tracks. This was the southwest corner of Sizemore County, where the hills gave way to the rolling plains of the Arkansas River valley. A couple of cows gazed sadly at me over a sagging wire fence, maybe trying to make me feel guilty about all those burgers.

Half a dozen miles west of the Redbud city limits, a paved road turned off to the left. There was no sign, not even a number, even though the side road was at least as wide as the main highway and in considerably better repair. I wondered, as I shifted down and braked, whether this was the turnoff I wanted; but I swung left and up and over the railroad right-of-way, and almost immediately saw a white plume against the sky. A couple of minutes later I was driving past the main gate of the Echota Creek nuclear reactor site.

It was on the right side of the road, and I didn't get much of a look before I was past. I went on up the road for a quarter of a mile or so and turned around and came back, driving slowly. The road shoulder looked clean and solid; I pulled off and stopped, square across from the main gate, and had myself a look.

The place wasn't nearly as big as some of the atomic plants I'd seen, but it was still pretty damn imposing, especially out there in that empty open countryside. There were three big main buildings and a considerable collection of smaller ones; the whole complex, in fact, had to be the largest group of man-made structures in Sizemore County except for the town of Redbud itself. In terms of sheer ground area, I wasn't even sure Redbud was all that much bigger.

I couldn't actually see much from the road; the plant complex lay a long way off, across an open field. The only structures nearby were the high chain-link outer fence, hung with warning signs and topped with razor wire, and, next to the big main gate, a small white-painted guard shelter. A man in a gray uniform was standing at the door of the guard shack, looking at me.

I popped open the glove compartment and got out my old Nikon binoculars and rolled down the side window for a better view. The 7 × 50s pulled everything close enough to let me make out details; I could even see individual workers doing something next to a string of freight cars that sat on a long rail siding. A yellow forklift was rolling slowly along what looked like a loading dock. Automotive windshields glinted in the morning sun, row on row, across a big parking lot.

The hell of it was, I still didn't know what I was looking at. The biggest building had a funny-looking tower or stack on top, from which white smoke or steam was streaming; I assumed that was where they kept the reactor itself, but even that was only a guess. For all I could swear to, this might have been the Acme Corporation's main plant, where they made all the giant springs and magnets and suchlike for Wile E. Coyote.

There was a large sign beside the gate and I turned the glasses on that, but it wasn't very informative. Red letters, not all that big, rather grudgingly admitted that this was the Echota Creek Nuclear Facility, a division of Hardesty Industries, Inc. Smaller black lettering spelled out the rules: employees must show identification at gate. Security badges must be worn at all times within compound. Vehicles must bear clearance stickers. Visitors must obtain passes and wait for escorts. All vehicles and persons subject to search and detention. Unauthorized persons entering grounds will be prosecuted for criminal trespass.

I aimed the glasses at the guard shack. The uniformed man was standing in the doorway, talking into a cellular phone. He was still looking my way.

I lowered the glasses and sat for a few minutes with them in my lap, looking at the plant. A black-and-white car appeared on the long curving drive, moving rapidly toward the gate. As it came closer I put the Nikons on it and saw that it was some kind of cop car, complete with overhead light bar. The paint scheme wasn't that of any Oklahoma police force that I knew, though.

The black-and-white stopped briefly at the gate and the guard came out of the shack and spoke briefly to the driver. He didn't point at me but he looked in my direction. The car rolled on through the gate after a minute and stopped on the shoulder of the road, across from where I sat.

A big beefy-faced man in a gray generic-security-guard uniform got out and walked across the road toward me. "Morning," he said. "Like to show me some identification?"

"No," I said after hardly any reflection, "I don't think I would."

He looked puzzled and then angry. "I'll have to ask you to step out of the car."

I gave him a warm smile. "Up yours," I said pleasantly.

After that the quality of our dialogue fell off rapidly. He told me to get out of the car and place my hands on top and consider myself under arrest. I suggested he have sexual intercourse with himself. He put his hand on his pistol holster and I explained that if he pulled a gun on me he should be prepared either to use it or have it inserted in an uncomfortable place.

He stood there staring at me for a moment and then he turned and went back to his car and reached for the microphone. I watched as he talked, rather agitatedly, into the mike. The fancy emblem on the door of the black-and-white incorporated the words HARDESTY INDUSTRIES SECURITY UNIT.

He replaced the mike and came back as far as the middle of the road. "Stay where you are," he shouted. "Don't try to leave." He went and sat in his imitation fuzzmobile, probably sulking and chewing his lip.

I sat and waited, wondering what the hell I thought I was doing now. I wasn't even sure why I'd wanted to see this place to begin with, except that I'd been hearing so much about it that my curiosity had been mildly aroused. Now I'd had a look at it, there was no logical reason to be hanging around, beyond a prickish compulsion to bait a uniformed asshole. Not much of a motive, when you thought about it, for a grown man.

Finally a white car, without markings, came up the plant drive and through the gate. It stopped behind the black-and-white and a man in a suit got out and walked over and said something to the beefy-faced guard. A moment later the black-and-white pulled out and around in a tight, unnecessarily noisy U-turn and roared back through the gate and disappeared in the direction of the complex, while the man in the suit began walking unhurriedly across the road toward me.

He stopped beside the Camaro and bent down slightly and smiled at me. He was a short, rather lightly built guy with a sharp face and pale skin; his hair was dark and getting thin in front, though I didn't think he was past his thirties. The suit was a damn good one, better than anything I'd ever owned, and it fit him like a son of a bitch.

"Hi," he said. "My name's Bob Cross. I'm guessing you're Taggart Roper."

I said, "Now why would you be guessing a thing like that?"

His smile got wider. It was a very white, even smile, easily as pricey-looking as the suit.

"You'll have to make allowances," he said. "I'm afraid everyone here is a little on edge when it comes to security. We've had some unfortunate experiences lately. Certain people would like to disrupt our operations."

His accent wasn't local or anywhere close to it; there were distinct Eastern Seaboard intonations, not New York but possibly Pennsylvania or the more civilized part of Jersey. He'd been to a good school, too, or else put in some serious work learning to sound like it. I wondered what sort of mistake an upwardly-mobile corporate ramrod had to make to get himself sent to a place like this.

"When the guard saw you," he went on, "parked here like this, studying the plant through binoculars, he called the main security office, and they sent a man to check you out. When you refused to identify yourself, and became hostile—"

"This is a public road," I pointed out. "On this side of that fence, I don't have to answer any questions from your private muscle. In my book he was the one who got hostile."

Cross nodded. "And you're entirely right, of course. Our security people don't have any legal authority on public property. The standard procedure, in a situation like this, is to call the local police. As it happened, Sheriff Mizell took the call, and was able to identify you from the guard's description."

He chuckled softly. "You seem to have made quite an impression on the sheriff," he added.

Sheriff? Well, maybe he knew something I didn't. "What did he have to say about me?"

"Among other things, he used the word 'attitude' a couple of times," Cross said blandly. "I believe the term 'smart bastard' came up as well."

"Man's got a way with words," I admitted.

Cross put his hands in his pockets and tilted his head to one side. Now I noticed, he looked a bit like some kind of well-dressed bird.

"There's only one small point that worries me, Mr. Roper," he said. "According to Mizell, you're a professional writer, studying the recent murder case with an eye toward doing a book. Which I can certainly see—I'd probably buy a copy myself—but what's your interest in this facility? I don't see the connection."

I shrugged. "Personal curiosity. This place does figure in the background of the story, after all. It seems to have been the focus of a lot of hostility, and not just between Sheriff Jordan and Chris Badwater."

"Oh, yes." Cross quit smiling. "We've definitely had some ugly scenes at this gate. That's why I wanted to meet you," he said. "I imagine you've had a chance to talk with some of Badwater's friends by now. Maybe you've gotten an idea for a different sort of book. Some of these self-appointed protectors of the environment can be very convincing. Don't misunderstand," he added quickly. "You've got the right to write whatever you believe. But you ought to give us a chance to tell our side."

He gestured toward the plant. "I can offer you a guided tour of the facility, and interviews with people who can answer your questions properly. You really don't have to resort to sitting here with your binoculars."

Christ, that was all I needed: a corporate dog-and-pony show. I said, "Believe me, I'm not planning to write that type of book. I wouldn't even know how."

"Oh?" Again that birdlike tilt of the head. "Well, if you should find yourself needing information—" He took a card from his breast pocket and handed it to me. "Give me a call."

I took his card and he stepped back and raised a hand in a little half-wave. He stood there watching as I started the car and pulled away. Just before crossing the railroad tracks I looked in the mirror and saw him walking back across the road toward his car.

I turned left at the intersection and gunned the Camaro on down the blacktop. A little while later I was rolling across the high old bridge above the Arkansas River, out of Sizemore County. I wondered if I'd ever go back.

13

WILEY HARMON SAID, "God damn it, Roper, I *told* you not to go dicking around down there in Dogpatch. Told you those shitkickers were liable to hand you your ass, didn't I?"

He dragged at his cigarette and gave his balding head a disgusted shake. "I mean, did I tell you or what? For somebody that keeps coming around with questions and paying hard bread for the answers, you sure as shit don't listen very well."

We were sitting in his parked car outside a Hardee's on the south side of Tulsa. Usually we met at a local cop hangout called the Copper Bottom, but it was midafternoon and Harmon, who was supposed to be on duty, hadn't wanted to risk running into any of his superiors.

"You better stop by a church, light a couple of candles," he continued, "give fucking thanks all you got was the shit beat out of you. If half what I been hearing is true, you picked an authentically bad place to go jerking people's dicks."

He took the remaining smoldering inch of cigarette out of his mouth, scowled at it, rolled down the window, and flipped the butt out onto the parking lot. A gust of dry autumn wind came in long enough to blow away a little of the accumulated smoke, but the atmosphere inside the car was still well past the toxic level when he rolled the window back up.

"Fucking overpriced shit," he grumbled. "I got to quit. You know, I figured out the other day, tobacco's got to be the stupidest dope there is. You don't get off on it, never anything beyond a nasty buzz when you smoke too many on an empty stomach, and yet if you don't get that butt on time you get a jones nearly as bad as a regular junkie. And the only reason anybody ever starts, no matter what they say, is that they think it makes them look cool. Jesus Christ, people are assholes. I include my noble fucking self."

I said, "Is it really that bad?"

"Are you serious? I know you don't smoke anymore, but you got to remember . . . oh, you mean about Sizemore County. Yeah," he said, "it's that bad all right. County heat down there, that's one rotten bunch of cops. Guy I talked to said Jordan was so tough he ate nails and so crooked he shit corkscrews, and the others are just as bent."

A good many people around the Tulsa area, I reflected, would have been more than mildly amazed to hear Wiley Harmon criticizing the moral standards of other cops, his own virtue being notoriously elastic. Rita often referred to him as the crookedest cop in the Tulsa PD; that was perhaps a trifle excessive, given the level of competition, but he was undoubtedly finalist material.

"I know what you're thinking," Harmon said. "Hey, when did I ever claim to be a straight arrow? But those bastards in Redbud make me look like Roy Rogers. Hell, from the shit I been picking up, they make me look like fucking *Mister* Rogers."

He turned half around in his seat and leaned back against the car door, facing me. "You got to understand," he said, "none of what I'm about to tell you is one hundred percent solid. Sure as hell isn't anything anybody could take to court—most judges wouldn't even accept it as probable grounds to issue a warrant, these days. It's all kind of loose, you know? Like I ask a guy I know in a certain department if he's ever heard anything about Sizemore County, he tells me something he got from somebody else who's usually reliable but might be full of shit this time."

"That's not really important, Wiley," I told him. "Right now I'm just trying to get the general picture."

In fact I wasn't even doing that anymore; but Harmon had clearly done a certain amount of work on this, and he'd expect to be paid, so I might as well hear his report. Besides, I still had a certain residual interest in Sizemore County; it wasn't the sort of place you forget quickly.

"Yeah, well, all I'm saying, some of the bits and pieces may be wrong. Still, the general picture, as you say, comes out pretty clear. Jordan was dirty, the whole fucking Sizemore County Sheriff's Department was dirty, and nobody believes they've gotten any cleaner since somebody wasted the main dirtbag. We're talking serious dirt, too, not just the standard petty-ass hick-town shit. I know," he said, "I told you that much before you went down there. Now, though, I actually know what I'm talking about. More or less."

"And?"

"And it's nothing very original. Dope, mainly. Quite a bit of the gross national product of certain countries where they say *sí* when they mean yes," Harmon said, "would seem to have been passing through Sizemore County, with the assistance of the late Rowland Jordan and his stalwart fucking minions."

I said, "I wouldn't think there'd be all that much of a market in a place like that."

"There's not. Actually, Jordan always kept the county pretty damn clean when it came to local smoking and snorting. Got his picture in the paper more than once, busting some good old boy for growing a little happy weed on the back forty. Word is that some worthwhile bits of cash and property got confiscated in the process, too, and you know how that works. Even if the original bust was so bogus the judge throws it out of court, the bustee almost never succeeds in getting his home and his pickup truck and his life savings back again. Nice little sideline for a lot of cop departments around the country, and legal as hell, too. But I digress."

He took his cigarette pack from his shirt pocket, made a face when he discovered it was empty, and said, "Shit." He wadded the empty pack up and tossed it over his shoulder into the backseat, where it landed atop a pile of German porno magazines featuring enormously fat blond women in black stockings. "Excuse me," he said, and leaned past me to open the glove compartment. Reaching inside, he hauled out a heavy-looking blue-steel revolver and laid it on the seat between us. After a bit of pawing within the glove box, he came up with a fresh pack of Camels. I noticed there was no tax stamp.

He started to replace the pistol and then he stopped and looked at me. "Hey, you in the market for a good piece? Colt Trooper, a little old but still clean. Took it off this punk—"

I shook my head. "I don't know what I'd do with it. Anyway, if I need a gun I've got one."

"You mean that old three-eighty? Shit." His voice dripped scorn. "I can't believe you've still got that puny little pissant. You ever shoot somebody with it and he finds out about it, he might get mad and kick your ass in."

He shoved the gun back into the glove compartment and began tearing open the pack of Camels. When he had one lit he said, "What I was saying about dope in Sizemore County—I didn't mean retail sales. According to reliable sources, as they say, the name of the game is warehousing and distribution. Lots of isolated cabins and barns along those country roads, you could stash enough shit to string out the whole Midwest. Places for labs, too, that's serious business in itself. Good location, within easy hauling distance of a lot of major cities. You got the Arkansas River running along the southern and western edges of the county, makes it simple to bring shit up by boat all the way from the Gulf. And I wouldn't be surprised if there was a cow pasture or two big enough to land a small plane."

"And that's what Jordan was running?"

"Yeah. Not that he and his boys necessarily got any white stuff under their own fingernails," Harmon said. "Way it was told to me, Jordan made his territory available to certain people who had certain needs. For the right price, you got a safe business location and a guarantee of invisibility. They'd even tip you off if state or federal heat came nosing around."

He puffed at his cigarette. "It wasn't only dope," he added. "Hot merchandise, stolen cars, all kinds of interesting shit wound up in Sizemore County at one time or another. One guy even told me there was a setup in a farmhouse for a while, running off pirated music tapes and videos. But the main money, as usual, was in Andes nose candy."

I said, "What about now? Since Jordan's death, I mean."

"Nobody's sure. Too soon to tell, really," Harmon said. "So far it looks like business as usual. Man I know in the state rackets unit, he said if there'd been any sudden stampede out of Sizemore County he'd have heard about it. Might be some people lying low, though, waiting to see how things go under the new management."

"Mizell?"

"Everybody assumes he's stepped into Jordan's shoes. Again, nobody really knows anything. Or if they do they aren't telling me."

He gave me a yellow-toothed grin. "That's what you been fucking with, Roper. Tell you something else," he said, "I wasn't the only one asking questions this week. Some people were inquiring, discreetly as all hell, about *you*. I think this Mizell asshole got a little bit worried."

"He told me he'd made some calls."

"Well, he knows some damn good phone numbers. Fucking Captain stopped by my desk, talking about football and crap like that, like he just wanted to shoot the shit with the troops. Finally asked me, so casual it made my nuts hurt, if I wasn't buddies with this guy Taggart Roper who used to write for the *Courier*. Said somebody'd told him we hung out together at the Copper Bottom now and then. Wanted to know whether you did anything besides write, what your angle was on cops, like that. Claimed he'd read one of your books and wondered what you were like." Harmon snorted. "Last book that dumb son of a bitch read, probably had pictures of talking ducks inside."

"What did you tell him?"

"That you were kind of a harmless loser."

"Thanks."

"My pleasure. What I'm trying to tell you, this isn't just some twisted bunch of local cops. The connections run all over. No other way they could have run a setup like that all these years without getting nailed."

"You think there's collusion at state level?"

"Why not? Christ, Roper, this is *Oklahoma*. The fucking governor has spent most of his term trying to beat a series of indictments, finally had to plea-bargain to stay out of jail. Somebody in the state treasurer's office seems to have walked off with six million dollars. That kind of shit, you can find out about for the price of a newspaper," Harmon said. "So figure what life's got to be like behind the woodwork. . . . But why stop at state? You seriously believe there aren't dirty feds too?"

He cleared his throat. "Speaking of official corruption," he said pointedly.

I took an envelope from my jacket pocket and passed it over. He stowed it in his own pocket without looking inside. I said, "Not going to count it?"

"What is a human relationship without that essential fucking ingredient of trust?" he said piously. "I trust you, Roper."

"I'm honored."

"Honest men have to stick together," he said.

It was getting well down in the bottom of the afternoon by the time I headed for home. There was barely time to make it ahead of the quitting-time vehicular stampede. That was all I needed, a session of Tulsa rush-hour traffic-busting; if Wiley Harmon was right, I'd been living dangerously enough for the last few days. In the interest of safety, then, I held the Camaro around eighty-five until I was across the river and coming up on the Yuchi Park exit.

Yuchi Park appeared to have survived my absence reasonably well. I stopped at Mr. Berryhill's place to collect Harry, who wasn't all that excited to see me; Mr. Berryhill always spoiled the stupid bastard. "He's been a real good boy," the old man said, scratching Harry's ears. "No trouble at all. Hey, I got some mail for you."

He went into his little frame house and came back a moment later with a stack of letter-sized envelopes and a couple of big yellow parcels. "Figured I better not leave this stuff sticking out of your mailbox," he said. "Got some people around here, steal a hot stove."

I thanked him, tossed the mail onto the front seat, made Harry get in back—he didn't like that; he preferred to ride up front, but Rita had had more than one blouse and skirt ruined with black hairs—and drove slowly down the gravel drive to my trailer.

Harry didn't want to go in right away; he wanted to celebrate our homecoming by running frantic, tongue-lolling laps around the yard. I sat on the fender and let him lope while I looked through the week's accumulation of mail.

One of the envelopes contained a welcome item: a check from Swallow Street Press, the final installment of my advance money for *Black Water*. There was a letter from the Yuchi Park library, asking if I'd be willing to come and read from my work at their annual Friends of the Library fundraiser. There was also a chain letter mailed somewhere in Florida, an invitation to enroll in a health club in Broken Arrow, a flyer advertising a new pizza establishment, and a J. C. Whitney auto parts catalog.

I stashed the check in my wallet, pocketed the library letter with a mental note to call and find out what, if anything, they intended to pay—lots of people assume that writers love nothing better than making free public appearances—tossed the other junk onto the Camaro's hood until I could get at a wastebasket, and turned to the two parcels.

One bore the logo of Swallow Street Press on the mailing label. It contained a stack of typescript, neatly rubber-banded together and the pages festooned with little yellow stick-ons bearing tiny scrawled notations. A note was attached to the top sheet:

> Dear Tag—
> Herewith the edited ms of STAKED PLAIN, and let me say (again) what a pleasure it's been to work on a book of this quality. If BLACK WATER is up to the same standard, I can hardly wait to get started on it.
> You'll find I've edited *very* lightly—just a few minor changes, mostly for clarity.
> I need this back by November 1. Can do????
> Marcia

And here it was, the moment every writer learns to dread. I stared at the manuscript, wondering how many times I was going to say shit in the next few weeks.

For reasons known only to an inscrutable God who lives somewhere in Gramercy Park, many editors have a very strange concept of their part in the literary process, seeing themselves virtually as co-authors. The author, they seem to believe, is little more than a fumbling idiot-savant cranking out baskets of rough castings, which have to be machined and polished and fitted by the skilled hands of the editor before they have any value.

So a forty-some-odd-year-old professional writer, with a couple of decades of experience in writing English prose for pay, spends over a year on a manuscript—sometimes writing the same page over and over again for a week, trying to get it exactly right—and then a twenty-some-odd-year-old editor, six months out of NYU, spends part of a weekend going through it with a red pencil until the God-damned thing is barely recognizable, rearranging word and sentence order, diddling with the punctuation, deleting Politically Incorrect words and phrases and now and then inserting entire sentences and passages of the editor's own devising . . . and all of it, or nearly all, for no discernible reason beyond sheer meddling for the sake of meddling.

A determined author can, except at the sleaziest houses, get the text restored to something like its original state; but this is at best a huge pain in the ass, and uses up bitch points that may be needed later on when raising hell about things like doofus covers and sales-and-promo departments that couldn't sell life jackets on the *Titanic*.

And you never get all the footprints out. You go over and over the mangled manuscript, grinding your teeth down to the gums and printing STET (Latin for "let it stand"; Author for "put it back the fucking way I wrote it") twenty times to the page, but then a year later the book comes out and the first thing you see when you open that advance copy is some bit of editorial syntax-scrambling that somehow got past you and now it's too late, and you go straight up in the air screaming and scare hell out of the dog. Although I think Harry's used to it by now.

Not all editors engage in this sort of thing, thank God; but the ones who do represent a major curse of an already excessively curse-ridden profession. And the ones who *loved* the book, and wouldn't *dream* of changing a *thing*, are the most certain to go into red-pencil feeding frenzies. "I've edited very lightly" doesn't mean squat, either; they all say it, even the ones who rewrote the entire last chapter to make the ending happier and changed the main character's name from Bob to Artie because they thought it sounded friendlier.

I sighed and laid the manuscript on the fender beside me. Whatever Marcia Grimshaw had or hadn't done to my novel, I didn't feel like looking at it now. One savage beating a week is enough.

The other package bore my name and address, printed in oddly formed letters, and a New York postmark. I ripped the end open and another bundle of typescript slid out. This manuscript, however, wasn't from my desk; it was typed on very thin, pulpy-looking paper, and the language was nothing I recognized. I couldn't even identify the alphabet; it looked a little like frat-house Greek, or maybe Cherokee.

Paper-clipped to the top page was a handwritten note on hotel stationery:

> Taggart my friend,
>
> Here is a copy of the translation of *The Last Bugle*. I am having someone mail this from New York City, New York.
>
> As I have told you, it is a great honor for me to do

this work. I hope that soon I can send you my translation of *Steps of the Sun*. Please be patient, the mail service here is very bad.

In respect,
Vladimir

For God's sake, I'd completely forgotten about my fan in Russia. I studied the ragged-edged pages with fascination and a sense of dyslexia. I wasn't even sure I had it right side up.

"Come on, Harry," I said. "Let's see what's in the refrigerator."

That evening, over after-dinner drinks, I gave Rita my final report on my efforts in Sizemore County. She listened attentively, and when I was done she reached across the table with both hands and took hold of mine. Gazing into my eyes, she said softly, "Bullshit."

I think I may have looked surprised; even shocked, perhaps, though it wasn't as if the word had never before come up between us.

"Tommy told me all about it on the phone last night," she said. "Damn it, Tag, I was afraid something like this would happen."

By now I knew what she was talking about. I'd done a little editing of my own; I hadn't told her about getting beaten up and jailed. She probably thought I was trying to spare her feelings, but that wasn't it. I simply hadn't been able to find a way to tell the story without sounding like a braggart telling heroic tales to impress the lady, or else a quitter making excuses for dropping out of the game.

"Why did you let me talk you into going down there?" she said.

I finished my drink and went to put the glass in the sink. I'd wanted to get together at her apartment, but she'd insisted it would be unfair to leave the poor dog alone on my first night home. From the front end of the trailer, Harry's snores registered his appreciation for our company.

"It was no big deal," I said, coming back to the table. "Anyway, it's over. For what it was worth . . . damn, Rita, the whole thing was such a waste all around."

"You did more than anyone else," she said quietly. "More than I could have done."

"Yeah, but it doesn't help Chris Badwater, does it?" I sat down. "See, there are basically two ways to beat a rap like that: prove the defendant couldn't possibly have done it, or prove somebody else did. But Chris isn't talking, so there's no getting an alibi out of him, and nobody else seems to have seen him that night."

I put my elbows on the table and rested my face in my hands for a moment. I felt incredibly tired.

"As for proving somebody else killed Jordan," I said, "you could probably pack Skelly Stadium with people who had solid reasons to want the son of a bitch dead, but that's a long way from knowing which one did it, let alone getting proof. Maybe a team of professional investigators could accomplish something, if they had enough time and resources. Me, I wouldn't even know how to start."

I looked up at Rita. "There's something else. According to Wiley Harmon, Jordan was doing business with some extremely heavy outside parties. It's possible this was a hit, rather than a personal homicide. If so, there's almost no chance of finding the killer."

"Or even surviving the attempt."

"Believe it. So any way you look at it, Chris's chances aren't great. I wish I could be more helpful."

Rita nodded. "You did all you could," she said, and reached for her purse. "Let me reimburse you—"

"No way. Look." I pulled out my wallet and showed her

the check from Swallow Street Press. "I'm flush for once. Got to remember to go by the bank on Monday."

"Not Monday," Rita said. "Holiday, remember? The Great White Asshole."

"Oh, yeah, Columbus Day. I keep forgetting. That's right," I said, "those people in Tahlequah were talking about holding a demonstration at the Echota Creek site on Columbus Day. I wonder if that's still on."

"It better be. I'm supposed to go down there and cover the event. My socially sensitive bosses," Rita said, "felt I was the obvious person to write the story."

She reached for her own drink and then stopped. "Hey," she said, "want to come along?"

"Back to Sizemore County? Charming, friendly Sizemore County, with its lovable folk and their quaint ways? Hell," I said, "I can hardly wait."

I reached into my jacket pocket and pulled out the Hohner and gave it a couple of experimental honks. Rita said, "What in God's name are you doing?"

"Trying to remember the changes to 'Dear Hearts and Gentle People.' Perhaps it would help," I said, "if you would go get me another Jim Beam on the rocks. Hold the rocks."

"You've had quite enough to drink," she said, and reached across the table and took the harmonica away from me and laid it on the table. "Let's go to bed."

"Let's," I said.

14

•••••••••

UTUMN GOT SERIOUS OVER the weekend; a great bulge of cold air, like the sag of a pregnant buffalo's belly, rolled down out of Kansas and turned the sky gray and roily for a couple of days, though there was still no rain. By midday on Monday the clouds were gone but the chilly wind remained, slashing across the flatlands of the Arkansas River valley and flattening the high grass in the fields along Echota Creek. Even the ragged-blown plume from the reactor stack looked cold.

"Hell," Rita groused as we got out of her car. "All those fine days I've spent sitting in that damn office, wishing I could get out. Then they finally give me an outdoor assignment on the first butt-freezer day of the season. I wish I could think of somebody to sue."

"Looks like a good turnout, though," I observed.

"Better be. With what this wind is doing to my sinuses, there better be a Pulitzer-grade story here today."

There was indeed an impressive collection of people in front of the Echota Creek plant. I thought there might be as many as thirty or forty demonstrators, though it was hard to tell with most of them bunched up and milling around in a tight little herd at the main gate.

They weren't the only figures in the landscape. The Size-more County Sheriff's Department had turned out in force for the Columbus Day festivities. The other side of the road was lined with brown cruisers—not a great many by urban stan-dards, about what you'd see at the average city holdup-and-homicide scene, but more than I'd have expected Sizemore County to own. Uniformed deputies formed a skimpy cordon around the demonstrators, though there weren't enough of them to stop people from passing freely through the line in either direction. Several more uniforms, standing close together and gripping nightsticks, barred the approach to the gate. I thought I recognized Pace's Jurassic shape in the middle.

Besides the deputies, a number of plant security guards were lined up on the other side of the fence, watching the demonstrators. At the gate, next to the guard shack, stood a loose group of men, talking with each other or speaking into hand-held phones. I saw Mizell, looking like a cop-academy poster in a crisp dress uniform, and Bob Cross, who was glancing here and there with an air of alert concern.

Moving among the demonstrators, or spotted about the area, were men and women carrying cameras and camcorders and microphones, with one female reactionary scribbling in a plain old low-tech notebook. "More of a press presence than I'd have expected," I said as we crossed the road.

"There was a tip," Rita said, "one of those anonymous things that somehow everyone hears about without anyone being sure of the source. Something special is supposed to happen here today, something more interesting than a bunch of placard-waving idealists staging yet another unpopular protest. And it's been a slow week for state news. You know how it works."

Rita held up her press card as we passed through the Thin Brown Line, and the nearest deputy nodded to her, but I didn't think he paid much real attention. He was a nice-looking young guy, and obviously very nervous; his face was shiny with sweat above the collar of an ill-fitting uniform blouse, despite the chill of the day. I hadn't seen him before.

No doubt Mizell had called up a lot of part-time and reserve deputies for the occasion.

"Do you see Tommy anywhere?" Rita asked me. "I thought he'd be here by now."

I scanned the crowd, looking for Tommy. I didn't see him; I didn't see anybody I recognized, not right away, but then it was difficult to pick out individual faces in that close-packed mass. "I don't see him either," I said, "but I'm not sure I'd spot my own mother in this bunch."

The majority of the demonstrators looked relatively young, though there was a sprinkling of gray or graying heads. Most wore vaguely outdoorish clothing, down vests and jackets, checkered shirts, and hiking boots; I guessed there were a good many L. L. Bean and Eddie Bauer labels on hand. There seemed to be slightly more women than men. Despite popular images, only a few of the demonstrators carried signs: END NUCLEAR INSANITY. LOVE YOUR PLANET, IT'S THE ONLY ONE YOU HAVE. STOP, YOU'RE KILLING ME.

Most of the faces were white, too; but over at the edge of the crowd a group of young Indians, maybe a dozen or so, stood in a tight, defensive-looking cluster. I said, "Maybe they've seen Tommy."

"I doubt it. College kids, I think, they wouldn't know him—I don't know any of them, either." Rita flipped her jacket collar up to shield her neck from the wind. "But what the hell, might learn something useful all the same. They probably know Chris."

She moved through the crowd toward the Indian caucus, and after a moment's hesitation I followed. I stopped a couple of paces away, though, not wanting my Caucasian presence to inhibit the conversation. I heard Rita speak to them in Cherokee and saw looks of embarrassed incomprehension appear on their faces. After a minute she said in English, "I'm Rita Ninekiller. Do any of you know my brother Tommy?"

A hand touched my shoulder and I turned and found myself facing Bianca Ford, the lawyer I'd met in Tahlequah. "Hi," she said. "Come to join the movement, or just curious?"

Her face was reddened by the wind and, I thought, a flush of excitement as well. She wore a knitted navy doofus cap and a G.I. camo field jacket. All she needed was a shopping cart and a mumble.

"Hey," she said, "Lester gave me something for you. Actually he said to give it to Tommy and tell him to give it to you, but Tommy hasn't showed up yet."

She handed over a folded sheet of yellow legal-pad paper. I pocketed it without looking at it, which seemed to disappoint her. I said, "When do the fun and games start? You know, the speeches or group singing or slogan-chanting or whatever you do?"

"We're waiting for, uh, some people." Her voice went suddenly I've-got-a-secret evasive. "You're going to love this . . . but listen, I have to get some stuff ready. Catch you later, okay?"

She turned and dived back into the crowd. A bearded young man in a peacoat was passing out handbills printed on pink paper and Bianca Ford took his arm and began talking to him. At my elbow Rita said, "I didn't know you knew Bianca. Getting to be good friends, are you?"

In Rita's voice Panzer divisions crossed the Polish frontier, Mitsubishi Zeroes appeared over Pearl Harbor, somebody shot the Archduke Ferdinand. I said quickly, "I don't really know her. Met her last week at Lester Bucktail's place." I pulled out the paper she had given me. "She had a message for me from Lester."

"Ah." The incipient-massacre expression left Rita's face and my own internal muscle groups relaxed a bit. I didn't know why she was being jealous; in the years we'd been seeing each other, I hadn't gone in for fooling around on the side, and I sure as hell wouldn't have started with Bianca Ford, who wasn't even in Rita's league. But I knew better than to say anything; the one thing more life-threatening than making Rita jealous was accusing her of being jealous.

I unfolded the note. Lester Bucktail had written, or rather printed in block letters:

FELICIA JORDAN IS AT SOMETHING CALLED
GREEN HILLS, I THINK IN OR NEAR
JENKS. PRIVATE HOME FOR MESSED-UP
TEENS AND NO VISITORS EXCEPT FAMILY.
NOTHING ON PAULA JORDAN EXCEPT SHE
LIVES SOMEWHERE IN TULSA.

The signature was in Cherokee. I passed the note to Rita, who read it and looked up at me. "Going to follow up?"

I shrugged. "I don't know what good it would do. Even if I found one or both of the daughters and—"

There was a sudden mild commotion among the demonstrators, people talking excitedly and looking back toward the road. The deputies were looking that way, too, and shifting stances as if anticipating trouble. I turned around, while Rita said softly, "Oh, shit."

Down beside the road, getting out of a dark blue van with an eagle painted on the side, were Marvin Painted Horse and Vince Lacolle. A moment later the van's rear door thumped open and Nehemiah Harjo dismounted, followed by Linda Blacksnake and the Cottonwoods. All of them were dressed much as they had been the last time I'd seen them, except for Linda Blacksnake, who wore a billowing purple dress that made her look like an enormous bruise.

Bianca Ford came out of the crowd and gave me a grin.

"Our mystery guests," she said, "and I *know*, but listen, Marvin Painted Horse is good for press attention anywhere he goes. Anyway, it's Columbus Day, and we had to have a Native American speaker."

Rita said something under her breath in Cherokee. Bianca Ford looked at her. "You're with the *Courier*, right? I'm sure I can fix you up with an interview. Got to go now, okay?"

She headed down the drive at a quick trot, wafflestomper soles thudding on the asphalt. A moment later she was shaking hands with Marvin Painted Horse, talking energetically and gesturing with her free hand in the direction of the plant gate.

Rita was digging in her purse, getting out a little pocket tape recorder. "Columbus Day, Echota Creek," she said, holding the recorder close to her mouth. "With Indians like this we didn't need Columbus."

She thumbed the switch and lowered the recorder. "I suppose this is the special event that was supposed to take place. Be still, my beating heart."

Marvin Painted Horse was striding up the drive now, the others falling in behind and beside him. I thought the deputies might try to stop him, but they stood aside. He didn't even look at them. He stalked onward, braids bouncing against his chest, face impassive as a boulder. You had to hand it to the son of a bitch; he had style.

The crowd parted to let him and his followers through. Everybody had gotten very quiet now; the only sound was the whine of the wind through the chain-link fence and, up by the guard shack, the sputter of a police radio.

He was heading straight toward the plant gate and for a moment I thought he meant to try to go in. I wasn't the only one; the squad of deputies blocking the drive were in ready-for-action mode, feet apart and batons slightly raised, while the private badges inside moved to cover the gate. Cross said something to Mizell.

But then at the last instant, just as Mizell took a step forward and opened his mouth, Marvin Painted Horse stopped and wheeled to face the crowd.

"Five hundred years ago," he shouted, "a colonialist pirate named Christopher Columbus came ashore in the Caribbean, thinking he was somewhere in the China Sea—because, being a typical white man, he had no sense of direction whatever."

A ripple of laughter ran across the crowd: nervous titters from the white demonstrators, delighted guffaws from the Indians. Marvin Painted Horse waited for quiet and then went on:

"His first official act was to kidnap several of the native people who had come in peace and goodwill to meet the strangers, and put them in chains for transportation back to Europe. In his report to the degenerate white rulers of Spain, he pointed out that the people were peaceful and gentle, and would therefore be quite easy to enslave.

"Five centuries later, we can see that his words were heeded well. Five centuries of unprovoked aggression and massacre, of calculated starvation and deliberately spread disease, of lies and betrayal and forced death marches—of genocide so nightmarishly effective that the leaders of the Third Reich made a study of the history of America's treatment of its native people, knowing they could get many useful ideas for the Holocaust they were planning—"

He swung his arm to point toward the nuclear plant. "And now," he cried, "when it seemed the white man could not possibly have any more evil tricks in his bag, we have this. After murdering and raping the people and the land, the master race has learned how to turn the sacred power of creation upon itself, to kill and disfigure not only the living but generations yet unborn. In Nevada, where they are careful to set off nuclear tests only when the wind is blowing away from Las Vegas and toward the Paiute and Shoshone reservations—"

There was a stir at the back of the crowd. I looked around in time to see a little convoy of vehicles coming up the road: four Oklahoma State Police black-and-whites and, in the lead, a plain white car with no markings of any kind. The cruisers weren't using their lights or sirens. Somehow that made their approach even more ominous.

Marvin Painted Horse was still speaking, but he'd lost part of his audience; a growing number of people were watching the latest arrivals. The five cars were coming to a stop on the road next to the plant entrance, not bothering to pull over, and doors were opening. Four men in dark windbreakers got out of the white car and started up the drive, while behind them uniformed state troopers began piling out of the cruisers.

They didn't try to go through the crowd; they didn't give any sign of noticing the demonstrators at all. They went around, walking up the slight slope beside the entrance drive, facing straight ahead, eyes hidden by dark blind-man shades. By now Marvin Painted Horse had stopped talking and you could hear the dry grass crunching under the cops' shoe soles.

The four men in the lead walked up to the War Party group and stopped, backs to the crowd. Their jackets bore the single word POLICE across the shoulder blades. Behind them the uniformed troopers deployed in a neat formation, half of them facing toward the crowd, the others facing Marvin Painted Horse's people. Meanwhile the line of deputies at the gate began moving quietly toward the War Party leaders from the rear. It was all done with impressive speed and efficiency; the whole thing had obviously been carefully planned.

One of the plainclothesmen took a step forward and produced a sheaf of papers. "Marvin Painted Horse." He didn't shout, but his words carried clearly. "Vincent Lacolle. Linda Blacksnake. You are hereby under arrest. Please turn around and place your hands on top of your heads."

There was a quick angry muttering from the crowd. Some of the young Indians began to move forward. Nehemiah Harjo said something.

One of the troopers carried a bullhorn. The cop who had spoken first took it and turned to face the crowd. "This arrest has nothing whatever to do with your demonstration." He had the bullhorn a little too close to his mouth, distorting his words. "These people are under arrest for conspiracy to distribute drugs. Please move back for your own safety until they have been secured."

Mizell came up beside him and took the bullhorn. "Listen," he shouted over the still-growing noise from the crowd. "There is nothing political about what you see—"

Somebody yelled, "Bullshit!" There were cries of general agreement.

"These officers are from the State Bureau of Narcotics," Mizell continued. "Please move back and let them do their jobs. Once they're out of here with their prisoners, you people can go on with your demonstration. Let's stay calm and nobody gets hurt."

A skinny woman standing near me, her gray hair done up in a single long braid, screamed, "Pigs!" It shook me a little; I hadn't heard that one since I was in college. It was like hearing somebody say, "Aroint thee, varlet!"

The plainclothesmen were speaking in low voices to the War Party people, maybe reading them their rights, maybe trying to get them to turn around and let themselves be cuffed. Nobody had drawn any weapons yet, unless you counted the deputies' batons. Nehemiah Harjo was still talking and nobody was paying any attention.

Suddenly Vince Lacolle yelled something in a language I

didn't recognize, and then, in one I did, "Fuck you, white-ass!" And took a swing at the nearest plainclothesman, who promptly grabbed Lacolle's wrist in a professional takedown hold and tossed him onto his face on the asphalt.

Linda Blacksnake spat out some non-Indo-European sylla-bles of her own and lunged at the plainclothesman, who was bent over putting handcuffs on Vince Lacolle. She had fast moves for such a big girl. A couple of uniformed troopers nailed her from behind and Nehemiah Harjo took a step in their direction, raising his hands and shouting, only to be seized and dumped on his ass by Pace, who was the only per-son on the scene who looked happy. Marvin Painted Horse stood quietly while the narcs cuffed him.

The young Indians at the front of the crowd charged, then, shouting and cursing and raising fists, and immediately ran into the troopers, who proceeded to knock the shit out of them. By now the crowd was surging forward and the depu-ties on the perimeter were moving nervously in, while Mizell called orders over the bullhorn.

From that point on the situation did nothing but deterio-rate. Quite a few of the demonstrators decided they wanted no part of what was going down, and tried to break for the road, only to meet the reserve deputies, who were swinging at everything that moved. The plant guards came rushing through the gate, apparently on their own—I saw Bob Cross waving his hands frantically at them, but they gave no sign of noticing—to add their efforts to the developing melee. At first there was only a lot of shoving and yelling, but then a night-stick flashed briefly and then another, and there was a sicken-ing whacking sound that I recognized all too readily.

By this time I had stopped watching and started looking for the egress. Rita had tucked in tightly behind me, her hand hooked in my belt. I put my head down and led with my shoulder like an offensive lineman, and rammed and plowed and trampled as necessary until we got to the edge of the battlefield.

A panicky-looking young deputy appeared, blocking our escape route. Rita reached around me and waved her press card and called, "Press, press, Tulsa *Courier,*" but he was oblivious. He raised his nightstick and I got ready to kick him in the crotch and then the woman with the gray braid walloped him in the face with a leather purse barely small enough to qualify as carry-on luggage. As he turned to face the unexpected flank attack I broke past him on the other side, dragging Rita behind me. "Fascist," the gray-haired woman was screaming. "Power to the people."

A moment later we were loping briskly down the grassy slope toward the road and Rita's car. Behind us Mizell's bullhorn-amplified voice boomed on, torn to bits and fragments by the wind: ". . . disperse . . . leave the area . . . subject to arrest. . . ."

We sat in the car and watched the rest of the farce. That wasn't my idea; but Rita wanted to stay, and it was her job, after all, and her car. So I sat and watched with her, wishing I'd brought my binoculars. We didn't talk a lot.

It wasn't much of a rumble, though some of the newspeople later made it sound like a failed version of the Storming of the Winter Palace. I'd seen far worse in my cop-reporter days, covering rousts in North Tulsa pool halls or raids on teenage beer parties. The demonstrators, except for a handful of veterans, clearly hadn't had much practice at this sort of thing, and, luckily, neither had most of the deputies. The troopers, who might have lent a bit of professionalism to the brawl, were primarily occupied in getting the War Party arrestees away from the scene. There was a lot of pushing and scuffling and grappling and a certain amount of the ever-popular hitting, but nobody appeared to be getting seriously injured.

Still, it was nothing any normal person would enjoy watching. Especially a person of my generation, who had somehow had the idea that all this was long behind us.

I thought somebody might come and run us off, but nobody paid us any mind at all. At last, when the fracas had died down and the last demonstrators were getting into their cars or being hauled away by the cops, Rita announced that she was going back up to the gate to ask a few questions.

I told her she'd go over my dead body. So she killed me and went anyway.

I watched her walking determinedly up the drive, press card in one hand and recorder in the other, and thought any number of admiringly exasperated thoughts. Instinct said go with her, but logic said I'd only screw up the job for her—Mizell would not be happy to see me right now, or to talk to anyone who was with me—and for once I let logic win.

It was late afternoon by the time we finally left the Echota Creek area. Crossing the railroad tracks, Rita said, "I still wish I knew what's happened to Tommy. Maybe we should go by old man Badwater's place, see if he's there."

"Take a right up here," I told her. "I think I've got an idea where we might find him."

A few minutes later, heading down the main road toward Redbud, Rita leaned back in her seat and let out a long and very tired sigh. "What a mess," she said. "Remember that time you and Wiley Harmon got into that fight with those bikers? A cluster-fuck, he called it. I've never understood that expression before today."

When Rita started quoting Wiley Harmon it was time to check the sky for signs of Judgment Day. I said, "Find out much?"

"Only the official basics. Marvin and Vince and Linda are

all charged with conspiracy and possession—some coke was found, allegedly, in their van after the arrests. Nehemiah Harjo is down for obstruction and interfering and resisting and the rest of the standard package. As are a number of other people of various races and affiliations."

She made an angry face. "The whole thing reeks, of course. Oh, I wouldn't be surprised to learn that the War Party leaders were involved in drug dealing—there have been rumors to that effect for a long time—and it's even possible that the dope found in the van was theirs and not a cop plant."

"Stranger things have happened."

"Yes. But the way the whole business was handled—Christ, Tag, you've been around police business a lot more than I have. Can you think of a worse possible time and place to make an arrest like that?"

"It would be difficult," I admitted. "Too many people on the scene, all crowded together—you'd have had a bloodbath if Vince Lacolle had come up with a gun—and all kinds of racial and political tensions in the air even before the narcs arrived. Just about perfect conditions to guarantee maximum brouhaha . . . and no reason at all for it, of course. It would have been dead easy to wait and pick them off on the highway as they drove away."

"And the whole thing isn't going to be worth a damn in court."

"Oh, hell, no. Conspiracy to distribute is practically impossible to prove unless you actually catch the suspects with the dope and the money in their hands. Even if you set up a sting, it takes really expert planning and execution to keep from blowing the whole case. And whether or not that shit in the van was a plant, the defense can point out that the van was parked and unattended in an area where all sorts of people were milling around."

I looked off up the road, thinking. "You know, it doesn't make any sense. The bust itself was handled as professionally as I've seen. So why the waterheaded timing?"

"Unless the idea was to send a message," Rita offered. "Maybe nobody really wanted a legitimate arrest. Up until recently, War Party hasn't had much of a presence in this state. This could have been meant as intimidation."

"Like a warning shot across War Party's bows?"

"Right. And it might have been considered too risky to actually put a man like Marvin Painted Horse behind bars, where he would make a perfect symbolic martyr figure—"

"So they deliberately screw up the bust, so he walks after a little stay in jail and maybe a quiet visit from some faceless people who explain that next time things might not go this way. My God, Rita, that's so twisted I almost admire it."

"Don't forget," she said, "the state can still confiscate all their funds, not to mention odds and ends like that van. Even if the charges don't hold up it'll take years and a lot of expensive court time before any of it gets returned—if they ever see it again at all. A neat way to cripple War Party, by grabbing its treasury, which doesn't look nearly as bad in the news as physical harassment."

Her voice was calm, but her knuckles were dead white where her hands gripped the wheel.

"I'm a journalist, God damn it," she said, "and I know all about objectivity and professional detachment. But I stood there listening to that bullshit and running my little recorder and keeping up my little smile for the bastards, and all the time all I wanted to do was scream and scream and scream."

As I'd guessed, Tommy Ninekiller's car was parked in front of Charlie's Foxhole. Tommy himself was parked inside, sitting alone at a table in the back, drinking beer. There was a nearly empty pitcher on the table in front of him and his face had a flushed, loose look.

Rita started to speak. "Fuck it," Tommy said without looking at either of us. "I heard about what happened at their fucking chickenshit demonstration. Who cares?"

He drained his glass and slammed it down on the table so hard I winced, expecting it to shatter. "Fuck Marvin Painted Horse," he said in a bitter monotone, "and Bianca Ford and her *yoneg* tree-huggers and my crybaby cousin Chris Badwater, may they hang his sorry ass from a tree full of well-fed pigeons. Fuck Mizell and all other cops everywhere, and, with all due brotherly regard, fuck both of you, too. Did I miss anybody?"

He turned, then, to look up at us. I saw that there were red rings around the whites of his eyes.

"Old man Badwater's dead," he said.

We both stared, unable for the moment to speak. Tommy nodded, a bit jerkily.

"I found him," he said in a softer voice. "I was going to go out to Echota Creek to meet you, but I thought I'd go by and see if he needed anything. He didn't answer the door when I knocked but he was nearly deaf so I went on in. The door wasn't locked."

Tommy hunched his shoulders and put his hands together as if suddenly feeling cold. "He was just sitting there at the table," he said wonderingly, "with his head bowed on his chest, and I thought he was asleep, and I reached out and touched him on the shoulder, and he sort of toppled over and slid down onto the floor, and then I saw he was dead."

15

T HERE ARE MANY WAYS to go about finding a person in a city the size of Tulsa. The techniques are familiar to private detectives, investigative journalists, collection-agency skip tracers, and other nosy bastards; and, with today's almost universal use of information technology, only the very rich and the very poor can vanish and make it stick. Credit card and finance companies, banks, public agencies, doctors and lawyers—they've all got computerized records nowadays, invariably containing a lot of personal information that was never any of their business, and any competent computer hacker can get at it with laughable ease. So can anybody else willing to slip some money to the right people; it's merely a matter of learning how to spot and approach the bribable employees, and this isn't as difficult as it might seem.

I knew quite a bit about the subject, since finding people, and finding out things about them, had constituted the greater part of my unofficial second job over the last few years. I even had contacts already in place—at the phone company, for example—so I didn't need to waste time shopping around for advantageously placed greedheads.

Sometimes, though, you start by trying the easy way. I looked in the Greater Tulsa phone book and sure enough, there was a Paula Jordan listed. Only one, too. How about that.

Of course there was no guarantee she was the one I was looking for. I'd never known a Paula Jordan, but I didn't suppose it was a terribly uncommon name; it wasn't as if I were looking for Evangeline Grunch or Wladislaw Syzygy. And the listed address was clear over on the east side of Tulsa, farther than I cared to drive without more than a name to go on.

I thought about it for a little while and then dialed the number. It was five in the afternoon and I wondered if anybody would be home, but after the second ring a woman answered with a slightly breathy, "Yes? Hello?"

I said, "Paula Jordan?"

"Yes. Who is this?"

"Hi, Paula." I put a big dollop of silly-ass warmth into my voice. "This is Willis Cranford. Remember me? We went to Redbud High together. I'm in charge of planning the class reunion—"

"Forget it," she said sharply. "I don't want to talk to you."

"Excuse *me*," I said stiffly, not quite doing Steve Martin.

"Look," she said, sounding a little less hostile, "it's nothing personal, okay? It's just that I never have anything to do with that Redbud scene. I left there years ago and I don't even like to think about it. Anyway, I didn't graduate. Why would I go to a reunion of a class I got kicked out of?"

"Well," I said, "could I at least ask you a few questions?"

"No time. I've got to finish doing the dishes and then I have to start getting ready for work. Say," she said, "what did you say your name was? I don't remember—"

"Thank you," I said hurriedly. "Have a nice day."

I hung up and sat there for a moment on the couch, considering. Harry came padding up and laid his head in my lap to have his ears scratched. "There you have it," I told him. "Another piece of brilliant investigative work by the human bloodhound, Taggart Roper."

Harry whined softly as my fingertips hit a sensitive spot. I said, "Okay, now I know where she is. So what, if anything, do I do about it?"

Harry didn't offer any response beyond a brief snuffle.

"Lot of help you are," I said, and stood up and stretched. "Least you could do is give me a little input now and then. Since you won't get a job, or even do your share of the housework. Look at this place."

Harry said he didn't want to look at the place, it depressed him. I couldn't really blame him. Things were in an even bigger mess than usual, staggering as that concept might be. I'd spent most of the weekend going over the edited manuscript of *Staked Plain,* and I hadn't felt like diverting time and attention to domestic details. Marcia Grimshaw hadn't done as much to my text as I'd feared—in fact she'd meddled less than any of my previous editors—but I'd still had to do a certain amount of stetting and scribbling and saying shit, and in the process a good many beer cans and food wrappers had wound up on the floor, as well as enough spilled coffee to wake up a mummy. Then yesterday there had been that grotesque affair at Echota Creek; I hadn't gotten home till late at night.

And maybe, I reflected, that was why I was diddling around with this pointless business of finding Paula Jordan. Maybe it was no more than a way of putting off the cleanup work. That was as good a reason as any; it certainly made as much sense as, oh, say, trying to assuage an irrational surge of guilt that hit me every time I remembered an old man asking me if I wanted more fish.

Damn if she didn't live in a trailer, too.

It sat in the approximate middle of a big dusty lot full of trailers, all of them up on blocks, most fitted with side awnings or tacked-on porches. There was more space between the trailers than in the average Tulsa-area park—the one I'd lived in before moving across the river had been like so many tin cans on a supermarket shelf—and several trailers were surrounded by silly little picket fences. I didn't see any plastic flamingos, though.

It was late now, dusk coming down fast, but there was still plenty of light to let me find Paula Jordan's place. Her trailer was smaller than mine but quite a bit newer. She hadn't done much to the exterior—it was still an honest trailer, not tricked out in imitation-real-house drag—but there were several clay pots, containing struggling bits of vegetable life, lined up beside the door.

Of more immediate interest, there were no lights on and no car in the parking space, and when I knocked there wasn't any answer either.

Well, she'd said she had to go to work; I'd known there was a chance of missing her, and I'd driven as fast as I could all the way from Yuchi Park. But traffic had been heavy, and I'd had to waste a lot of time crawling along at seventy or so. I stood looking at the trailer, wondering what next, and then a voice behind me said, "Looking for Miss Paula?"

I turned and saw a short, chubby old guy standing in the door of the next trailer. He was bald and red of face, and he wore a light blue polo shirt and checkered pants pulled up almost to his armpits, secured with a white belt. White shoes, too. Tommy Ninekiller often said that there was nobody on earth who could dress as goofy as an old white man, and this one was living proof. He had a friendly smile, though, rather than the suspicious scowl that trailer-park people often aim at strangers.

"She's gone to work," he informed me. "You her boyfriend?"

"Cousin." It was the first thing that came to mind. "Haven't seen her for over a year, been working overseas. I guess I should have called ahead."

"Uh-huh." He looked sympathetic. "Well, she always goes

to work around this time, except Sundays. I think you just missed her."

"You know Paula pretty well?"

His smile got wider, revealing impressive bridgework. "She's a real friendly girl," he said. "Nice looking, too, if you don't mind me saying so." His eyes held a distant look, as if remembering something he'd forgotten a long time ago.

I said, "I don't suppose you know where she works."

"Oh, sure. Foxy Ladies, that's the name of the place—"

A woman's carbide-tipped voice came from within the trailer. "Walter, who are you talking to?"

The old guy glanced nervously around. His grin was gone now, replaced by a harried expression that looked to have a lot of miles on it. I said, "Do you know the address?"

He looked back at me. "No," he said abruptly, and stepped back into the trailer and closed the door with a distinct bang. As I started to walk away I heard the woman's voice again: "Walter, who was that? Walter?"

I hadn't gotten enough sleep the night before; I'd stayed up till three in the morning, finishing the last pages of *Staked Plain*, and then I'd gotten up at nine to haul the manuscript to the post office and the check to the bank. That must have been why my mind was working so poorly. I can think of no other explanation.

I crossed the street to a little convenience store and asked to see their phone book. I had no idea where to look in the yellow pages, but the white-page business listings had a Foxy Ladies, located on the other side of town. I was going to have to drive another six or seven miles, most of it back the way I'd just come. Uttering a couple of perfunctory oaths, I yanked the Camaro around in a fast and illegal U-turn. Resist much, obey little; I think Walt Whitman said that. Or maybe it was Keith Richards. I forget.

Driving back along the expressway, blinking against the still-painful last rays of the expiring sun, I wondered what sort of place Foxy Ladies was and what Paula Jordan did there. Women's fashions, or one of those lingerie shops? But she'd just gone to work, and most retail clothing stores in the Tulsa area closed down about six. Maybe Foxy Ladies was a beauty shop; maybe Paula was a hairdresser.

That's what I mean about my brain not working worth a damn. I was less than a block from the place when the shorted-out lights finally came on in my head, and even then it was the big sign above the entrance—FOXY LADIES in bright red, flanked by hot-pink outlines of female bodies—that did it. Well, okay, I hadn't been looking forward to visiting a hair salon anyway.

It wasn't quite dark yet but the parking lot beside Foxy Ladies was already nearly full—guys getting off work, no doubt, having a drink and a bit of titillation before heading homeward. I parked across the street, in case I needed to leave in a hurry. A woman on the front porch of a small frame house gave me a dirty look. Tulsa is odd that way; there is no established zone, as in most cities, for strip joints and porn shops—the Bible Belters would never stand for that sort of blatant official tolerance of sin—so they wind up scattered all over town, occasionally in residential neighborhoods, to the severe chagrin of the people who live there.

Foxy Ladies was a sizable establishment, with big glass front doors flanked by displays of eight-by-ten color glossies of nearly naked women. The interior was about what you'd expect: grope-around lighting, low ceiling, tables crammed too close together. A long narrow stage ran down the middle of the room.

Near the end of the stage a short, busty brunette was backed up against a shiny pole that rose from stage to ceiling. She was moving her hips from side to side, rubbing her slightly plump bottom against the pole, while running her hands up and down the insides of her thighs. All she had on was a pair of white fishnet stockings with matching garter belt, black fuck-me pumps, and a G-string. Hidden speakers filled the place with a recorded neo-disco arrangement of "Dance With Me." As I crossed the room she turned, raising her hands to grip the pole, and began rubbing her crotch against the gleaming metal in a series of knee bends.

A thin black waitress, wearing a red satin outfit that didn't cover much more than the dancer's rig, came over and met me while I was still deciding where to sit. "Welcome to Foxy Ladies," she said, smiling. "Do you want a table, or would you rather sit by the stage?"

I told her I'd take a table, which obviously pleased her; the guys who perched on the stools beside the runway would use up most of their tip money stuffing bills into stocking tops and G-strings. When she had seated me and taken my order—beer; I'd have preferred Jim on the rocks but the hard liquor here was sure to be watered—I asked my question.

She frowned. She wasn't, she said, supposed to identify the dancers by their real names. "No offense," she said, "but we get these weirdos, follow the girls around. Sometimes family, too, they can be the worst. Not too long back this one girl's daddy showed up with two of her brothers, great big old rednecks, going to take her home whether she wanted to go or not. Wrecked the place, took a bunch of cops to get them out. You want to meet one of the dancers, have her come to your table for a drink or a private dance, okay, but you got to ask for her by her stage name."

I slid a folded twenty across the table. "Like I told you," she said, "you ask me about this Paula Jordan, I can't help. But now if you wanted to meet, oh, just for example *Ashley*—why, you could ask me about *Ashley* and no problem, I could tell *Ashley* there's a gentleman wants to meet her."

She gave her nose a pointed little wiggle, just in case I was unusually thick. "You wouldn't be interested in *Ashley,* would you?"

"Why, yes," I said. "Now you mention it, Ashley sounds very nice."

She palmed the twenty. "She's about to go on. When she's done I'll fetch her. Any name you want me to give her?"

"Just a gentleman admirer."

"Fine," she said. "I'll get your beer. Enjoy the show."

I sat and nursed my beer—at five bucks a pop I wasn't doing any chugging—and watched the brunette finish her routine, rolling and hunching frantically on the floor in an excess of ersatz ecstasy. There was applause and a good many customers reached up to stick bills into her garter belt as she pranced off.

A female voice came from the speakers: "And now for your enjoyment, the lovely, the exciting—*Ashley!*"

The curtains parted at the end of the stage, while the music began again, this time a fairly decent "Hot Child in the City." At the end of the four-bar instrumental intro, Paula Jordan appeared.

She was tall, five-six or more, and a lot of that was very fine leg. She wore sheer black lace-topped stockings, a skimpy black garter belt, and a black lace teddy cut high to show off her buttocks. Her straw-blond hair was tied up in a high ponytail that switched and bounced as she strutted down the runway. Everybody applauded and some testosterone-stupid cowboy yipped and howled like a coyote.

She grabbed the pole and swung around it and began to dance.

In all the books and movies, when the detective finally finds the Mystery Woman dancing in a sleazy club, she always turns out to be far and away the best dancer in the house: too good for such a cheap dive, a pale flame leaping gazellelike about the stage, so magnificent that even the rowdiest lechers in the audience fall silent from sheer worshipful awe. . . .

Paula Jordan, however, simply wasn't all that good.

Oh, she was all right; she stayed with the music and she had some reasonably good moves. But she was a big girl, and inclined to lumber, and half the time she didn't have a clue what to do with her hands. Her routine was no more than a series of uninspired standard bits—hot-squatting, humping the pole, crawling on hands and knees—with absolutely no surprises.

But then, with her looks, she didn't need much of an act. The clientele certainly loved her; she must have had as much money tucked into her costume as I usually had in the bank.

Halfway through, she slowly undid the black garment and wriggled out of it, leaving nothing but stockings and garter belt and a G-string that barely covered her labia. She had large, heavy breasts, with nipples so dark I decided she couldn't possibly be a natural blonde.

When she finished and strode offstage to loud and sustained applause, my waitress walked past my table and gave me a nod. I saw her vanish through a door beside the stage. About twenty minutes later Ashley/Paula came out the same door, wearing a black dress. She walked across the room toward me, pausing here and there to acknowledge greetings and compliments and fend off drunken passes. When she sat down at my table I got a good many resentful looks from her admirers.

"Roberta said you wanted to talk to me," she said in that breathy voice I remembered from the telephone. "Buy me a drink? It's the only way they'll let me sit with you."

I nodded and waved the waitress over. After the traditional ritual had been carried out, and Paula had a cocktail glass of tea in front of her, I introduced myself and trotted out my shopworn cover story.

She was shaking her head well before I was done. "No way," she said decisively. "Look, man, I don't know how you found me, but you wasted your time. First place, I don't talk to *anybody* about my family. I'm sure not going to dish out a lot of personal stuff about my father, with him barely in his grave, to some stranger trying to make a buck writing some damn book. And besides," she added, "I couldn't tell you anything. I left Redbud when I was seventeen and I haven't exactly stayed in touch. Like I told this geek who called me this afternoon, I don't even want to think about that town anymore."

I tried to look sympathetic and sincere. "Of course I understand how you feel about your father's death. Did he know about—" I gestured toward the stage, where a pale, essentially naked redhead was doing a spirited dirty boogie. "Your work?"

She snorted. "Boy, what is it with you? You don't listen, or you don't quit? But yeah, sure, of course he knew what I did for a living. He was a *cop,* for God's sake. And no, I don't guess he liked it, but we never really discussed the subject, okay? Or much of anything else." Her eyes were getting shiny. "Now are you happy? Going to put that in your book?"

"I'm sorry."

"No you're not." She sipped her tea. "Listen, if you do write that book, could you leave me out of it? I mean, do you have to even put me in it at all? I'd appreciate it if you wouldn't."

I made a noncommittal shrug. "No, really," she said. "This is important to me. There's . . . I'm not figuring to be working here, doing this kind of shit, much longer, okay? And I don't want people reading about me and finding out that I ran off when I was a kid and wound up stripping."

She made eye contact. "What I'm saying, if you could leave me out of your book, I'd *appreciate* it. You understand? That's how much it means to me."

My mind flashed up a picture of her as she'd looked a little while ago, wearing only black stockings and a spotlight. I said, "Um, ah—yes, I see." I cleared my throat unnecessarily. "Well, as I say, I don't even know whether I'm going to write the book."

I stood up. "Thanks for the conversation, anyway. By the way, have you been to see your sister Felicia? Isn't she—"

"You son of a bitch." Paula Jordan's voice was low and harsh and her eyes were flat as a rattlesnake's. "Don't you go near my sister. Don't even think about her. God damn you, leave her alone!"

A large man in a suit materialized beside the table. "Everything all right?" he asked Paula.

"Get him out of here," she said, almost whispering. "Please."

He turned to look at me. He was as wide as Pace and most of a foot longer. His face consisted mainly of scar tissue. I said quickly, "I was just leaving."

"Know that already, do you?" He folded his arms and shook his head. "Too bad. I was hoping you'd make me explain it to you."

"You went *where*?" Rita said that night. "Taggart Roper, if you're going to start hanging around those places—"

"It was where she was," I said defensively. "Would you rather I'd visited her at home?"

"I don't want you anywhere within a mile of her."

"No need to worry about that. She doesn't want to talk to me and there's no reason to think she knows anything anyway. Which," I said, "would seem to eliminate my last possible lead, since there's no point in even trying to get into Green Hills to see the other daughter. Sorry, Rita. Looks like I struck out again."

"Never mind. I appreciate the effort."

She stood up. We were spending the evening at her apartment in south Tulsa. It was still early and we hadn't gotten past the drinks-on-the-living-room-couch stage yet.

"So you like exhibitions?" She walked to the center of the living room and turned to face me. She had on a cream-colored silk blouse and a short tan skirt and just now she also wore an odd, sly expression. Her tongue came out and licked her lips and then her right foot began tapping out a steady, insistent rhythm. "Got your instrument with you, Maestro? Give me something to work with."

"My instrument?" Then I got it. "Oh. Yeah—"

I took the harmonica from my jacket pocket and put it to my mouth and swung into a standard twelve-bar blues, doing some reed-bending down on the low notes. Rita's hips began to roll with the beat. "All right," she said.

She started to dance, little close steps at first, then her whole body getting into it, fluid and graceful as a swimming mink. Her hands rose slowly to the buttons of the silk blouse, while her eyes stayed locked on mine. "Don't stop playing," she said urgently.

She took her time undoing the buttons, teasing me a little, as I switched to a down-and-dirty "Summertime." Turning her back, she shrugged the blouse off, looking at me over her shoulder, hips swaying, dancing a few steps away and back before turning back to face me. She held the silk blouse in front of her for a couple of bars and then tossed it away. Rita seldom wore a bra, but tonight she had on a little mauve number that cradled her small firm breasts like a pair of loving hands.

She reached for the skirt's zipper and ran it up and down a few times with the music. By now I was into "The Lady Is a Tramp" and my lips were getting tender, but I wouldn't have stopped if the Hohner had been radioactive. She undid the skirt and let it drop, stepping neatly out of it as it crumpled to the floor. She wore a mauve garter belt and matching stockings and wispy mauve panties that she played with a little, snapping the elastic waistband, before turning her back again and reaching back to unhook the bra. That was nice; no doubt front-hook bras are handy but there are few sights as erotic as a beautiful woman reaching back to unhitch a bra. Something about the way it curves the body—

The bra came free and she danced a little longer with her back to me; which was okay too, backs being a fine and underappreciated item of female anatomy. At last she turned half around and bent, pointed breasts dangling like little bells, to slide the panties down off her hips. A moment later she stood facing me, feet apart, arms raised and spread, a big dirty triumphant grin all over her face, while I blew a loud and sincere fanfare on the Hohner. "*Yes!*" she cried happily.

After that there was nothing to do but carry her into the bedroom, where a very good time was had by both.

16

T HEY HELD GRANDFATHER Badwater's funeral on Thursday, at a little Indian Baptist church not far from his home. The old building was packed; the deacons finally had to set up some folding chairs in back to handle the overflow. I hadn't realized he'd been so well known.

Chris Badwater was there, sitting in the front row, flanked by a pair of Cherokee Nation cops. I wondered how they'd worked out the jurisdiction on that. I couldn't tell, from behind, whether he was wearing handcuffs.

I sat with Rita and Tommy up near the front, on the aisle, and listened as a skinny old man in a bad suit led the congregation in a series of hymns. The singing was all in Cherokee but I recognized a couple of the tunes—"Amazing Grace" and "Sweet Hour of Prayer"—though I knew, from Rita, that Cherokee hymns aren't necessarily translations, many being original lyrics set to familiar English tunes.

They sounded good to me, even though I'm not usually much on church music. I didn't see any hymn books and there was no instrumental accompaniment, yet everybody came in together in four-part harmonies, often quite complex. They sang in slightly lower keys than a white choir—most of the songs, as best I could tell, were done in G—which gave added power to the bass voices. Inside that small wooden building, the effect was more than impressive.

The preacher was a man about my age, with powerful-looking shoulders and a dark, hawklike face. He spoke at some length in Cherokee, his soft high voice rising and falling in musical cadences, and then switched to English in what I took to be a translation. It was a fairly standard funeral sermon, for the most part, telling about the life and good qualities of the deceased. Toward the end, though, he said something that stuck with me:

"Every time one of our elders dies, the definition of all of us—of what it means to be Cherokee—changes by that much. When they are all gone, what will we be? Who will be left to help us remember who we are?"

After the sermon everybody stood and sang a final song, one I'd never heard before, very slow and stately and somehow moving even though I had no idea what the words meant. The voices split on the chorus, first the sopranos and tenors—some of the old women had astonishing range and strength; the hair fairly came up on the back of my neck when they hit and held the high notes—and then, repeating each phrase in response, the basses and altos:

> *Ogajeliga* . . . . .
>   *(Ogajeliga* . . . .)
> *jaguhwiyuhi* . . . . .
>   *(jaguhwiyuhi* . . . .)

Then, at the end, they went back and sang the chorus again, this time in brisk and spirited tempo. Later Rita explained that this was a very old song, traditionally sung at funerals. On the Trail of Tears, when as many as a third of the Cherokees in the world died—a worse toll than the Bataan Death March; a higher percentage than the Holocaust—it was sung so many times that it became almost a national anthem.

The graveyard was about a mile away. We rode in Rita's car—the Camaro's nonstock pipes would have been a bit loud for the occasion—but I drove. Rita was crying silently.

"They said it was heart failure," Tommy said from the

backseat. "The hell. He just didn't want to live anymore, so he quit living. Those old full-bloods can do that. They get ready to go, they *go*."

At the graveyard there were a couple of customs I'd never seen before. First everybody stood around the grave and, one by one, various people stepped forward and told little anecdotes about the deceased—some pretty funny, too, not at all what white people would consider appropriate at a funeral, and there was a good deal of laughter. Then they all lined up, while a young man held a shovel full of loose dirt, and filed past the grave, each person taking a handful of earth and tossing it onto the coffin.

The two Indian cops escorting Chris Badwater, I noticed, took a handful apiece with everyone else. Maybe they were relatives. Chris had on handcuffs, all right. "Probably a condition those bastards in Redbud insisted on," Tommy said in a low voice, "before they'd let him be escorted by his own people. You know, in the old days, when a Cherokee got the death sentence, they gave him a year to provide for his family and set his affairs in order. Then when it was time he came and turned himself in for execution. Never was a single case of a man failing to show up."

I'd thought I was the only Caucasian present, but at the cemetery I saw Bianca Ford in the crowd. After the ceremonies were done she came over and put out her hand. "Good to see you again," she said.

"You knew Grandpa Badwater?" Rita asked her, a trifle skeptically.

"I met him once. He was a sweet old guy. But mostly I came out of sympathy for Chris." She looked off across the cemetery, where the tribal cops were leading Chris Badwater away. "They wouldn't let me speak to him just now, even though I'm his attorney. But at least he saw I was here. I hope that means something to him."

Tommy said, "What do you mean, you're his lawyer? I thought Nehemiah Harjo was his mouthpiece." He frowned. "No, that's right, they've got the Crapulous Creek in the slammer too, don't they?"

"Actually Nehemiah made bail yesterday. So did the others."

"Really?" Rita said. "All of them?"

Bianca nodded. "I was surprised, too. You'd think they'd go for no-bail, the charges they had against Marvin and Vince and Linda."

"Especially with Vince's prison record," Tommy mused. "And all of them with a history of violent rhetoric and preaching resistance to the white man's law. Somebody probably decided they were more dangerous in jail than out of it, given the way such things usually work."

"Where'd they get the money?" I asked. "Since I assume the War Party treasury got impounded as possible drug profits."

"The Cottonwoods mortgaged their house."

Tommy groaned and Rita cursed. Bianca said, "Anyway, Nehemiah came by the jail and explained to Chris that he wouldn't be able to handle his case any longer. Said he had to devote all his time and effort to defending the leaders. Came right out and said that Marvin Painted Horse was more important to the movement than Chris. Chris asked where that left him and Nehemiah said everybody had to be willing to make sacrifices in the cause of racial justice."

This time I added a few expletives of my own to the chorus. "So," Bianca said, "that woke Chris up a little, and now he wants me to defend him. I think he's ready to take part in a real defense."

"Took him long enough," Tommy growled. "Too bad he didn't wise up sooner. That old man might still be alive."

Bianca sighed. "I don't know how much good it's going to

do him. There doesn't seem to be a single bit of evidence in his favor, and he still hasn't offered any alibi for that night."

She looked at me. "Have you got anything yet?"

I shook my head. She said, "Want me to certify you as engaged in investigative work for the defense? It would at least give you some legal status."

"No," I said. "I'm clear out of ideas."

That wasn't strictly true. But the one idea I had left was nothing I wanted to talk to Bianca Ford about; and besides, there was no way she or anyone else could make what I had in mind remotely legal. If I did it at all, I'd have to do it on my own, out there with my solitary ass bare to the wind.

But hell, I ought to be used to that by now.

The Green Hills Care Home was located on a county road more or less west of Jenks. It wasn't an easy place to find; it took some exploring just to get on the right road, and then I almost went past it before I realized it was there. All that was visible from the road was a lot of young second-growth hardwoods in need of thinning, and set back a little way from the left side of the road, a kind of ornamental gateway.

At least I assumed it was ornamental; it certainly wasn't functional, there being no fence or wall on either side or, as far as I could see, any means of closing it. There were merely a pair of truncated brick ramparts, like giant bookends, flanking the beginning of a narrow blacktop lane that wound off through the trees. The one on the right bore the discreet legend GREEN HILLS in not very large iron letters. Driving by, if you noticed it at all, you'd have taken it for the entrance to a housing development, or possibly a private estate belonging to somebody with money to blow on pretentious crap.

I aimed my rented Toyota between the bookends—there were reasons why the Camaro wouldn't do for today's business—and rolled slowly down the drive. The woods turned out to be a Potemkin forest; right around the first turn, less than a hundred yards from the road, the trees ended with abrupt finality, giving way to open ground covered with neatly mowed grass. Now the place looked more like a country club; but up ahead was another gate, a serious one this time, with a high chain-link fence stretching off on either side. It might have been put up by the same people who had installed the Echota Creek atomic plant's defenses.

There was a guard shack here too, and a sign: ALL VEHICLES MUST STOP. When I stopped mine, an elderly man in a blue uniform came out of the shack, carrying a clipboard. "Visitor?" he asked.

I nodded. He glanced at my license plate and made a notation on his clipboard. "You'll have to check in at the front office," he told me.

"Thanks. I hope I'm in time for visiting hours."

"No problem," he assured me. "That's only for regular visitors. You can come any time, Father."

I thanked him again and drove on through the gate, resisting the urge to bless him. Well, my false colors had passed their first test. Damn well should have, considering my investment; the black shirt and the white dog-collar had cost me something over forty bucks at a religious-supplies store in Tulsa. I'd wondered if the general public could buy them, and had come prepared with a tale about getting a present for a nephew about to enter the ministry. But evidently anybody with the money, or a major credit card, could acquire holy threads with no questions asked. I'd been a bit shocked.

Green Hills Care Home appeared ahead. There was a big, two-story red-brick building, a bit like a college dormitory, with several smaller but still sizable structures scattered over the hillside beyond. I could see a tennis court, where a couple of girls in white outfits were batting a ball back and forth, and a volleyball net. The whole scene was quite peaceful; I might have been looking at the campus of a small and exclusive prep school. But then I got close enough to see the bars on the windows.

The drive terminated in a large parking area in front of the big building. I stuck the Toyota into a slot marked VISITORS, got out, and paused to straighten my best dark suit—the overall effect of my ensemble wasn't bad, I decided; well, they do say that a man of distinction always looks good no matter what he wears—before starting for the front entrance. At the last moment, going up the steps, I caught myself whistling "I'm Too Sexy for My Shirt." I gave myself a mental kick in the ass and went in.

I'd come prepared to face a certain amount of suspicion and even hostility, but the stout woman at the front desk was cordial enough. I identified myself as the Reverend Willis Cranford, of St. Luke's Episcopal Church, and asked if I might be allowed a brief visit with Felicia Jordan.

The stout woman poked at her desktop computer, studied the screen, and said, "Ah—we don't have your name listed, Father. Of course we're happy to have visits from the clergy, but according to our records Felicia's religious affiliation is Methodist."

I gave her a warm forgiving smile. "I know. You see, my church is in Hot Springs, Arkansas, where several of Emily Jordan's relatives are among my parishioners. I happened to mention that I was going to be in Tulsa at a ministerial conference, and they asked that I stop by and see Felicia. For their peace of mind, you understand."

She bought it; I didn't even have to produce the phony letters and other props that I'd spent half the night fabricating. "Certainly," she said, reaching for her phone. "You can wait in one of the visiting rooms. Or we've got a little visiting area in back of this building, if you'd prefer that. It's such a pretty day today."

"That sounds very nice," I said. "Which way?"

The visiting area was merely a bit of lawn, about the size of a small highway rest stop walled off from the rest of the grounds by a high wooden fence with a padlocked gate. There were several redwood picnic tables and a lot of metal lawn chairs. I sat at one of the picnic tables and waited, wishing I'd worn a topcoat. The weather had warmed up a good deal since the weekend, and the sun was bright in a clear sky, but the breeze still had a full set of teeth.

After about fifteen minutes the door behind me opened and I turned to see a tall gray-haired woman in a white uniform ushering a wispy young girl toward me. I stood up and the woman said, "Here's Felicia now, Reverend. Naturally there's no time limit in your case, but it might be best to keep this visit as brief as possible. She has a group session later."

I nodded, not really paying attention. I was looking at the girl beside her.

Felicia Jordan might have weighed ninety pounds with her shoes on, but I wouldn't have bet on it. She was one of those unnervingly thin early-teen kids, all legs and arms and spidery fingers, and her skin was so pale you felt you could see all her insides if you got the sun behind her. Her hair was blond and a little stringy. She wore a white blouse and a gray skirt that I guessed must be a sort of uniform.

Her eyes were blue and enormous, with dark semicircles underneath, and they stared at me with an expression of resigned horror, a raccoon caught in the headlights. Here, the eyes said, was yet another strange adult who was going to do or say something to make life even more dreadful than it already was, but there was nothing to do but get it over with.

And that was when the day turned on me. I'd been treating this whole thing as something of a lark: dressing up in an outrageous disguise and bullshitting my way into their little private cuckoo's nest, what a laugh . . . but I looked into Felicia Jordan's eyes and suddenly it wasn't funny anymore. The truth was that I had lied my way into a mental institution, disguised as a Christian minister, in order to question a disturbed child about the brutal murder of her father, and I hadn't given ten minutes' thought to the emotional damage I might do. When you laid it out that way, this wasn't a moral high point in my life.

I came close to tossing the whole wretched imposture, then; but I remembered a kid in a cell and an old man in a box, and I put on a big false smile and said, "Hello, Felicia. You don't know me—"

The gray-haired woman disappeared back into the building while I spun my introductory line. Felicia Jordan was still staring at me, unblinking. When the door closed she said suddenly and clearly, "Bullshit."

I suppose I did a double-take. She said, "Mama's family are all super-heavy Arkansas Baptists, with a few Nazarenes. There's not one of them would even talk to a man with his collar on backwards. I've heard them all say so enough times."

She sat down at the picnic table and, after a moment, I sat down on the other side, facing her. "So," I said, "who am I, then?"

Unexpectedly she giggled. It was a strange giggle; it sounded like a perfectly normal postpubescent female titter, yet nothing happened on her face to back it up. She simply opened her mouth and the sound came out.

"I don't know," she said, "but I'm glad you came. You got me out of a session with this dikey bitch of a shrink. I'd rather talk to you than her, no matter who you are or what your game is." Again that eerie detached giggle. "Besides, you're kind of cute."

I saw now that her pupils were dilated. Stoned to the hair roots, of course, on whatever zombie-maker drugs they used here to keep their expensive charges quiet—Thorazine, maybe, or Lorezapam.

"I bet you're some kind of a repc*ter," she went on. "Trying to get a story about what happened to Daddy, huh? Or maybe you're with one of those TV shows, like Geraldo. I hope you haven't got a hidden camera on you. My hair is totally gross. The shampoo they give us here is all wrong."

Screw this. "Felicia," I said, "if I tell you the truth—"

"I won't rat on you. Jesus Christ," she said, "it'll be cool to have somebody level with me for a change."

So I told her, in basic terms, what I was up to. She listened attentively, though there was still a definite spaciness about her. At the end she said, "Wow. So you're trying to get Chris Badwater off. I hope you make it. Everybody gets all bent out of shape when I say so, but I never did believe he killed Daddy."

"Any particular reason?" I asked, and held my breath.

"Well, for one thing, just *look* at them. I mean, of course you can't look at Daddy, but did you ever see him when he was alive?"

"No."

"If you had you'd know what I'm talking about. He might have been kind of, like, old, but you wouldn't believe how strong he was. Tough, too. And you've seen Chris. Daddy would have broken him in half, tomahawk or no tomahawk." Again that giggle. "Besides, Chris couldn't kill a potato bug. He's just a big old *mouth*."

It was a disappointment, but not a heavy one; I hadn't really expected more. I said, "You know Chris?"

"Oh, sure. I mean, I don't really *know* him, not well, but

I've met him. He gave me a ride home from a powwow one time and Daddy just about took the roof off. Of course Daddy wasn't too happy about me going to the powwow in the first place. He didn't like Indians," she said, and sighed. "Didn't like me being friends with them, but I feel like, you know, somebody's cool, they're cool. Who cares about all that race shit?"

She put her skinny little elbows on the table and rested her chin in her hands. "So are you, like, going to get him off?"

"It doesn't look good. Chris won't say where he was that night, and nobody else seems to have seen him anywhere. As for finding the real killer—" God, how to say it to her? "There are too many possibilities," I finished lamely.

"Tell me about it," she said. "Lots of people didn't like Daddy." Once more that skulled-out giggle. "Lots and *lots* of people. I know what you're saying."

She sat up and tilted her head to one side. "I tell you what, though, if you want to know where Chris was the night Daddy got killed, you ought to talk to Judy Littlebear."

It was a new name. "Who's she? His girlfriend?"

This time Felicia Jordan managed a small but genuine laugh. "His what? No, no. They weren't, like, *going* together or anything. Between you and me, I always kind of suspected Chris might be—" She made a limp-wrist gesture. "I don't think he knows it, though."

She pushed a wind-whipped strand of hair from her face. "I shouldn't say stuff like that. Like I told you, I don't really know him that well. He's so much older than me," she said seriously. "I don't know Judy either, except to speak to. See, her sister goes with this boy I know, *his* sister is in my class—"

She went into a labyrinthine explanation of extended teen-age relationships. I didn't try to follow it. "Anyway," she went on, "Chris and Judy both go to NSU—well, okay, he dropped out this spring and I think she just started, but you know what I mean—and they're both into a lot of, you know, political things. Indian stuff, pollution, like that. They sort of hang out together, okay? Only they have to be cool about it, because her family doesn't like him."

"You think she might have been with him that night?"

"If she wasn't," Felicia said, "I bet she knows where he was. Anyway, you ought to talk to her."

"Thanks," I said sincerely. "Any idea where I can find her?"

"She's in college. You ought to be able to find her around NSU."

I looked at my new watch. A ten-buck Wal-Mart digital wonder, plastic band and all; it didn't go worth a damn with the high-church imposture, and I couldn't believe I'd forgotten to take it off, but apparently nobody had noticed. I stood up. "I better go," I said, "before somebody thinks to call your mother and ask about me. Thanks again, Felicia."

"Oh, hey, wow, that's cool." She stood up too, swaying for a second and blinking. "It's been fun getting to talk to somebody besides family and shrinks. These people here are such a pain in the ass."

Her voice was bitter and there was serious pain in the huge eyes. "When they're not treating us like criminals they're treating us like retarded children," she said. "And they keep us doped up till we turn into potted plants. You know, half the kids in this place are here because of drugs, so what do these assholes do? Give them drugs, that's what."

She grinned crookedly. "There's this boy my age, got into big trouble last week. They've got this sign on the shrink's office door, says THERAPIST in these, like, metal letters, you know? And he sneaked out one night and somehow he moved the letters over so it said THE RAPIST. He caught hell, but if you ask me he was just telling it like it is. Glad you came to see me," she said. "You seem like a pretty real dude. Wish I could have helped you."

"You did," I told her. "It may even turn out that you saved Chris Badwater's life."

"I hope so. He's okay, you know," she said. "He just needs to, like, get over himself. Like a lot of people I know."

17

* * * * * * * * * *

TOMMY NINEKILLER SAID, "Well, so much for another promising idea. This is getting to be a drag."

"Maybe she's got something," I said over my shoulder. "Don't be so eager to give up."

"Huh uh," Tommy said definitely. "Look at her face."

We sat in the parked Camaro on a winding Tahlequah street with the evocative name of Goingsnake and watched Rita coming back toward the car. Behind her, in the doorway of a little frame house, a stocky young Indian girl stood gazing curiously at us in the midafternoon sun.

Tommy was right; Rita's face wore a tight-lipped expression of frustration, and her boot heels were hitting the concrete walk with a little more than necessary force. She stepped down off the curb and yanked the door open and slid in beside me. "They haven't seen her since yesterday," she said. "No suggestions, either."

"So what do we do now, gang?" Tommy said from the backseat. "Put an ad in the paper? Hire a skywriter?"

"Shut up, Tommy," Rita said crossly. "Damn it, I was afraid of this. Saturday afternoon is a terrible time to try to find a college student." Then, after a minute, "But it's a good question. What *do* we do next? I'm all out of ideas."

We'd been looking for Judy Littlebear since noon. So far we'd learned that she'd moved out of her dormitory to share a duplex apartment with a couple of other girls; we'd located the apartment, with a certain amount of difficulty—Tahlequah's streets seemed to be laid out according to no humanly comprehensible plan—only to find nobody home and no clues as to when somebody might be back. A couple of kids at the Native American Student Association, over at the NSU campus, had given Rita a few names and addresses of Judy's acquaintances but this was the last one on the list and none of them had done us any good.

"Let's go back to Lester's," Tommy said. "Maybe he's found out something by now."

It was another bright wind-whipped day, a good deal warmer than the preceding one; people were walking along the streets of Tahlequah in shirtsleeves, and a few endothermic teenagers even wore shorts. At this time of year, in eastern Oklahoma, a rise in temperature after a cold spell usually means rain on the way, but the sky was still clear.

Lester Bucktail was in his front yard, picking up litter, when we drove up. "Damn college kids threw all these beer cans over the fence last night," he groused as we came through the gate. "Least the little bastards could have done was toss in a few full ones for me." He shoved a handful of crushed cans into a black plastic trash bag and knotted the top. "Come on in. You guys look like you could use a drop yourselves."

We all trooped up the outside stairway and into the living room. Billy Greenstick was sitting cross-legged on the floor with a stack of comic books. "Look at that," he said, pointing to a violently colored panel. "They came up behind this guy and held this chloroform rag over his face. You think that would work?"

"Wouldn't work on me," Lester Bucktail told him.

"Sure it would," Tommy said. "They'd just have to say, 'Here, Lester, try this.' "

Lester led the way back to the kitchen and opened the re-frigerator and took out a couple of cans of Old Milwaukee.

Rita shook her head and, after a glance at her, so did Tommy, but I took one gratefully.

"Did a little calling around," Lester Bucktail said, opening the other can. "Nobody knows much about Judy Littlebear. She doesn't have any close family around this area and she doesn't seem to be much of a campus social mixer."

"Does Billy know her?" Tommy asked.

"He says not. Thinks they have some mutual acquaintances, but he couldn't reach any of them by phone. These kids on weekends, they don't stay in one place for long."

"Maybe she went home," Rita suggested.

"No, that's the one thing I did turn up. Several people remembered hearing her say she wasn't going home this weekend. The impression I get, her father's pretty strict, old-fashioned Creek Baptist—"

"I thought she was Cherokee," I said.

"Her mother is. The Littlebears are Creek, though."

"Quite a few of them around Tulsa," Tommy said. "I didn't know there were any in Sizemore County. Didn't know there were any Creeks down there at all. Well, that goes some way to explain why the old man didn't want his daughter hanging out with Chris."

Lester Bucktail swigged beer, wiped his mouth, and nodded agreement. "That's the picture I got. Anyway, the best suggestion anybody came up with was to check out the powwow tonight, down at the community building. Almost everybody I talked to said that there was a good chance Judy'd be there, and if not there would still be people around who might be able to tell us something."

Tommy looked at Rita and grinned. "Powwow? Hey, sis, you up for a little Southern Plains hip-hop? Listen to the boys banging on the old drum and yowling like coyotes in heat, maybe get out there and do the intertribal boogie—"

"Actually I wouldn't mind," Rita said thoughtfully. "I

haven't been to a powwow in a long time. Might be fun . . . and it does sound like our best chance to find Judy Little-bear." She touched my arm. "But if you don't want to stay so late, Tag—"

"Sure," I said.

The community building was a big barn of a place down on the south side of town. It was around seven when we got there and the parking lot was full; I had to park a considerable distance away and we walked back up the sidewalk toward the bright lights of the entrance. A couple of young guys in bright-feathered fancy-dance outfits came from behind a van and walked in front of us, laughing and talking animatedly in some brittle-sounding language. I caught the words "Kim Basinger," though.

The BLAM BLAM BLAM BLAM of a big Plains drum met us as we came through the door. Voices rose above the drum in a high-pitched monotonous song. "Boy," Lester Bucktail said, "that sound sure takes me back. Haven't been to one of these in years. Not since I quit dancing."

Inside, people sat or stood or milled around outside a large open arena, its perimeter marked off by board-and-block benches. In the center of the circle, sitting on folding chairs, half a dozen men bent over the drum, faces taut with concentration, their long whippy drumsticks rising and falling in unison. So did their voices, with a little less success in the unison department.

"I don't recognize any of these guys," Lester Bucktail said, "but they're probably eastern Indians—Shawnees, Creeks, Cherokees, whatever. I doubt if any of the regular drums would come to a little affair like this. More likely this is just a pickup group."

"These young guys from eastern tribes," Tommy added, "they learn those Kiowa and Ponca songs from memory. Although there might be one or two Plains boys in there, students from over at the college. See, this powwow stuff isn't really part of our tradition—our people picked it up from the Plains tribes in modern times—"

"For God's sake, you guys," Rita said. "Tag knows all that. We used to go to powwows around Tulsa all the time. Quit treating him like a tourist."

We worked our way through the crowd until we had a clear view of the arena. Around the drum, scattered about the floor in no apparent formation, a dozen or so gourd dancers moved in small mincing steps, shaking long-handled rattles made from metal containers or bell gourds, holding feather fans in their left hands. The swishing *shick-shick-shick* of their rattles cut softly but insistently through the booming of the drum and the wailing of the singers. Most of them were older men, their dark faces relaxed and expressionless as they danced.

"Warriors' dance," Lester Bucktail said to me. "Used to be for returning war parties. Now it's mainly for Indian veterans. But that's right, I guess you know about that."

The gourd dancers were moving in to surround the drum now, coming up on the balls of their feet and bouncing on their heels, shaking their rattles furiously. Some of them let off shrill yipping cries. Lester Bucktail's face was wistful as he watched them. "That's what I used to do," he said. "Never was much into the rest of the powwow stuff, but gourd dancing was a way to be with other veterans, help me deal with some things. Were you in Nam?"

I nodded. "Me too," he said. "Ia Drang, back in sixty-six. Way back when it was still possible to believe in the God-damned war." He looked at me as if waiting for me to say something, but when I didn't he gave a little shrug and went back to watching the dancers.

"I'm going to circulate," Tommy announced. "See if I can

locate Judy Littlebear. You realize we don't even know what she looks like."

"I'll go with you," Lester Bucktail said. "I see some people I know."

The song came to an end, the drummers following up with a flurry of arrhythmic bangs to signal the end of the set. The gourd dancers broke ranks and began leaving the arena, shaking hands and talking among themselves. The drummers were lighting cigarettes, casually ignoring the prominent NO SMOKING signs. Up on the stage a seriously overweight man began a series of announcements. His voice came over the speakers in a mumbling drone and he seemed addicted to the phrase "At this time." So much for the proud traditions of Indian oratory.

"Let's get something to drink," Rita said. "This weather's got me permanently dry."

I followed her over to the concession stand and paid for a couple of slushy Pepsis. A horse-faced Indian woman stopped and spoke to Rita in Cherokee, and they talked for a few minutes while I stood holding the Pepsis and watching the ice melt.

"My Aunt Minnie," Rita said after the woman moved away. "She knows Judy Littlebear, but she hasn't seen her tonight." She took one of the Pepsis and grinned at me. "She says you're cute. She says if I don't want you she'll take you off my hands."

The announcer was calling for a round of intertribal dancing. The drummers began bashing and yelling again and costumed dancers poured into the arena, eagle feathers jerking with the rhythm, brass bells jingling at knees and ankles. Straight dancers stalked along in bright cloth outfits and Northern traditional dancers crouched and stooped in their feathers and paint, while fancy dancers whirled and leaped like hummingbirds on speed. Women stepped daintily in white fringed buckskin dresses or gyrated in fancy-shawl out-fits, with quite a few coming out of the crowd in street clothes, shawls held over their shoulders, to join the growing swirl.

"It's all gotten pretty bogus," Rita said. "Tommy's right, hardly any of these people have any legitimate tribal connection with these songs and dances. And a lot of the outfits are about as authentic as Buffalo Bill's Wild West Show, and the powwows lost any right to talk about preserving traditional Indian values when they started having cash-prize dance contests. But hell, it's fun, and there's not enough of that around nowadays for Indians or anybody else. I wish I'd brought my shawl. I'd like to dance."

"No time for that," Tommy said, materializing at her side. "We have to go to Redbird."

"The stomp ground?" Rita asked him. "She's at a stomp dance?"

"That's what I hear from usually reliable sources." He looked at me. "You know how to get there?"

I shook my head. "Never mind, kimosavee," Tommy said. "Your faithful Indian companions will guide you. Come on, we've got to rescue Lester. There's this two-hundred-pound Choctaw woman, has him cornered over by the side door, looking at him like he's all of the basic food groups. He's a goner if we don't get there quick."

"Turn right at the light," Tommy said from the back seat as we cleared the parking area. "Head south out of town. Get on eighty-two."

Quite a few people were driving into or out of Tahlequah that evening. Down past Keys, though, the traffic began to thin out; and beyond the new bridge across the north end of Lake Tenkiller, we had the road mostly to ourselves. That was just as well, since the vehicles that did appear tended to be operating pretty erratically, and with no more than modest lighting equipment. In the backseat Tommy and Lester began singing a Forty-nine song, English words to a Plains tune:

> *"I don't care if you are married*
> *I will love you anyway*
> *I'll take you home in my one-eyed Ford*
> *Ya hey ya ho yo hey—"*

—till Rita finally turned around and told them to shut up.

The old two-lane got very squirmy going over the hills, dropping down off Buckhorn Mountain to cross the Sequoyah County line at Snake Creek. Another snaketrack uphill and then the lights of a country store appeared up ahead. "Hang a left," Tommy instructed.

A long roller-coaster straight and a couple of sweeping curves, the Camaro heeled down hard on its shocks and the tires grabbing blacktop—I was enjoying myself now; you could do some serious driving on this road once the ancients had turned in—and Rita said, "There. Take that side road on the right."

The side road was narrow and bumpy, its pavement crumbling and treacherous with potholes. A couple of miles on, a rough gravel road led off to the right. All my passengers said, "There."

A large sign, unevenly lettered on a four-by-eight sheet of plywood, appeared in the headlights:

REDBIRD SMITH
NIGHTHAWK KEETOOWAH SOCIETY
RELIGIOUS CEREMONIAL GROUNDS
ABSOLUTELY NO ALCOHOL OR DRUGS ALLOWED

The legend was repeated in Cherokee subtitles. "Sloppy work," Tommy said. "Who the hell did that?"

"Paint them a new one," Lester suggested.

"Huh-uh. Nighthawks scare me. I always feel like they *know* things."

The dirt road wound through a grove of big post-oak trees and emerged onto a broad grassy field. In the middle of the field a good-sized fire was burning, with shadowy figures moving around it in a counterclockwise orbit. I parked the Camaro under a huge oak and we all got out and walked across the field toward the fire. The sky was blue-black and clear, lit by an enormous moon.

Post-oak arbors formed a circle around the dance area. Indian families sat on wooden benches under the arbors, or in folding chairs, or on the hoods and fenders of cars and pickup trucks, watching the dancers circling the fire.

Next to the fire, his face lit eerily by the leaping flames, the dance leader crouched and gesticulated as he called out the syllables of the ancient song. Behind him, men in wide-brimmed hats followed in a flat-footed trotting step, singing the response chorus in unison. There was no drum; instead women and girls of varying ages, interspersed among the men, carried the rhythm with turtle-shell rattles tied to their legs, moving their feet in a curious double shuffle to produce a steady pulsing *shaka-shaka-shaka-shaka* beat, like a gigantic rattlesnake leading a rhumba band.

"Damn," Tommy said, "I've got to start coming to these things again. You live in the city too long, you forget."

"Yeah," Lester Bucktail agreed. "That powwow scene, it's just something to do for laughs. This—" He swept an arm in a gesture that included the fire, the dancers, the entire area. "This is who we are. This is where it lives. This is what's real."

Both of them, I noticed, were speaking in quiet, subdued

voices, with nothing of their usual cranked-up smart-assed style. Tommy's face in the firelight was actually peaceful.

"Excuse me," Rita said. "I couldn't agree more, but didn't we come here tonight for a particular reason?"

"Right," Tommy said. "Let's go over to the tables and ask around. Those old women know everybody. Besides, I'm getting hungry."

Nearby, lit by several undersized electric bulbs, stood a large open arbor where people sat talking in comfortable old chairs and women tended long board tables loaded with pots and bowls and dishes of food. "Help yourself," Rita told me. "Everything's free."

I looked at the nearest table. There was chicken and fried pork and chili and dumplings and various vegetable dishes; there were more kinds of pie than I could identify, and piles of fry bread. "Jesus," I said involuntarily.

"Dig in," Tommy advised. "Join us poor starving Native Americans."

I took a paper plate and let a smiling old woman load it with grape dumplings. *"Jiyosihas, chooch?"* she asked. "There's coffee over there."

Tommy went over to speak to an old man who sat smoking a short-stemmed pipe. The old man wore a black Western hat with a beaded band and a large eagle feather sticking out behind. " *'Siyo, eduji,*" Tommy said. *"Dohiju?"*

They began talking in Cherokee. Rita was already engaged in conversation with a trio of elderly women and Lester Bucktail had drifted off in the direction of the fire. I got a foam cup of coffee from a big electric pot and sat down on a bench and tried the grape dumplings. They were almost unbearably good. If I hung out with these people on a regular basis, I thought, I'd have to buy a new trailer. One with wider doors.

Down by the fire, the leader's voice rose in a high loud whoop, ending the song. The dancers scattered, several of them moving toward the food tables. A pretty young woman in a big skirt came out of the darkness and sat down at the next bench, looking tired. The turtle shells tied to her legs must have had an aggregate weight of twenty or thirty pounds. She glanced my way and gave me a shy smile, but she didn't speak.

Rita came back from talking with the old women. "She's here," she said to me. "Come on."

Judy Littlebear didn't look like any sort of bear, big or little. She was almost as small as Felicia Jordan, with fine facial bones and huge dark eyes; if she'd been a model the fashion writers would have been overusing the word "waiflike."

She was never going to be a model, though. She was attractive enough, might even have been considered beautiful if you liked the type; but when she spoke she revealed cruelly malformed teeth. Nothing that a good orthodontist couldn't have fixed, but I doubted if there had ever been any chance of that for Judy Littlebear; few Indians make that kind of money, especially in a place like Sizemore County, and the Indian Health Service would hardly be likely to take any interest in something so "nonessential" as braces for a developing young girl. Marvin Painted Horse, I thought, ought to have a picture of this kid smiling; it would do more to make his point than any amount of florid rhetoric.

Just now, though, she wasn't smiling at all. In fact she was pretty close to tears.

"I can't help you," she said for maybe the twentieth time. "I'm sorry, but I can't tell you anything. Please quit asking me, all right?"

But of course we couldn't do that, not when she put it that way. Up to this point we'd been on a fishing trip, in a pond that had looked odds-on to be ecologically dead. Now, however, it was obvious that Judy Littlebear did know something, and was hurting from the stress of carrying it inside her.

"You know what's happening to Chris, don't you?" Tommy said to her. "And what's going to happen if somebody doesn't help him?"

"I know," Judy Littlebear said hopelessly. "I just *can't*."

We were standing under a big oak tree off near the edge of the field. Long leafy branches cut off most of the light from the moon and stars, but it was still easy to see the sheen of tears on her face.

"This is bad," Lester Bucktail said in an undertone. "This place is sacred. We're not supposed to be doing this here."

The stomp dancers were circling the fire again. *"Honawiye, honawiye,"* sang the men, and *shaka-shaka-shaka* went the turtle shells.

Rita stepped back and turned, looking toward the dance area. "Lester's right," she said. "Everybody ease up. I'll be back."

She walked away into the darkness and the rest of us stood for a time without speaking. I ran my hand over the thick trunk of the tree. Something—lightning, I supposed—had split it clear down to waist level, yet it was still very much alive and in the tree business. I wondered how old it was.

Finally Tommy said, *"Na,"* and there was Rita coming back across the field toward us. A second human figure accompanied her. "Okay," she said as she joined the group under the tree, "let's all clear off. Somebody wants to talk with Judy."

"Somebody" was an old man in a black hat. I thought he might be the one Tommy had been talking to earlier, but I couldn't really tell. He went up to Judy Littlebear and began speaking to her, so quietly that I couldn't even tell what language he was using.

"Come on," Rita insisted.

We all moved away. For want of a better objective we wandered back to the dining area and stood under the arbor drinking coffee and listening to the music.

"Who's the old guy?" I asked. "Medicine man?"

"Jimmy Birdshead. He's—" Rita shrugged. "Medicine man, all right, but more. He's an elder. I don't think I could explain all that means."

Quite a bit of time went by. The dancers finished their song and dispersed. A man with an amazingly powerful voice began shouting in Cherokee, apparently exhorting the congregation to renew their efforts. After a bit some people went out and started another song. Or maybe the same one again; what did I know?

I didn't see or hear the old man coming; all of a sudden he was simply there. His face, in the bad light from the bare overhead bulbs, looked as folded and grainy as an old saddle.

He said, "Judy will talk to you now."

18

‹•••••••••›

CHRIS DIDN'T KILL anybody that night," Judy Littlebear said. "He was at Echota Creek, breaking into the plant. I know. I was with him."

We all stared at her. It was a good thing it was dark; our facial expressions must have been very short on dignity.

"He had this idea of getting into their offices," she went on. "Looking for evidence that they'd been faking their environmental reports, covering up accidents, anything that could be used against them. He was going to do it by himself but I made him take me along."

"You actually got inside?" Lester Bucktail asked incredulously. "How? Over the wire?"

"Chris picked out this white guy from Redbud who drove a camper pickup and worked the midnight shift at the plant. I don't know how he found out about him, where he lived and all, but anyway we went to the guy's house that night and sneaked into the back of the truck and hid, and we rode right through the gate like that. They're supposed to check the backs of trucks and vans, but they never do if it's one of the regular crew."

I held back an admiring whistle. Chris Badwater hadn't made much of an impression on me up to now, but clearly the kid had more potential than I'd realized.

"We waited till after the shift changed," Judy Littlebear said, "and then we slipped out of the truck and used the parked cars for cover till we got to the plant itself. But the administration section was all locked up for the night. We couldn't get into the building, let alone any of the offices. There was a guard prowling around and Chris didn't know how to pick locks anyway."

"So what did you do?" Rita asked. "Go home?"

Judy Littlebear shook her head. "Chris said we'd come too far to give up without accomplishing something. He said we could make trouble for the company if we could show how bad their security was. I mean, it's a nuclear plant, they've probably got stuff somebody could use to make an atom bomb or something. Makes them look pretty bad if a couple of kids can get inside that easy."

"True," Tommy remarked. "The federal people are jumpy as hell about that sort of thing."

"So," she said, "what we needed was proof we'd been there. We spent, I guess, a couple of hours sneaking around that place. We got inside a storage building and took some papers off a bulletin board, and then we slipped into this other place—it was all lit up and there were people working, I thought for sure we were going to get caught but we hid behind some machinery and nobody saw us—and Chris took a warning sign off the wall, with one of those radiation symbols on it, he was really proud of that. And I boosted a few time cards out of the rack beside the clock where the workers punch in and out."

The despair had left her voice now; she was speaking fast, with pride and excitement, and she was looking directly at us for the first time. "Chris had a camera," she said, "a really good one that he'd saved up and bought, with super-fast film. He had it because he was hoping to photograph documents if we got into an office, but he took a lot of pictures inside the plant buildings. We took turns, too, photographing each other. Of course we didn't show our faces, we had these bandannas tied on like old-time bank robbers, but I bet that wouldn't stop anybody who really wanted to prove it was us."

"How did you get out?" Tommy wanted to know.

"Went back and hid in the same guy's truck till morning. It was a little scary getting out in broad daylight right beside his house, but we got away all right."

"Far out," Lester said approvingly. "You still got all that stuff you took?"

"It's back at my place in Tahlequah. We still hadn't decided how to use it when he got arrested. The film hasn't been developed, but it's safe." She bowed her head suddenly. "And I knew it would save Chris, but I was afraid of going to jail. I had this older cousin, she did a year for possession and when she got out you could barely recognize her. Looked ten years older than when she went in."

"Holy God," Tommy said. "That's why Chris went stonewall. Being the hero, taking the heat. I think this is the first time I've ever actually been proud of the silly son of a bitch."

"Chris isn't exactly in the clear if we use this," Rita pointed out. "Of course blackbagging a nuclear plant isn't in the same class with murdering a cop, but he's still looking at jail time. He can't expect much leniency from the court."

"You got that right," Lester affirmed. "Still, it beats getting life. Let alone death."

"Hang on," I said.

They all looked at me in surprise. I'd been keeping a low profile throughout the conversation; I think they'd forgotten I was there.

Rita said, "You've got an idea?"

"I'm not even sure it qualifies as an idea," I said. "Just something that might be worth a try."

* * *

"You understand," Billy Greenstick said, "there's absolutely no guarantee this is going to work."

"Understood," Tommy told him.

"In fact if you guys weren't all bigger than me I'd say it's a stupid idea."

"Jesus *Christ*, Billy," Lester Bucktail said, "just get on with it, will you?"

"Okay, okay." Billy Greenstick made soothing motions with both hands. "Soon as Damian gets back with the software, okay?"

It was Sunday afternoon. We were gathered in the Roadkill Publications editorial office, waiting for Billy's friend Damian to bring some mysterious but supposedly essential items. Rita had borrowed the Camaro and driven off with Judy Littlebear to the supermarket for humbler but equally vital supplies; it was almost certainly going to be a long afternoon and quite possibly an even longer evening.

The front door opened and closed. "That'll be Damian now," Billy said.

"Let's hope so," Lester grunted. "One of us ought to go watch the front. Anybody could walk in."

"Senility has made you paranoid," Tommy told him.

"The hell. What if Bianca Ford takes it into her idealistic head to pay a visit? There are, I would remind you, very important reasons why it won't do for her to find out what we're up to. Especially if we pull it off."

Damian came through the office door. He was a tall, cadaverous white kid, maybe seventeen, with a pale long face covered with zits. He wore baggy-assed pants held up by wide suspenders and an oversized long-sleeved shirt in a toxic shade of green. He had an extremely strange haircut that made his head look like a small nuclear explosion. Large pink shades hid his eyes.

"I swear I'm going to get me a zoot suit," Lester Bucktail mused. "With a drape shape and, if at all possible, a reet pleat. For this we lost a continent? No offense, Damian."

"I got the stuff you wanted," Damian said to Billy, ignoring Lester, "but Dennis says tell you he's got to have that random digit disk back by tomorrow."

"All *right.*" Billy sat down at Lester's desk and began doing things to the computer, while Damian rummaged through the contents of a large blue backpack. "Now let's see how good the bad guys are—"

Damian pulled up a chair and sat down beside him, gazing at the computer screen. "Are you going to shozbot the wangleborg," he asked, "or just let the bimbleplud tribble out on the throckles?"

"Not with that yocknapatawpha," Billy Greenstick replied absently. "Have to arbuthnot the paradiddle and hope the dinkenspiel doesn't demosthenes."

"Klatu mirata nikto," Damian agreed.

I mean, that wasn't what they *said;* it only sounded that way to my terminally ignorant ear. No doubt they were speaking English, but it might as well have been Cherokee, or Serbo-Croatian, or Sanskrit. This was definitely turning out to be my month for feeling left out of conversations.

After a few minutes I walked out of the office and through the house and stood on the porch, watching some kids across the street doing insanely dangerous things with skateboards. I took the Hohner from my jacket pocket and honked a few bars of "Harbor Lights" but I couldn't get into it. The dry wind was still blowing. If we didn't get some rain soon, the whole state was going to go up in brush fires.

Lester Bucktail came out and joined me. "You understand any of that stuff they were talking about?" he asked.

I shook my head. "Me either," he said. "I just barely know

how to work a computer for legitimate purposes, if Billy helps me. The kind of techno-burglary those kids are up to in there, I don't have a clue. I feel practically fucking prehistoric."

He laughed. "Tommy's standing around trying to look hip, but I don't think he knows any more than we do." He leaned back against one of the cracked wooden columns that more or less supported the sagging porch roof. "You use a word processor?"

"Typewriter."

"Huh. I thought all the novelists were into word processors now. Except for the ones in the movies and the soap operas, and they don't even know to double-space their manuscripts . . . conservative, are you?"

"I tried a word processor once. A loaner from a friend." Actually it had been one Wiley Harmon had acquired from a fence as part of a payoff-in-kind deal, but there was no need to burden Lester Bucktail with the details. "I don't know, it was too fast, too handy. Apparently I need something to slow me down and force me to think about what I'm doing. Call me a dinosaur."

"Oh, I don't know. Sure has been a lot of bad writing published since people started using the damn things. Of course there was a lot of bad writing published before—" His voice trailed off. Then, "You think they can do it? Get into the Echota Creek plant's computer hookup?"

"I'm damned if I know. It seems pretty improbable on the face of it." And more so every time I thought about it; this was one of those ideas that look brilliant at midnight but pathetically flimsy in the daylight. "Even if they get inside the main system, you know, that doesn't necessarily mean they'll be able to do us any good. Hardesty Industries has got to have all the good stuff stashed away in the electronic equivalent of Jack Benny's safe."

"You'd think so, wouldn't you? But then you wouldn't

think a couple of goofy college kids could penetrate a nuclear plant's physical security that easily, either."

He shoved his hands into his pockets and grinned at me. "Come on, Roper, let's go upstairs and see if there's any beer left. Not a damn thing we can do down here but hang around and feel stupid, and I get enough of that in my life as it is."

The afternoon wore on. I sat in Lester Bucktail's living room and drank beer while he talked about the Ia Drang campaign. To my relief he didn't try to get any war stories out of me.

Rita and Judy came back with bags of sandwich materials, assorted snacks, and plastic bottles of Bubba Cola. Rita caught me looking into one of the bags as I carried them upstairs. "What did you think," she said, "the little ladies would be in the kitchen whipping up a feast while the menfolk attend to the serious work? Dream on, my love."

Behind me on the stairs Judy Littlebear giggled. "You aren't going to get those two boys away from that computer long enough to eat a real meal anyway. Something they can eat one-handed without taking their eyes off the screen, that's all they want. I know guys like that from school."

She was half right; Billy all but ignored the tray of food that Rita placed on the desk beside the computer, but Damian tore in with the enthusiasm of a Somalian refugee. "Thanks," he said with his mouth full of corn chips, and sneaked a look at Rita's bottom as she turned away.

"Getting anywhere?" Rita asked Billy.

He made a vague frustrated sound. "Sort of. I'm inside the main system—that was easier than I expected, I know bubblegummers who could have done it—but the kind of stuff we're after, that's another story."

"Security codes?" Tommy said from over by the window.

"Actually that hasn't been too much of a problem yet," Billy said. "But the whole setup is sort of weird. Even if you had the codes, you could spend a lot of time finding what you wanted. See, this is a small operation, but it's part of a big conglomerate corporation. So a lot of what I'm getting here is Hardesty Industries, not just this particular plant. It makes things more complicated."

"Christ," Lester said, "I actually understood what you said. Somebody hand me another beer, quick."

Rita came around the desk and looked over Billy's shoulder at the screen. "What have you got there?"

"That's the oogenshploogen from the hogusbogus," Billy told her. Or something like that.

"Kamehameha ungawa," Damian added helpfully.

"Oh, shit," Lester said. "Are you guys going to start doing that again?"

Rita dragged up a chair and sat down next to Billy. "Take it slow and simple," she said. "I'm weak on the terminology."

Billy scratched his head. "Basically, the front door was locked so I tried going in a window. Sometimes you can get at the files you want by way of something else that isn't as heavily guarded. I was into the financial records, thought maybe I'd find a weak point there."

"That's how we did it last month," Damian put in, "when we—" He saw Billy glaring at him and shut up.

"Anyway," Billy told Rita, "I screwed up some way and now I'm deep into this." He gestured at the screen. "And I'm not sure how I got there, so I have to be careful how I get out, or I could blow all my work."

Rita studied the display. "Hm. Excuse me." She reached past Billy and poked a couple of keys. More gibberish appeared. "Hey, that can't be right. . . ."

I said, "I think we need more chips."

Rita waved a hand, not taking her eyes off the glowing digits on the screen. "Get some pickles while you're up there."

* * *

Judy Littlebear was in the kitchen, making herself a sandwich. "Anything happening yet?" she asked me.

"How the hell should I know?" I said grumpily. Then, remembering, "Don't worry. I'm sure they'll find something. They know what they're doing, hard as that is to believe."

She laughed. "That Damian kid is such a geek. Billy's really sort of sweet, though."

She got a glass from the shelf above the sink and poured herself a Bubba. "Of course," she said, "even if your idea does work, I'm still in big trouble. My father's going to kill me when this comes out."

"Maybe not."

"Ha. You don't know my father. Super-uptight Creek Baptist, deacon in the church and all, you wouldn't believe it. I don't even get to wear shorts at home in the summer. He'd go ballistic if he found out I was at that stomp dance last night. According to him that's a huge sin. 'Devil worship' he calls it. Boy."

She sipped her Bubba. "And he'll be mad because I was with Chris at all, never mind what we were doing. Last weekend when I went home he made a big deal out of showing me the newspaper, went on and on about how he always said Chris would come to a bad end. If it was up to my old man Chris would already have a rope around his neck. I mean, he said so."

"How's he feel about the nuclear plant?"

"He's been trying to get hired there ever since it opened." She set her glass down. "Was there something you wanted?"

"Just looking for the pickles," I said. "Seen them?"

The sun went down with a slightly corny display of reds and purples; some clouds were finally beginning to move in, down on the horizon. I sat on the front porch blowing harmonica and watching the lights come on up and down the street. The cat came padding across the yard, sat down, listened to the first half of "Stardust," and got up and went under the house, tail twitching. "Everybody's a critic," I said to an audience of none.

A little after dark, the door opened and Tommy stuck his head out. "Come on," he said. "They've got something."

I followed him back through the house to the office. Billy Greenstick was still fooling with the computer and Damian was leaning over the desk giving advice and commentary, but Rita was looking happy and waving sheets of computer printout.

"I *knew* there was something funny about those figures," she said when I came in. "I may not be a computer genius, but I didn't spend a year on the financial page for nothing. Look at this."

She handed me a sheet of printout. I looked, saw, did not comprehend. "Rita," I said. "Rita, come on. You know I'm even more hopeless on financial matters than I am with electronics. I take it this is good news."

"The pension fund, damn it," she said impatiently. "The Hardesty Industries employee pension fund. I'd bet my life savings on it."

At the desk Billy made a satisfied sound. Damian said, "Awesome." The printer began cranking out more paper, making a horrible cicada sound.

"They're ripping off the pension fund?" I asked, dazed. "For God's sake, I thought that went out with the old Teamsters—"

"No, no, nothing that crude. Every bit as illegal, though, if I'm right about what's going on. Look," she said, "the pension fund for an outfit the size of Hardesty Industries represents big money. Big money means big temptation for a certain type of mind, especially in times like these. And it looks as if some people haven't been resisting hard enough."

"This sounds hot," Lester said. "Talk to us."

"For one thing, they're underfunding the pension plan—which isn't illegal, oddly enough, though some people in Washington are working to try to change that. It wouldn't be great for the corporate image if it came out, but basically it's no big deal—just one of those ethically rotten things that everybody does. But there's more."

Rita tossed the printout onto the desk. "What you've got there are the figures on the pension fund investments. And they're bullshit," she said flatly. "There's no way in hell certain of those stocks can have lost the kind of money they're claiming. In fact there's no way some of them can have lost at all. And others damn well should have paid more than they admit here."

"Back up," I said. "They're playing the market with the pension fund for a stake? Can they do that?"

"Of course they can. Nothing wrong with it as long as they report everything properly. But," she said, "that's speaking of regular market-type investments. There are certain no-nos."

"Such as?" Tommy asked. "Dope?"

"Jesus, you people." Rita made a disgusted face. "Speculating in foreign currency, that's the present favorite. You can make lots of money doing that in today's world. But you better not get caught doing it with the employee pension fund, because that's against federal law."

I said, "That's what they're doing at Hardesty? You're sure?"

Rita shook her head. "Foreign currency is only my best guess. There are other possibilities. The important thing is that they're doing something shady with some of the pension-fund money, something that would get them in trouble if it came out, and they're diddling the numbers to cover it up. Specifically, they're underreporting returns on certain investments, or claiming losses, and using the difference for whatever they're doing."

"Doesn't somebody eventually ask where the money went?" Tommy wanted to know.

"Not necessarily. If your speculation pays off as expected, you can do the same trick in reverse to replace the stake you used. As long as the bottom line gets evened out, nobody's likely to get inquisitive."

"You can prove this?" Judy Littlebear asked. "Just from that stuff Billy and Damian hacked into?"

"Not directly. But give any competent federal investigator a look at these numbers, and I guarantee he'll know instantly that they're doing something naughty. Finding out what," Rita said, "shouldn't be a big problem."

"I love it," Lester Bucktail chortled. "This beats hell out of anything we were hoping for. Falsified emissions reports, unreported accidents, safety violations—hey, since when has anybody really got hurt for that kind of crap? Hardesty Industries gets caught doing the dirty to the environment two or three times a year, all over the country, and nothing ever happens beyond maybe a chickenshit fine. But something like this, hoo boy. We're talking major pain, gang."

"Understand," Rita said, "there's no way to know who's actually doing this. Has to be a certain amount of high-level guilt; this isn't something a handful of greedy junior execs or bent clerks could put together—but it doesn't matter. In the end, the corporation gets clobbered. Not only in the courts," she added. "Do you have any idea what this could do to Hardesty stock?"

"Got some more numbers coming up," Billy called.

"Run it all," Rita told him. "No, wait. Tag, how about it? We've already got enough to nail them a dozen times over."

"Run it," I agreed. "We're not building a legal case here, we're making a club. When I hit the bastards with it, I want to be sure I get their attention."

19
....

BOB CROSS FINISHED studying the last sheet of printout and looked up at me and said, not for the first time, "You son of a bitch."

"I take it the material speaks for itself," I said. "I mean, surely there's no need for me to point out the implications. Wasted time, mutual embarrassment, we can cut past all that, right?"

I hoped to hell he agreed. Despite hours of explanations and coaching from Rita, I still wasn't sure I understood what was going on. If Cross called my bluff—

He didn't. He looked at the stack of printout again and said softly, "The bastards. The worthless greedhead bastards. They couldn't leave it alone."

His face held enough anger for a Balkan civil war, but I didn't get the feeling it was directed at me. He raised his head and stared out the window of the Camaro. We were parked beside a dirt road a mile or so from the Echota Creek plant, but the white plume from the reactor was still visible against the overcast sky.

"So it's true," he said. "You know, Roper, there have been rumors about something like this. Well, not really rumors, nobody would have dared to go that far—because if it's true, it has to include people you don't want to piss off. Let's say if you were in the right position at the right time, you might have noticed a few very small straws in the wind."

His fingers began tapping a little tattoo on the stack of paper in his lap. "God damn it," he said, "why do they do it?

I can understand how some hungry hustler, working on the edge and without a net, might figure he had no choice but to get a little dirt on his hands. But you see these people who already have it made by any standard—money, authority, prestige, all the right friends in all the right places—getting up to these gonif games like any bunch of street-gang punks."

"They say there's no such word as enough."

"Evidently not. No, hell, Roper, it's not the money. Anybody with the brains and knowledge to set this up could have made as much or more off legitimate investments, and with half the work."

He half-turned in his seat and faced me. "I know this one guy," he said, "he's got to be part of this pension-fund racket. Has a wife who makes Christie Brinkley look like Evander Holyfield. Father-in-law's one of those hammerhead-shark Dallas lawyers. And fifty-two weeks out of the year, the son of a bitch is carrying on these stupid low-rent affairs. I'm not talking about keeping a high-class mistress, either. He gets into every secretary in the office—or tries to, I don't know why he hasn't been hit for sexual harassment by now—even when they're regular Rottweilers. And that's how these people are, Roper. I've spent my adult life around them. They have to feel they're getting away with something. It's the dynamic of their lives."

His face changed suddenly. "Shit," he said, and reached out and slapped my chest with both hands. His right palm found the bulge over the left side of my ribcage. "What's this? What are you trying to pull?"

I knocked his hands away, not hard. "Don't do that," I said mildly.

He sat back, white-faced, and watched as I flipped my jacket open and reached into the inside pocket. "See?" I said, showing him the Hohner. "Don't make me use it."

I dropped the harmonica back into my pocket and pulled

the jacket back farther and let him see the shiny .380 Colt stuck into my waistband. "Maybe this is what you thought you'd spotted," I added.

He looked at the gun for a second and then he laughed, a sour little laugh that didn't make it higher than his upper lip. "Hell, no. I thought you might be wearing a wire, that's all. What's with the popgun? Afraid I might get crazy and try to take you off?"

"The thought occurred to me."

"You think I'm a complete fucking idiot? If you're smart enough to get those figures—however the hell you did it— you're damn well smart enough to make backup arrangements. Say a floppy disk left with a friend, maybe that environmentalist lawyer in Tahlequah, to be turned over to the appropriate agency if anything happens to you. Or you might have set something up with one of your journalist colleagues. You need a gun right now like you need an extra elbow."

His lip curled. "Especially a toy like that. What is it, a thirty-two?"

"Three-eighty."

"Oh? Remember last winter when they had that mass shooting in east Tulsa? Some nut shot up a Wendy's—I think he worked there; it's getting so I don't know how anybody gets up the balls to fire anybody—with a three-eighty like that. Six victims and every one of them survived. I don't even think they were seriously hurt."

He shrugged. "But never mind the cowboy nonsense. What are you after? I assume you do want something. Of course," he said, "you understand I can't do anything for you myself. All I can do is pass this on. Something I'm not looking forward to, by the way . . . let's have it."

I told him.

When I was done he said, "I'll be damned. That's all?

That's *it*? Hell, I thought this was going to be something serious."

"That's it," I affirmed. "Hardesty Industries doesn't press charges against Chris Badwater and Judy Littlebear for anything they did on company property that night. And if they catch any trouble at all for their little adventure, you'll find out how serious this is."

"I can't guarantee anything," he protested. "Oh, sure, the company won't press charges, I can promise that much right now. What the hell, it's not as if they set off a bomb or took hostages. But I can't control what the local authorities might decide to do."

"Bullshit. You're trying to tell me you and your bosses don't have any influence with the people who run this county? Hardesty Industries buys and sells places like this out of petty cash."

"Okay, okay. Point taken. I'll . . . handle it."

He gave me one of his birdlike tilted-head looks. "And you're not after anything else? Hard to believe, Roper. Why not cut yourself a little piece while you're shaking us down? You've got material here, should be worth quite a bit to some people to have it buried. Blackmail is such a tacky word," he said, "but you could call it a consulting fee. Why no cash demands?"

"I didn't think of it," I said honestly.

Bianca Ford wasn't at Charlie's Foxhole when I arrived, but she showed up half an hour later. "Sorry I'm late," she said, sliding into the booth. "This better be good, Roper. I got a ticket on the way down here."

"Tovin's working the roads again?"

"Tovin?" Her forehead wrinkled. "I don't know anybody named Tovin. I got the ticket on the way out of Tahlequah.

Really, they ought to make those stop signs bigger if they expect people to notice them."

She folded her hands on top of the table. "So what's happening? You sounded so mysterious on the phone."

I gave her such information as she needed to know, suitably edited in the interests of discretion. Her eyes went wide. "Oh, wow. Why didn't I think to talk to Judy Littlebear? I've met her. She came to a couple of demonstrations with Chris . . . she'll definitely go through with it? Make a statement, give testimony in court if it comes to that?"

"So she says. Lester's got the evidence, by the way, at his office. You'll have to have the film processed."

"Hm. I hope it's not fogged. They were sneaking around a place with a history of radiation leakage. Well, no matter," she said. "With or without the pictures, I shouldn't have any trouble getting Chris out. I don't expect we'll have to go to court with it. Stinson won't want to endanger his conviction record. He's up for reelection next year."

She gave me a thoughtful look. "And you're certain Hardesty Industries isn't going to press charges against Chris and Judy?"

"It's been seen to."

"But you won't tell me how. Oh, wait. There's something I don't want to know about."

"I don't think so, no."

"Say absolutely no more. I appreciate the consideration. As long as it's not something that's going to come out of the woodwork and bite me on the ass some day—"

"No."

"Then thanks. Whatever you did, thanks for doing it. Boy," she said, "it's a load off my mind. I didn't have the first idea how I was going to defend Chris. We wouldn't even have had a shot at plea-bargaining down to manslaughter. Between you and I, it was looking like all I could do just to beat the death penalty."

"Glad to be of service."

"Who do you think did do it?" she asked.

"I don't know. I don't particularly care."

I drained my beer glass and got up. "Let's go see what's on special at Donna's. I already missed lunch and I don't want to drive all the way back to Yuchi Park on an empty stomach."

It was after four when we came out of Donna's. "I better get on over to the courthouse," Bianca said. "I won't be able to get Chris out tonight, maybe not tomorrow either, but at least I can let him know he's going to be all right."

She put out her hand. "Take care of yourself, Roper. Look me up next time you're in Tahlequah."

When she was gone I walked across the street and climbed into the Camaro and sat for a few minutes with my hands on the wheel, looking off down the street at nothing in particular. I wasn't contemplating any heavy insights; I was merely thinking how God-damned tired I was.

The pistol in my waistband was digging at my hipbone and, after a quick glance around, I took it out and laid it on the seat beside me. I couldn't think why I'd carried it around this long; I hadn't had any need for it after finishing up with Cross.

I looked down at the ridiculous weapon and wondered why I'd packed it at all. It had been an impulse thing; I'd grabbed it that morning at the trailer while I was getting my keys—and guns really aren't good things to pick up on impulse. Harry should have said something.

Cross had never been a credible threat, and if he had been I wouldn't have done myself much good with a pocket .380. I ought to sell it, I reflected; it should be worth some money. It was something of a collector's item, after all, being at least half a century old, and its chrome plating was still shiny and clean.

It had been a gift from a friend, and I'd hung onto it because there had been a few times that I'd felt the need. It was handy to carry, being flat and light, and didn't make an indiscreet bulge under my clothes.

But it was just enough gun to get me into trouble and not enough gun to get me out. Back when I'd acquired it, I'd bought a box of special hollowpoint cartridges that were supposed to greatly increase its effectiveness, only to discover that they invariably jammed the old-fashioned automatic mechanism every third or fourth shot. And the standard jacketed factory rounds that it held now were decidedly on the wimpy side. The Badwater family tomahawk was undoubtedly a superior weapon.

Shaking my head at myself, I started the Camaro and pulled out onto the street. A short time later I was rolling past the city limits, where a battered metal sign informed me that I was LEAVING REDBUD and advised me to DRIVE SAFELY and COME AGAIN SOON.

All day long the sky had been gray and grim. The clouds that had moved in during the night now stretched from horizon to horizon, ponderous and low-bellied. When I drove out of Redbud it was still well before sundown, but great masses of roiling storm clouds filled the western sky and masked the sun, so that the light was already beginning to grow dimmer. The woods and fields looked somehow strange and things seemed not to have their proper shapes. The atmosphere was heavy and dense, so humid that my clothes felt damp.

Screwy things were happening to the air pressure, too, and there was an unpleasant feeling of electric tension. I was starting to feel edgy, a little wired, impatient to get home. Easy to yield to temptation and stand on the gas at a time like this; I kept one eye on the speedometer needle and the other on the road ahead, watching the shoulders and side roads for lurking cops. Another ticket, that was all I needed, now that I was almost out of this damn county for good. . . .

All of which may explain why it took me a few miles to realize that I'd acquired a shadow.

I never knew exactly when or where they got on my tail. The road was hilly and winding, and lined with dense woods along most of the way: the kind of road that makes it easy to follow another vehicle without being spotted. Even when I did see the car behind me, there was only a brief flash in the rearview mirror as we both hit the tops of little rises at the same time. It was some miles on before the road straightened out long enough to let me identify the brown object as a police cruiser.

I believe I uttered a scatological expletive or two. But I told myself to stay cool; there was no reason to assume they were stalking me. This was, after all, one of the main roads in the area, and even in a place like Sizemore County there is such a thing as legitimate cop business. Most likely they were simply going the same way—

No they weren't. It took only a few simple experiments—slowing down, then accelerating cautiously without going over the limit—to settle the point; they were definitely trailing me, and not trying to be very subtle about it. The cruiser stayed back there at a constant distance no matter what I did. We might have been the engine and caboose of a short invisible train.

Well, there was still no cause for serious concern. Mizell would surely have heard by now that I'd been seen in Redbud again; he might well have assigned somebody to tail me and report on my movements, or to make sure I was leaving. Or that could be my old buddy Tovin back there, trying to spook me into giving him grounds for a semi-honest score this time.

Even when the lights started flashing and the cruiser suddenly came charging up from astern, I wasn't terribly alarmed. Another citation, another fine and possibly some eventual effect on my insurance premiums; but nothing worse, nothing heavy—because, after all, there was no longer any reason for it. Whatever happened in Sizemore County after today, my part was done and nobody had anything to gain by leaning on me.

Still and all, I did give half a second's consideration to standing on it. The Camaro might not have the flat-out power of a police cruiser—though it would be damn close, after the work I'd had done on that old mill—but it was lighter and would corner faster. Anyway, on a road like that, pure speed is less important than skill and the willingness to go all the way to the edge. If I couldn't outrun the bastards, there was still at least an even chance I could outdrive them, and it was less than half a dozen miles to the county line.

But I was tired and feeling out of it, and, as I say, I still wasn't taking the situation seriously. So I began braking and shifting down, looking for a place to pull off, while the cruiser swung over into the other lane and came roaring up alongside me. Pace grinned at me through the side window and I had a moment's regret that I hadn't made a run for it; but I saw Mizell behind the wheel, and relaxed a bit. Mizell might be an evil son of a bitch, but he hadn't impressed me as the kind to go in for recreational brutality.

The old blacktop had skimpy gravel shoulders, but there was a place up ahead where a dirt road came out of the woods and met the pavement, and I pulled off there and stopped. The cruiser went past me and slammed to a gravel-grinding halt a little way in front of the Camaro's bumper. I sat and waited while Mizell and Pace got out and walked toward me, thumbs hooked in their holster belts.

It occurred to me that this was a very empty stretch of road. There were no houses for miles and at this time of day, on a Monday, there was almost no traffic. By now I was beginning to feel a good deal less easy about what was happening.

Pace stopped near the front of the Camaro and stood watching me through the windshield, still grinning. Mizell came around to the left side of the car and bent down to look in at me, while I rolled the window down. "Afternoon," he said. His voice and face were friendly. "Like you to step out of the car for a minute, please."

When I hesitated he put a hand on the window frame and said, "Don't worry, Roper. This is just a routine matter. We'll have you on your way again in no time."

I didn't believe a God-damned word of it. But I opened the door and got out; it was too late for anything else. As my feet hit the ground I remembered that idiotic little .380 lying there on the passenger seat, in plain sight and impossible to miss. Son of a bitch.

And sure enough, almost immediately, Mizell said, "*Hello.* What have we got here? Pace, look what this man's got."

Pace came up and peered in through the open door. "Weapon," he grunted. "Want me to get it?"

"Please," Mizell said.

Pace bent and reached, his massive shoulders disappearing inside the Camaro. A moment later he pulled back and straightened, holding the .380.

"Is it loaded?" Mizell asked.

Pace was already popping the clip and racking back the slide. A stubby little brass cartridge hopped out through the ejection port and fell to the shoulder. Pace stooped and picked it up and thumbed it back into the clip. "Fully loaded," he reported unnecessarily.

Mizell looked at me. "This is a serious offense," he said gravely. "Firearms carried in motor vehicles are supposed to be unloaded and locked in the trunk. You should know that."

"Might be stolen property, too," Pace suggested. "We ought to run a check on the serial number, Chief."

"Good point," Mizell agreed. "Cover him, Pace."

A couple of minutes later I was being pushed into the back of the cruiser. It was a clumsy business, but I'd done it before. Nobody had explained my rights to me. That was just as well; I wasn't in the mood for humor, anyway.

The door slammed shut behind me. Mizell came around and got behind the wheel. "Pace will bring your car," he said over his shoulder.

I sat in uncomfortable silence as he hauled the cruiser around and headed back down the road toward Redbud. Through the back window I saw the Camaro following close behind.

"You shouldn't have come back to my county, Roper," Mizell said. "Things seem to happen to you around here."

I'd thought we'd be going back the way we'd just come. But a mile or so down the road Mizell slowed the cruiser and swung left, onto a gravel side road that I didn't recognize. And, not far along, he turned off again, this time taking a narrow unmarked track that wound off through the woods. Dust rose up in dense clouds behind the cruiser; I couldn't see whether Pace was still with us or not.

"Hey," I said, not unstupidly. "This isn't the way back to Redbud."

"Noticed that, did you?" Mizell half-turned and gave me a big smile. "Not much gets by you, does it, Roper?"

Well, hell.

20

•••••••••

"I GOT A PHONE CALL a few hours ago," Mizell said conversationally, "from a guy I know, works for Hardesty out at Echota Creek. I think you know him too, don't you? Man named Cross."

He paused and maneuvered the cruiser carefully around a large pothole. By now we were creeping along in low gears; a good runner could almost have kept up. The road was in bad condition and, from the look of it, had never been much to begin with; a logging road, perhaps, kept open by deer hunters and the like. The trees grew thick along both sides, their lower trunks obscured by heavy brush. Here and there the spreading limbs reached out over the road from either side, creating a dark, claustrophobic tunnel effect. There were no man-made structures in sight, except for the road itself; there weren't even any fences.

"Couldn't let well enough alone, could you?" Mizell said. "We had that fucking Indian kid down cold, nothing left but to go through the motions of a trial and ship his ass off to McAlester. Then everything would have gotten back to normal around this county. The troublemakers would have had themselves a martyr, good for stacks of white-liberal guilt money for years to come. Everybody would have been happy."

"Except for Chris Badwater."

"Who was all charged up over his big chance to be a hero. No, there was satisfaction all around on this one. But then you came along and started screwing around, and everything went to hell."

The cruiser lurched as a tire found a bad spot. "Shit," Mizell said without heat. "You know, Roper, I really tried to do this the easy way. You wouldn't believe the ass-chewing I gave Pace for working you over that night. I've had my dealings with writers and journalists. I knew any attempt to intimidate you would only convince you there was something worth digging up. Lean on this guy, I told Pace, and he'll sink his teeth in like a God-damned alligator and no telling what he's liable to bite into before he's done. Pace wanted to kill you," he added. "I told him that wouldn't accomplish anything but bringing a horde of your colleagues down on us. Like the time the Mob hit that reporter out in Arizona."

"Thanks for the concern."

"Hey, no need to be sarcastic, Roper. As I say, I tried to go the other way. Thought I'd give you a certain amount of harmless cooperation, play the hang-out game, even help you a little—I had a hell of a time persuading Emily Jordan to talk to you—and you'd give up and go away. And it almost worked, didn't it?" he said. "You looked at a few files, paid a meaningless little call on Emily, went by the plant long enough to jerk Bob Cross's chain, and that was it. You drove out of Sizemore County without looking back, didn't you? What changed your mind?"

"An old Indian," I said. "He gave me some advice on fishing."

"What the hell?" He glanced back at me. "You're a weird son of a bitch, Roper. Anybody ever tell you that?"

I said, "It's too late now, Mizell. Whatever you're planning to do to me, it won't change anything. Too many other people know the score. There's even physical evidence to back up Chris's alibi, and I'm not the one holding it."

"So? Badwater walks, okay, he walks. Understand this, Roper," Mizell said, "I don't particularly care about the Badwater kid, one way or another. That asshole Stinson may have a political stake in convicting him, but that's his problem."

"And yours?"

"My problem," he said, "is that this is going to open a lot of cans that need to stay on the shelf. Because if that Indian punk didn't kill Jordan, then everybody's going to want to know who did. And that's bad news for me. Very bad news indeed."

"Because—oh." I saw it then, or thought I did. It wasn't a tremendous shock; I'd been nursing strong suspicions along those lines almost from the beginning. "So it was you. Sort of a hostile takeover from the inside? I suppose the rackets are lucrative enough to be worth a murder or two."

The cruiser swerved and Mizell's head jerked. "Jesus Christ, Roper, is *that* what you think this is all about? You do have some strange ideas."

He laughed. "Oh, all right, I'll admit I thought about getting rid of the old bastard, now and then. Who wouldn't? But I didn't do it," he said. "It wouldn't have made sense. There was enough money to go around, and I'm not a greedy man. And Jordan had a real talent for the political side of the job, which I've never had. Candidly speaking, I wish he was back. I'm not looking forward to having to do the glad-hand routine with the yokels. Election's next year, you know."

He paused, fighting the wheel, as the cruiser banged over a stretch of washboard. I hated to think what this was doing to the Camaro. Not that there was any reason to assume I'd ever be driving it again. Mizell wouldn't be talking this freely if he had any intention of letting me walk away from the conversation.

"I'll tell you the truth," he said. "I just assumed Badwater *was* guilty. Believe it or not, I honestly believed we had the right guy this time. Worries me more than a little, finding out he didn't do it. I mean, that brings up a lot of ugly possibilities, if you follow me. What if my late boss got hit for business rather than personal reasons?"

"Reasons which might come looking for you next."

"Exactly. I'm going to have to do some serious checking around, find out what's happening. It looks as if Jordan may have been into something the rest of us didn't know about. All very worrisome." He shook his head slowly. "I almost owe you, Roper. It may be that you've been responsible for alerting me to trouble that I didn't realize I had. Maybe it's just as well you were so persistent. Ironic, isn't it?"

The road dipped down and crossed a dry streambed, and then climbed sharply up a wooded hillside before leveling off. Mizell said, "This looks about right. . . . At any rate, my immediate problem remains. When they cut the kid loose, there's going to be an outcry to find and convict the real killer. An outcry that will be heard at least as far away as Oklahoma City," he went on, "and that means several varieties of potential trouble. We could well wind up with state investigators snooping around, not to mention news people asking questions and people like you turning over rocks. I can't risk it, Roper. We've got too many buried bodies in this county. And that's not merely a figure of speech."

"Bad for business."

"At the very least. After all, that's our main commercial attraction—a quiet, discreet place that nobody knows or cares about, where no questions are ever asked. A high-profile murder investigation involving the sheriff's office? With, inevitably, questions arising about possible police corruption?

It won't do," he said. "Already I'm under a lot of pressure. Certain people have made it clear: if I want to inherit Rowland Jordan's job, I'd better find a way to restore peace and quiet and obscurity."

"Silencing me won't do that."

"Irrelevant. You're merely a means to an end," he said. "The most urgent need is to wrap Jordan's murder up, fast. Since you've seen to it Chris Badwater won't do, I need a replacement killer."

"You've lost me."

"For God's sake, Roper, you're supposed to be a novelist. Where's your imagination?"

He brought the cruiser to a stop and turned to look back at me through the heavy steel mesh. "Turns out we got the wrong Indian," he said. "You'll be interested to learn that the murder was in fact the work of that bunch of assholes who took the dope bust last week. The ones you had the run-in with, that night at Charlie's Foxhole."

"War Party? That's crazy."

"And that's precisely the beauty of it, Roper. *They're* crazy. It's a matter of public record. No need to show a logical motive, because they wouldn't need one and everybody knows it. Not to forget their recently discovered involvement with dangerous drugs."

He made a disgusted sound. "I'd like to kick somebody's ass for that idiotic scene out at Echota Creek last Monday—more publicity that I didn't need, thanks to certain panicky fools in this state who still think the Indians are liable to go back on the warpath and start taking scalps again if we don't keep a tight rein on them—but it may come in handy."

I said, "I still don't see where I come into all this. Did I miss something?"

"Why, it seems your recent investigative efforts did more than clear Chris Badwater. Somehow, perhaps through your well-known contacts in the Indian community, you found evidence pointing to the War Party leadership. I think Vince Lacolle makes a good candidate for the actual hatchetman," he said. "But that's a detail."

"You want me to help you set Lacolle and the others up for Jordan's murder? Forget it," I said, amazing myself. "Even if I could do it, forget it."

Mizell chuckled. "Oh, you'll help, all right. You won't even have any say in the matter. You see," he said, "when those fanatical, drug-crazed redskins found out about the paleface journalist who was on their track, they took steps. With tragic consequences."

My skin felt very cold.

"Luckily," Mizell went on, opening his door, "they failed to find the notes the late Mr. Roper had hidden in his car. Which led, or rather will lead, to the issuance of warrants for their apprehension, for the murders of Sheriff Rowland Jordan and Mr. Taggart Roper. As I say, I owe you. I don't see how I could do this without you. Of course, if it weren't for you I wouldn't have to do it at all, but—"

He got out of the car and stood looking back up the road. There was a crunch of tires on gravel and the rumble of the Camaro's engine. Pace's voice called, "This the place?"

"Pull on around me," Mizell called back. "Easier to get out afterwards."

I watched through the side windows as the Camaro rolled slowly past. There wasn't much room to spare. Mizell opened the left rear door. "Out with you," he said. "Watch your head."

I climbed awkwardly out of the car, bumping my head despite Mizell's warning. I saw now that he had his revolver out, covering me. It looked like a very large revolver, but then my perceptions were less than objective at the moment.

"This should be as good a spot as any," he remarked. "Isolated enough to let us conclude our business in privacy, yet not too hard to find."

I looked around. We certainly seemed to be a long way from anywhere in particular. Off to the left, beyond the rough border of the road, the ground rose gently toward the forested crest of the hill. To the right of the road, the hillside fell steeply away into a brush-choked little draw.

"Hunting season's starting up," Mizell said. "There'll be a good many old boys using this road. Of course if need be I can arrange to have you found at the right time, but a little extra authenticity never hurts."

I said, "You'll never make this work."

"Sure I will," he said cheerfully. "You'll see. Well, that's right, you *won't* see, will you?"

"You're going to wind up with a big spectacular trial. Double murder, militant Indians—you're just asking for a media circus in Redbud. Exactly the kind of situation you're trying to avoid—"

"Trial? What trial? We can't permit anything as untidy as a trial, Roper. I'm afraid the suspects are going to be very foolish," he said. "I believe they're going to resist, leaving the arresting officers no choice but to employ deadly force. I wouldn't be surprised if various bits of incriminating evidence should turn up on their persons."

"Assuming you can find them. Odds are they've skipped."

"No, no. As it happens, they're staying with the Cottonwoods for the time being. Too bad about Jimmy Cottonwood and his wife," Mizell mused. "Solid citizens, credit to their race and all that. But it's what they get for harboring dangerous criminals and terrorists."

"There'll be a federal investigation. Civil rights—"

"Oh, grow up, Roper. Since when has the government given a shit about Indians' rights? The feds don't want to know," he said. "Their own hands are none too clean."

Something flickered behind the pale blue eyes. "Now if we were talking about a bunch of niggers, that would be another story. Believe me, I know all about that. How else did I wind up wearing a county-mountie badge, here in the asshole of the universe?"

Pace got out of the Camaro and came walking back toward us. "He give you any trouble?" he asked Mizell.

"No trouble." Mizell didn't take his eyes, or his gun, off me. "Mr. Roper's been a model prisoner. I can't understand why you and Tovin had so much trouble with him that night."

Pace guffawed. "You want to put the stuff in his car first," he said, "or take care of him, or what?"

Mizell smiled slightly. "I don't think we should make Mr. Roper wait any longer than necessary. It would be inconsiderate."

"Want me to get the shotgun?" Pace asked.

"I've got a better idea. What did you do with that little automatic he had in the car?"

"Got it right here." Pace pulled the .380 from his hip pocket.

"Hand it over. Then cover him. Careful, now."

Pace held out the .380 and Mizell took it, left-handed. Pace drew his own pistol and aimed it at me. Mizell looked at the little Colt for a moment. "Hate to have to stop a man with this," he remarked. "But for the present purpose, it'll do."

He pulled back the slide and released it. There was a soft clink as a cartridge slid into the chamber.

Pace said, "Going to do it with his own gun?" The thought clearly pleased him.

"It's a bonus," Mizell said. "When this piece turns up on Vince Lacolle's body, and they get a ballistic match—"

"Yeah." Pace licked his lips. "Hey, Chief, you sure you don't want me to do it?"

"No. I've seen you shoot, Pace. You're simply not accurate enough to do a clean job with a small gun like this."

Pace nodded. He didn't seem offended. "Take the cuffs off him first?" he inquired.

"Leave them on till afterward. I've got a roll of duct tape in the car," Mizell said. "We can tape his wrists and ankles. Mouth, too, that'll look good."

"Then plant the rest of the roll in those Indians' van," Pace suggested. "Ought to be possible to match the stuff up, little extra touch there."

"Not bad," Mizell agreed. "Not bad at all, Pace. We'll do that."

They stood there talking about it, and I stood there listening, and I should have been falling down begging for mercy or praying frantically or at least quietly urinating down my leg with terror. But it was the damnedest thing: I didn't feel any great rush of fear, didn't seem to have any strong feelings at all on the subject. In a very short time I was going to be dead, under circumstances that undoubtedly constituted a hell of a note, but the prospect wasn't as horrifying as it should have been. If nothing else, getting killed would simplify a lot of things; I'd never again have to look in a mirror and wonder what the hell I was doing with my life. Or drink myself to sleep at three in the morning because there were more questions than answers.

The sky was almost black now above the trees. There was a mumble of thunder. Mizell glanced upward. "Let's get this over with," he said edgily. "I don't want to have to drive this road in a rainstorm."

He looked at me and made a small gesture with the Colt. "Move away from the car, if you would."

I walked back past the rear of the cruiser and turned. I don't know why I didn't at least try to run, or why I felt the need to face Mizell. Some romantic notion of not wanting to get it in the back? That sounds about like me.

Mizell was standing beside the car, holding the .380 out at arm's length, like a duelist or a target marksman. "No brave last words, Roper? Good."

The pistol muzzle flashed bright orange in the graying light. There was a loud sharp report and an invisible fist punched me in the chest, very hard, a little left of center. The world went red and then black, and I stumbled backward and fell, rolling and tumbling down the steep hillside, crashing through the brush, to come to rest at last with a mouthful of leaves and dirt and no breath at all in my body.

21
◆◆◆◆◆◆◆◆◆◆

U P O N T H E R O A D M I Z E L L ' S voice said clearly,
"Shit!"

That expressed my own sentiments, pretty much. I was feeling severely confused: either I was still alive or death wasn't at all as I'd expected.

"God *damn,* Chief!" Pace cried dumbfoundedly. "He fell clear off the road!"

My vision was coming back, though there wasn't much to see but a lot of dead leaves just beyond the end of my nose. I struggled for breath, managed to force a few cubic inches of air into my lungs, and damn near passed out from the pain. The left side of my chest felt like a blast furnace.

"Go down and get him," Mizell called. "I want to put him in the trunk of his car."

"That ain't going to be easy," Pace complained. "Hell of a steep little climb, there, to be carrying a dead man. Wish we had a rope."

Thunder boomed again, this time much closer. There was a spattering sound in the treetops and something hit the leaves next to my face. "Hurry up," Mizell said irritably. "It's starting to rain."

There was a sound of heavy footsteps on gravel. "I see him," Pace yelled excitedly. "Hey, Chief, what if he's still alive? Do you want me to finish him off before I bring him up? Because if you do you better let me take that little gun—"

"Don't worry about that," Mizell said over the growing

drumming of the rain. "I got him squarely through the heart. He was dead before he hit . . . Where are you going now, damn it?"

"Get my raincoat. Hell, like you say, he's not going anywhere."

Mizell said something I didn't catch.

"Yeah," Pace insisted, "but it ain't just getting wet that I'm thinking about. With my slicker on I won't be as likely to get blood on this uniform."

"All right, but let's go—"

I didn't wait to hear more. I rolled over and sat up, fighting down a scream, and tried to get to my feet. The trees and bushes did a slow ballet around me and I fell again, this time on an unreasonably rocky spot. The hell with it; falling was faster than running anyway. I pushed off and let myself slide on down the slope like a luge jock, deeper into the undergrowth and farther from the road, while thunder banged and growled and rain rattled through the trees overhead and Mizell's voice rose in a high furious shout: "Pace! Pace, he's getting away!"

The brush was really dense toward the bottom of the slope; I had to do some kicking and shoving to get through, while limbs lashed my face and twigs clawed for my eyes. The slope bottomed out in a rocky little mini-ravine, the bed of a small stream, waterless from the long dry spell, though that wouldn't last long now. Here it was possible to get to my feet and walk, after a fashion—I was still dizzy from the fall, and my wind hadn't fully returned—and after a moment's hesitation, I headed up the draw, following the streambed, where the going was easier. I wanted to run, but the rocks underfoot were too treacherous for that; as it was, I stumbled repeatedly and gave my ankles a few painful twists.

All this time I could hear Mizell and Pace shouting back

and forth as they crashed down the hillside after me. They were having difficulty going, from the racket they made; the rain was coming down now in great driving sheets and the hillside would be soft and slick. I couldn't see them and I wasn't worried about their seeing me, as long as they didn't get too close. The rain and the failing light and the dense cover added up to the kind of visibility fugitives pray for. I didn't even have to be particularly stealthy; between the rain and thunder and the noise the two of them were making, they weren't going to hear me.

Once they got to the bottom, though, it would be another matter. They wouldn't have to be geniuses to figure out that the streambed was my obvious escape route; the only question would be which way I'd gone. And that would be an easy one to solve: split up. They were armed and I wasn't, and either of them could take me without help.

I didn't have much faith in the final outcome. I had enough of a head start to stay in front of the pursuit for a little while, but that was all. They were both in better condition than I was, and I was in considerable pain and having trouble breathing. The only hope was to keep ahead of them till dark—that wouldn't be long now—and then try to find a hiding place for the night and pray for the rain to continue. That might save me from being shot; it would also almost certainly guarantee I'd die of hypothermia, but you can't have everything.

But for now, for want of a better option, I kept moving, stumbling and lurching up the streambed, which was getting steeper and rockier all the way. The soil must have been thinner, too, higher up on the hillside, because the brush on either side was lower and sparser; I was starting to feel naked. Should have gone the other way, of course, the cover would be thicker downstream. And there, up ahead, where the creek crossed the road; I'd be an exposed target, getting across that open space—

The road. Of course; I remembered crossing a dry streambed, shortly before Mizell had stopped the car. I wondered how much chance I'd have if I took off down the road now. It was a tempting idea; running down an open road, I could build up quite a lead while Mizell and Pace were still struggling through the brush.

But it was no good. They'd spot my tracks right away in the rain-softened dirt, as soon as they came to the crossing, and then they'd simply go get the cruiser and come after me. And even if I made the blacktop—which had to be most of a mile away—what then? There was nothing there for me, no houses where I could ask for help . . . and, of course, almost no chance of finding anybody in Sizemore County willing to try to help me against Mizell and Pace.

There was, of course, one obvious move I could try. It was so dangerous it made my stomach hurt, but the situation wasn't exactly bristling with alternatives.

I turned and started running along the road, not back toward the highway, but the other way, up the hill. The grade was steep and the road ran straight up it, rather than zigzagging; my lungs were going nova by the time I was halfway up, and my legs felt like something from Chef Boyardee. All that kept me going was the knowledge that I was utterly exposed now; if Mizell or Pace came up that streambed and out onto the road just now, I was going to make one hell of a target, rain or no rain.

And, naturally, that was what did happen. I was grunting and puffing on up that road, nearly to the top and beginning to believe this was going to work after all, when there was a shout behind me and a gun went off. It wasn't any pocket .380; this was the heavy boom of a full-sized police service revolver. Something popped past my ear, a nasty snapping sound that I hadn't heard since Vietnam.

Pace's voice yelled, "Chief! Chief, he's up on the road! He's trying to get to the cars!"

There was another shot and gravel kicked up next to my right foot, stinging my ankle. But then I was over the crest and sprinting madly down the muddy road in the pouring rain, while thunder blasted and lightning cracked the sky into jagged pieces.

Up ahead the road curved to the left, following the contour of the hillside. As I reached the curve there was another bang behind me, farther back; Pace must have reached the top of the grade. This one didn't even come close, nor did the two quick shots that followed. He wasn't going to have much luck hitting a moving target with a pistol, at that range and under those conditions, but it was fine with me if he wanted to use up his loads.

I loped on around the bend, gulping air and trying to ignore the pain in my chest and legs. There they were, sitting in the rain, waiting patiently for everybody to finish this nonsense and come drive them home: the brown police cruiser and, beyond, the low-slung white shape of my old Camaro. I hoped Mizell and Pace had been in too much of a hurry to take the keys.

The keys were in the Camaro, all right; I could see them through the window. I was struggling to get the door open—the simplest tasks become difficult in handcuffs, but of course that's the idea—when a gun went off and Mizell's voice shouted, "Roper!"

He was coming up the steep hillside, a little way on down the road; he was almost to the top, and he could have had me if he hadn't paused to snap off a long-hope shot. He had his revolver out, aiming it one-handed while he clutched a sapling for support with his other hand. "Stop, you son of a bitch!"

he yelled wildly, and fired again. The Camaro's outside mirror exploded at my elbow.

This was getting too intense. I turned and dashed back the way I'd come, crouched low to put the road shoulder between myself and Mizell. But the prospects were no better in that direction; I could just make out Pace's bulky shape through the rain, coming around the curve at a dead run. I wondered if he'd paused to reload.

The cruiser's door came open at the first jerk; it hadn't been fully latched. I dived in headfirst, sliding across the front seat on my shoulder, hearing a startled wordless shout from Pace. The short-barreled pump shotgun came free of its vertical rack with less difficulty than I'd feared, but then things got hairy. A pump gun is a childishly simple device to operate, until you have to do it wearing handcuffs. Finally I held the buttstock between my thighs and worked the action with both cuffed hands. There was a lovely satisfying *klonk* as a shotshell slid into the chamber and I sat up and hopped out of the cruiser just as Mizell came around the front of the Camaro.

There was no way to hold the shotgun as it was meant to be held, and I didn't try. I held it by the pistol grip with both hands, like a huge handgun, and rested the pump forestock on the upper edge of the cruiser's open door. Mizell's revolver was just coming up on target when I fired.

I was going for a body shot, but the unorthodox position and my own haste combined to throw the shot high. The buckshot charge took Mizell squarely in the face. The gun in his hand went off, once, but I don't think he knew it. I couldn't tell where the bullet went. His feet did a strange little two-step and then he spun around and fell face-down on the muddy road.

I was already turning, bringing the shotgun clumsily around, when another gun banged, too damn close behind me, and a slug punched into the cruiser's door inches from my hip. Pace was standing in the middle of the road, no more than a dozen yards away, pointing his gun at me. I stuck the shotgun's butt between my legs again and clawed for the slide, knowing there was nowhere near enough time.

The sharp metallic snap came clearly through the sounds of the storm. Pace looked at his gun in amazement, cursed, and reached for the row of cartridges on his belt. He must have put in a lot of practice at emergency reloading; he had the cylinder open and a batch of fresh rounds in his left hand when I shot him in the chest.

The recoil nearly sprained my wrists, but I wasn't going to have to do that again. I tossed the riot gun into the cruiser and went over to where Mizell was lying with what was left of his face in a growing puddle of rainwater. I had to turn him over to get what I wanted. Movies and popular folklore have created an exaggerated picture of the destructive effects of shotgun fire; Mizell was still recognizable as Mizell. He wasn't anything you'd care to look at on an empty stomach, though.

It took a little frisking and digging to find the handcuff key, and a regular juggling act to unlock the cuffs with my wet, numb fingers. I went back to the Camaro and got in and sat behind the wheel for a few minutes, breathing painfully and trying to think. That was the hardest part.

Time for damage assessment. I pulled off my sodden jacket and ripped open my shirt and ran cautious fingertips over the left side of my chest. I couldn't detect any blood, but then my shirt and skin were soaking wet from the rain. Something hurt like hell, though, when I touched a spot a few inches left of my wishbone.

A switch closed in my head, finally. I said, "I'll be God-damned." And reached into the inside breast pocket of my ruined jacket and pulled out an oblong mass of splintered wood and twisted brass, the wreckage of a Hohner chromatic harmonica.

There was really no time to be screwing around like this, but I flipped on the Camaro's interior light and had a look. As best I could figure, the little jacketed .380 pill had hit the Hohner at an angle—maybe my jacket had been hanging crooked—and bounced off to God knows where, leaving me with nothing worse than a monster bruise on my chest. The harmonica hadn't survived the encounter.

A Bible would have made a better story, but hell, I'd take this and not complain.

I took the keys from the ignition and went back and opened the Camaro's trunk, where I kept a canvas bag with various emergency supplies. Back in the car, I dug into the bag and got out a thick navy sweater, a heavy-duty flashlight, a nylon rain poncho, and a plastic pint bottle of Old Crow—not, however, in that order. The bourbon hit my stomach with boots on and for a moment I thought I was going to lose the remnants of Donna's special, but then everything settled down and the warmth began to spread through me and I put the cap back on the bottle and stuck the Old Crow in the glove compartment very quickly. Any more and I'd start to relax, and that wouldn't do, not while there were still things left to be done out at the edge.

I stripped off the soggy shirt and pulled the sweater over my head, wincing as the rough wool touched my bruised chest. I climbed back out of the car, put the poncho on, and went to work.

Mizell was heavier than he looked; I did a certain amount of grunting and straining, dragging him up the road and then hoisting him into the back of the cruiser. I noticed the .380 sticking out of his waistband, considered, and pulled it free and put it in the Camaro's trunk, remembering at the last minute to clear the chamber. It was still a moderately valuable item of property, after all, and this had been an expensive evening.

Pace was an even harder job; I didn't have as far to move him, but he was a good two and a half hundred pounds of very literally dead weight, and I damn near ruptured myself getting him into the car. I dumped him on top of Mizell, not bothering with the trunk. If anybody got close enough to this car to see into the backseat, it was all over anyway.

Time to sanitize the scene. I got out the flashlight and spent a little time picking up various odds and ends off the road—the two revolvers, the handcuffs with their key, the cartridges Pace had dropped—and tossing them into the cruiser. I didn't bother with the various ejected cartridges lying around; on a back road in Oklahoma in the fall, empty shell casings are as common as beer cans and rubbers.

By now it was dark. The thunder and lightning had moved on but the rain was still bucketing down. Bullet-sized drops flashed in the cruiser's headlight beams as I pulled slowly around the Camaro and on up the road, looking for a place to turn around. There was no shoulder and the road was narrow; I had to stick the cruiser's nose into the bushes, finally, and nearly got the front end bogged down before I was clear.

The creek was already filling up and flowing fast as I drove across. After that, though, the dirt road made better going than I'd expected; for all its crudeness, it was solid and well-drained. The wet trees and bushes glistened as the headlights raked the woods.

A little while later I was turning onto the blacktop, aiming the cruiser in the direction of Redbud. There were no other cars in sight.

* * *

Where the river makes that big bend, Grandpa Badwater had said, a couple of miles before you come in sight of Redbud. I didn't have any trouble recognizing the spot. A one-lane gravel track led off through a stand of scrubby pine trees. The cruiser's headlights illuminated a bullet-riddled ROAD ENDS sign and then shone out into rain-laced blackness.

I set the parking brake and switched off the lights and got out, taking the flashlight from the seat beside me. It was a vertiginous little place; the track ended no more than a couple of car lengths from the lip of a sheer cliff. There was no guardrail, only a few widely spaced metal posts hung with plastic reflectors, and a line of white-painted rocks. Far below, a hundred vertical feet or more, the Arkansas River was a barely visible gray sheet. Deep hole there under the bluffs, the old man had said, must go halfway to China.

The ground was littered with cans and bottles and assorted trash; this must be a popular spot on more pleasant nights. A footpath led off into the darkness, vanishing at a steep angle down along the face of the bluff. That would be the trail to Grandpa Badwater's fishing spot, I guessed. A pretty damn rugged climb, from what I could see of it; that had been one tough old man.

The white rocks weren't all that big; it wasn't a hard job to roll a few of them out of the way. I had to do a little backing and wheel-cutting to get the cruiser lined up properly—that was spooky, with nothing but a few yards of level ground between the front wheels and that big dark drop—and then it was grunt time.

A full-sized cop car isn't the easiest vehicle in the world to push. The first couple of tries did nothing but rock the heavy cruiser forward a little on its shocks. But I turned around and dug my feet in and got my whole body into the effort, and after an interminable back-wrenching moment the car began to move, very slowly and then with increasing speed, while beer cans crumpled and bottles popped beneath its tires. The front end dipped as the ground began to slope away and now the cruiser was lumbering toward the rim of the precipice like a suicidal dinosaur.

I felt a touch of regret as it went over the edge; I'd have liked to leave the headlights on and watch the fall. The flashers too, even the siren—but I hadn't dared let myself have that kind of infantile entertainment. For one thing, I didn't know who might live on the other side of the river.

As it was, there wasn't much to see. The cruiser's front end dropped violently as the wheels cleared the edge; then there was an ugly tearing noise as the underside of the car scraped over the rocky rim. When the center of gravity was past the balance point, the car nosed downward, the back tires coming clear up off the ground. Then the whole heavy mass simply slid off into the darkness and disappeared. I walked cautiously over to the edge and listened. A huge booming impact floated up from the river.

Must go halfway to China. . . .

It was a long exhausting walk in the rain, miles and miles back up the highway and then the gravel side road and then the logging track. The hooded poncho kept my upper works fairly dry, but my feet were swimming inside my ruined dress shoes, and my suit pants were mere sodden rags plastered against my shivering shins. I wished I'd brought the bourbon along. Or, better yet, stayed home.

The highway was all but deserted. I walked along the shoulder for almost three hours and only two cars came by, both heading toward Redbud. Each time I dived off the road and lay in the wet ditch until the headlights had passed. There would have been nothing much for anyone to see—only a vague hooded figure trudging along in the rainy night, like some demented monk on an unusually harsh act of penance—but my mind was working in very Gothic channels by then.

The dirt road was rougher going, but the trees there did block off the worst of the wind and rain. It was almost totally dark in the woods and I had to use the flashlight to stay on course at all. When I came to the crossing I found the stream running high; I started to take off my shoes and roll up my pants, realized what an idiotic idea that was, and waded on across, the water rushing cold around my legs.

Climbing the hill used up nearly all of my remaining dregs of strength, but the Camaro was still sitting there on the road waiting for me. I fumbled the door open and scrambled gracelessly in, slamming the door and resting my head on the steering wheel and shaking hard for a lot of long minutes.

Finally I made myself sit up. A swallow of bourbon warmed my insides and, once I had the engine going, the heater began doing the same to my outsides. I got the car turned around—nearly going off the edge at one point, and too numb to feel more than mildly alarmed at the close call—and rolled slowly back down the road, remembering after a few minutes to turn on the windshield wipers. The Camaro had a little trouble negotiating the creek crossing, but we made it.

Late was turning into early when I finally got back to Yuchi Park. By the time I'd let Harry out to take care of business—he complained bitterly about the rain; I told him I didn't want to hear it—and peeled off my soggy clothes, there wasn't much left of the night. Well, the damn thing had gone on long enough.

I heated up some canned soup and made myself drink a cup of it, chased that with a big slug of Jim Beam, and went to bed. And you'd think I'd have had some strange and frightening dreams, but I didn't; I don't think I dreamed at all. I slept

clear through the day and on into the early evening; and I
might have slept longer than that, but the phone woke me up.

Rita apologized for disturbing me, but she thought I might
want to know that Emily Jordan had just confessed to killing
her husband.

22

KILLED HIM BECAUSE he would have killed me. He had already killed so much of me. Now he was going to kill what was left. So I stopped him."

That was what Emily Jordan said. Or that was what she was quoted as saying, in the single statement that she made to the reporters who flocked to Redbud to cover the story; but they probably got that part right. Having talked with her a couple of times, I thought the words had a certain ring of authenticity.

"I feel deep regret," she said, "but no remorse. I did what I had to do."

One thing was certain: Emily Jordan wasn't going to lack for an audience. Not that season, not with lines like that.

It was a strange, angry time. Several widely publicized court cases had focused public attention on the whole subject of domestic violence and abuse; and somehow this had metamorphosed, in certain quarters, into a general orgy of ovaries-good-testicles-bad rhetoric. The level of rage was at times downright scary. Educated, intelligent, cultured people went around saying the craziest things; and husbands all over the country began sleeping with one eye open, and going on very long fishing trips.

All of which was unfortunate or not, depending on your point of view, but it did guarantee plenty of sympathetic attention for a disabled woman who claimed to have axed her old man out of brutalized desperation.

"Emily Jordan," declared one prominent feminist leader, on a nationally televised panel discussion, "is every woman."

"Emily Jordan," said another prominent feminist leader on the same panel, "is what every woman ought to be."

And that was just the beginning; that was before the really *heavy* stuff came out.

As it happened, all these fascinating matters—Emily Jordan's confession, and the events immediately following—passed me by. For a time there, most of the viewing and reading public knew more about the story than I did.

I didn't, in fact, know much of anything. The long walk in the rain, coming on top of all the other physical and mental traumas of that night, laid me out worse than any beating; I hadn't been so sick in years. Rita came over Tuesday evening and found me huddled under every blanket I owned, shivering violently, with a temperature like a cheap woodstove. Or so she told me, later, but you couldn't prove it by me.

She got me through the night somehow, loaded me into her car next morning, and took me to see a doctor she knew. I have vague recollections of a waiting room with Tommy's paintings on the wall, and a nurse who stuck a needle in my arm and out through my elbow, and a tiny paper cup that I was expected to pee in when it was all I could do to hit a full-sized toilet, but that's all. I don't even recall what the doctor looked like.

The next couple of weeks were loathsome. The chills and fever went on through the rest of the week, breaking now and then—one night Rita changed the sheets six times in four hours—only to come back again and again. I was taking three different kinds of pills, but I couldn't tell that they did any good. Maybe they kept me from dying. At the time I was far from convinced that this was a plus.

Saturday afternoon, old Mr. Berryhill came by, bringing me

some misdelivered mail—the service had been terrible lately, but nobody felt brave enough to complain about any postal employee that year—and Rita talked with him for a few minutes. A little while later he came back and handed Rita a paper sack full of dried roots and leaves and bits of bark, with instructions to boil the mess in water and make me drink the liquid. Which she did, over my feeble objections, and that night the fever broke for good, and after that I started to mend. But it was still another week before I could get out of bed and move around on my own.

Later I found out that Rita had used up a year's accumulated vacation time, and had to hand over a high-prestige story to a rival on the *Courier* staff, in order to stay with me and nurse me. She said it was because somebody had to take care of Harry; it wasn't his fault that his owner was a damn fool.

So it was some time before I took much interest in current events, and by then the Emily Jordan story had already crested out. Most of my information, then, was acquired at second or third remove; despite my earlier intensive and near-fatal involvement in the case, I wound up like everybody else, knowing little more than what I read in the papers or saw on TV, and placing only limited faith in that.

"Twenty-five years," Rita mused. "I can't even imagine being *happily* married for that long. Twenty-five years of abuse? That's so dreadful my mind won't fit around it."

"If she's telling the truth about that—" Tommy began.

"If?" Rita's face went stormy. "Why do men always assume the woman must be lying?"

"Why do women always assume she's telling the truth?" Tommy said pointedly. "Getting so it's open season on guys. Any woman commits homicide or mayhem or whatever on her old man, all she has to do is claim he beat her up, and instantly she's got the other women rallying around her and screw the facts. On the other hand," he went on, over Rita's angry protest, "you won't have any trouble getting me to believe the worst about Rowland Jordan. And he put her in a wheelchair, that's pretty damn abusive, all right. . . ."

"He always referred to it as an accident," Emily Jordan told the reporters. "Perhaps it was, in a sense. He was in one of his rages, and he struck me, as he had so many times before. This time I happened to be standing at the head of the stairs, and I fell all the way to the bottom. He was genuinely sorry, I think, for what he had done. He was always sorry afterwards, but it never stopped him from doing it again."

According to Emily Jordan, life with the late sheriff of Sizemore County had been anything but the warm, tender relationship that had been presented to the public. He had begun verbally and then physically abusing her, she said, within the first few years of marriage. In the beginning the incidents had been relatively rare. Later he had begun drinking heavily in the evenings, and the abuse had gradually grown to be the basic fact of their lives.

"I endured it," she said, "at first because I was brought up to be submissive to men, and later because I hoped that Christian forgiveness would change him, and after that because I was ashamed. Finally I endured it because I was afraid. He said he'd kill me if I ever told anyone, and I believed he meant it. I still do."

The beatings had stopped for some time after her fall. She had had to undergo a considerable amount of surgery and physical therapy before she could even get around in a wheelchair, and Jordan had been helpful and kind during this time; she had told herself that the disaster had brought him to his senses at last. But then things had begun to deteriorate again: first verbal abuse and threats, then more direct cruelties.

She said, "It is true, as I said in my earlier statement, that he sometimes liked to carry me about the house like a child. He was equally fond of taking my wheelchair away from me and making me beg him to give it back. Or putting my personal possessions—even my medication—just out of my grasp, and mocking me as I struggled to reach them. By then he rarely beat me. He had learned subtler ways to degrade and terrorize me."

"All I was going to say," Tommy said, "if this is true, it must have been a hell of a thing for the children to live with."

"Except that she claims he never did any of this when they were around," I pointed out. "Says he was really careful about that, and she went along with it."

It was a couple of weeks since Emily Jordan's confession had hit the news. I was more or less ambulatory, now, but still pretty limp, and far too foggy-headed to do any writing. So I'd been passing the time by reading the various newspaper and magazine articles about the Jordan case, and going over the transcript—Rita had gotten me a copy—of her statement to the press.

"I bet they knew," Rita said. "Children always do."

"When did you get to be such an expert on children?" Tommy asked.

"Hey," Rita said, "I've got you and Tag around."

Rowland Jordan had, by his wife's account, gone clear over the edge in the last couple of months of his life. She felt it had been the anniversary that did it.

"Everyone was congratulating him," she said, "and he kept up a good front, but I could tell he was starting to brood. He began talking bitterly about spending twenty-five years in a bad joke of a marriage and still having no way of escape. Because, of course, there was no question of a separation. Under the circumstances, it would have been political suicide for him."

Then the verbal terrorism had begun: "He talked about getting rid of me, cutting himself free from the burden around his neck. He would talk for hours when he was in one of his moods, telling me stories about murderers he had known, men who had killed and gone free. He said there was nothing easier than getting away with murder, especially for a man in his position. At first I thought he was only trying to frighten me for his own sadistic enjoyment, but finally I realized he was serious. He meant to kill me."

"The special horror of Emily Jordan's situation," wrote one nationally syndicated columnist, "is that she did not even have the usual option of calling the police. The law may sometimes prove a flimsy shield, but at least the recourse exists. But in this woman's case, the man she feared *was* the law."

"A little on the wordy side," was Rita's comment. "But to the point, all the same. Talk about living a nightmare."

And so, one September night, Rowland Jordan had gone for it.

"He had been drinking," his widow said. "Not heavily, but sometimes it took only a little. He began working himself up into one of those blind rages that I knew so well. He said he'd had all he could stand, that he was tired of being tied to a useless excuse for a woman. He said he wished I'd broken my neck in that fall. Then he said it wasn't too late. He was going to carry me upstairs and I was going to have another accident. This time I wasn't going to survive."

"He came at her and she chopped him," Wiley Harmon said, the only time we ever discussed the matter. "Boy, you have to hand it to the old broad. She knew what to do and she didn't fuck around."

"I didn't plan what happened next," Emily Jordan said. "There was no time to think at all. The tomahawk happened to be hanging on the wall within my reach. When he came toward me I took it down and swung it at him, as hard as I could. I only meant to fight him off, but the blade caught him in the side of the neck and I realized immediately that I'd killed him. He staggered about for several seconds before he fell. There was a great deal of blood."

She had remembered to wipe the tomahawk handle for possible prints. She had rolled into the kitchen and gotten a trash bag, taken off her blood-spattered clothing and bagged it for future disposal, stashed the bag under the sink, and returned to the living room.

"Then," she told her listeners, "I got out of my chair and crawled out of the room and down the hall to the stairs. It was very slow and painful for me. I had to drag myself along on my hands and elbows, because I have no use of my legs at all. Going up the stairs was even harder, and getting into bed was almost impossible. It took me almost two hours to get from the living room to my bedroom, put on a nightgown, hoist myself into bed, and call the deputies."

And that, I think, was what did it; that was what stuck in people's minds, and made the Jordan case something more than just another battered-wife-kills-husband story. Beyond all the other lurid details, there remained that terrible and memorable image of a tiny, white-haired, naked woman pulling herself slowly up a stairway, step by excruciating step, dragging her useless legs behind her.

"It has to be true," Rita insisted. "Nobody would make up a story like that."

I wasn't altogether sure I agreed with her logic. People, in my experience, could make up some astonishing tales; witness the Elvis Presley sightings, or UFO encounters, or Oliver North's testimony.

And there was something that was bothering me, some memory lying in a dark corner of my hall-closet mind; but I couldn't get a grip on it to drag it out into the light. It wasn't, I told myself, as if it mattered.

"When I learned that Chris Badwater had been freed, I realized it was only a matter of time before the truth came out. So I called the prosecutor's office and made my confession."

That was the only reference to Chris Badwater in the whole transcript. As far as I could tell, nobody ever picked up on that aspect of the case. Emily Jordan had captured the sympathy and even admiration of a great many people; it would have been unseemly to bring up her apparent willingness to let an innocent Indian kid take the fall in her place. Very few of the news stories, and none of the opinion columns and magazine essays, mentioned Chris's name at all.

Nobody—at least nobody I knew—was greatly surprised when the Sizemore County prosecutor announced that Emily Jordan would not be standing trial for her husband's death.

"A clear case of self-defense, under the most extreme circumstances," Stinson told the press. "This woman has suffered tragically. No purpose can be served by subjecting her to the additional pain of a public trial."

The decision was widely hailed as an example of heightened awareness of the battered-spouse problem, and an enlightened official attitude toward abused women. A few cynical voices suggested that this was merely another case of the wheels of justice getting steered by the hands of media-hype hustlers. If Emily Jordan had been an unattractive, foul-mouthed biker mama, or a black alcoholic on welfare, would she have gotten off so easily?

Tommy Ninekiller, when he came by to tell me the news, had another view.

"She knows too much," he said. "Married to Rowland Jordan all those years, there's no way she doesn't know which closets the skeletons are in."

I said, "You think she blackmailed the people who run the county into dropping the case? Told them to have Stinson back off or she'd have to make some new statements to the media?"

"Hell," Tommy said, "I doubt if she had to. Those guys aren't stupid. And Stinson can't have been eager to touch the case anyway. Win or lose, he was going to come out of it looking like an asshole."

He grinned at me. "Hey, something else I heard, might interest you. Couple of friends of yours have disappeared."

"Oh?"

I thought I did that "Oh?" rather well.

"Mizell's vanished," he said. "So has that big ape-shape deputy who beat you up. Pace?"

"That's the name."

"Well, the bastards have split. At least that's the general opinion. Nobody's seen them since just about the time Emily Jordan sang her song. Lester says they probably figured she was going to tell a few good stories about the goings-on in her late old man's department, and they decided to haul ass."

"Hm." I did that pretty well too.

"On the other hand," Tommy went on, "there's a different theory floating around, depending on who you talk to. Quite a few people think Mizell did something to piss some heavy people off. Like maybe he got a little grabby when he moved into Jordan's shoes. And Pace, well, maybe he got caught in the crossfire. Who knows? Anyway, they're gone—along with a fully equipped cop car, I understand—and nobody expects to be hearing from them again."

He looked in the direction of the kitchen. "Got anything to drink, old Euro-American bro?"

"Jim Beam on the shelf above the sink," I said. "And bring me one too, will you? Make it a double and throw in some rocks."

He gave me a dubious glance. "I don't know, Roper. Rita said you're not supposed to drink while you're taking those pills."

"That's all right," I assured him. "I'll just cut out the pills."

I didn't mention Tommy's bit of news to Rita. But he must have told her himself, or else she heard it somewhere else. I can't think of any other explanation for what she said that night.

We were lying in bed, not talking or doing much of anything. I was feeling pretty good, having established, half an hour or so before, that at least part of me was back in working order. I was starting to nod off, in fact, when Rita said suddenly, "Tag? Are you awake?"

I said, "Mhmph," or something to that effect.

"You do realize I'm not blind," she said. "Or an idiot. I saw those cuts and bruises and scratches all over your body, that first night when I found you here."

"I had to change a tire in the rain. Slipped and fell down an embankment and into some bushes."

"And I'm Marlene Dietrich." She sat up and reached over to lay a hand on the left side of my chest. "There was a huge bruise here, so bad the doctor checked for cracked ribs. He wanted to know if you'd been in an auto accident."

She paused. This time I kept quiet.

"While you were running a fever," she said at last, "you kept singing—you don't remember any of this?"

"No."

"You'd sing, now and then. You sang, 'I Shot the Sheriff.' Only you always changed the words. You kept singing, 'And I also shot the deputy.' And then you'd laugh." She shuddered. "It wasn't a good laugh."

I still didn't speak. She lay back down beside me and turned her back.

"Oh, Tag," she said in a small choked voice. "What did I get you into? What did I do to you?"

I knew I was supposed to say something in response, but I couldn't come up with anything that wouldn't upset her even more. How to explain what had happened to me? "Rita, it's not that two men tried to kill me; they weren't the first to try it, or even the best. And it's not that I killed them; I got a medal once for killing better men, for poorer reasons—" No. No way in hell.

How to tell her that I'd seen my own death staring at me out of the muzzle of a ridiculous little gun? And that I'd learned something about myself in that moment, and it was going to take me a little while to figure out how to fit the knowledge into my life. . . .

I told myself she wouldn't understand. But maybe I was afraid she would.

23
◆ ◆ ◆ ◆ ◆ ◆ ◆ ◆ ◆ ◆

By the time i was up and even occasionally around, October was history and November was well under way. A wet, gray November it was, too; somebody seemed to be trying to balance the climatic books for the dry spell we'd had earlier, and adding generous interest. I didn't see much more of the sun when I finally got out than I had when I was bedridden.

I spent the rest of the month catching up on this and that. A gun collector from Bristow gave me a sizable check for the old .380, which turned out to be a relatively rare variant model; I used the money to replace my ruined suit and shoes, and had enough left to buy myself a new harmonica. I'd been thinking about going back to a regular non-chromatic job, a Marine Band or maybe a Blues Harp, as being cheaper and handier to carry; but in the end I bought another big chromatic, because after all you never know.

I didn't buy another gun, though. I'll admit I thought about it, but I didn't.

The Jordan story faded away and vanished from the public consciousness. The media found other matters of more pressing relevance: a professional-sports scandal, a rock-music scandal, a British-royal-family scandal, several more bizarre domestic murders. All the same, some interest must have remained, because I got a call from somebody at Swallow Street Press—not my regular editor, but a higher-up—wanting to know if I would care to write a true-crime book on the case. I declined, with thanks.

The offer did remind me of something, though.

Rita had cleaned up the trailer while caring for me, and picked up the mess, so that of course I couldn't find a God-damned thing anymore. It took quite a bit of pawing and rummaging around, then, before I located what I was looking for: the big manila file envelope that Lester Bucktail had loaned me, with the material on Rowland Jordan. I'd forgotten to give it back.

I bounced the heavy envelope in my hand, wondering whether to call Lester Bucktail about it or simply mail it to him. My hands still weren't completely steady. The file slipped from my grasp and hit the floor, scattering its contents around the living room. I said, "Son of a bitch," and hunkered down and began picking up clippings and photographs, stuffing them back into the big envelope, muttering imprecations at my own clumsiness.

A glossy black-and-white print lay under the coffee table. I bent and reached, got my fingers on it, and was about to shove it in the envelope with the rest of the file when I recognized the picture. It was the one Lester Bucktail had shown me that day in Tahlequah; the silver-anniversary photo, with Rowland and Emily Jordan posing together in their living room.

I sat down cross-legged on the floor and stared at the picture, while Harry sniffed inquisitively at the envelope. Emily Jordan's big sad eyes gazed back at me; was there fear in them, or was that no more than my imagination filling in from afterknowledge? And Rowland Jordan, now I noticed, had to be standing on or near the spot where he would one night end up inside a chalk outline. The furniture had been changed, but I recognized other features of the room—

I said, "Hey, Harry, look here."

Harry looked. He asked me what my point was.

"That's okay, Harry," I told him. "You don't see it, but

hell, you're a dog. What was my excuse? What was *everybody's* excuse?"

I didn't share my discovery with anybody but Harry. At the time I couldn't see that there was anything for me to say or do; it didn't have anything to do with me, not now. There were some interesting questions that came to mind, but I could live fine without the answers.

And for a time I put the whole business out of my mind. A cold front came in just before Thanksgiving and covered eastern Oklahoma with sleet; the roads were coated with ice and I spent the holiday alone, except for Harry, freezing my ass off in that old trailer. The only murder I wanted to think about was the one I planned to commit against that grinning jackass who announced the weather on the evening news.

But the front moved on, and the sun came out long enough to melt the ice and clear the roads. If you don't like the weather in Oklahoma, Mr. Berryhill often said, stick around a couple of minutes.

I remembered a bit of unfinished business, and realized that this might be my last chance to take care of it before the year ended. I've always had a thing about starting each new year with a minimum of loose ends.

So, one afternoon a few days into December, I fired up the Camaro and headed for Sizemore County once again. I should, I thought, have rented a car, but it would have been an extra expense, and I didn't really believe there was any danger. I doubted if anybody there remembered me at all.

Emily Jordan did, though. She said immediately, "Mr. Roper. Good evening."

She sat there in her wheelchair, holding the door open—there was no sign of Inez—and, if the light wasn't playing tricks, she was actually smiling at me.

"This is a surprise," she said pleasantly. "Please come in. It's such a cold night, isn't it?"

I walked beside her as she rolled down the hallway. The motor of her wheelchair made a soft high sound. "I'm afraid I was a little hostile when you were here before," she said. "Of course you'll appreciate my reasons, now. I must say that after dealing with certain members of your profession over the last month or so, I've come to remember you as a model of courtesy and restraint."

In the living room she wheeled to face me. "What brings you to Redbud again, Mr. Roper? I'd think you'd have seen enough of us."

I held up the large white envelope I was carrying. "I had some business in the area," I said. "Thought I'd come by and bring you this. Something you might like to have."

"Oh?" She took the envelope, examined the flap, saw that it wasn't sealed, and turned it up and gave it a little shake. A black-and-white photograph fell out and landed in her shawl-covered lap.

I wouldn't have thought her face could get any paler, her eyes any bigger, but she managed. She stared down at that dog-eared eight-by-ten as if it were a rattlesnake with a live grenade in its mouth.

"Mr. Roper," she said after a moment, "this is in very bad taste. I can't think why you brought me this. Please take it away."

I took the photo from her hand, which was trembling slightly. "You're sure? You really ought to hang onto it," I told her. "You never know. If it gets into the wrong hands, somebody else might see the same thing I did."

"I don't know what you're talking about." Her voice had gone dry and flat. "Please leave."

"Of course," I said, "you do have to know what you're looking at. This dark object in the background—" I touched the print with a fingertip. "It's not all that clear, is it? Most people wouldn't recognize it as a tomahawk. Let alone *the* tomahawk, recently celebrated in print, film, and over-the-top rhetoric nationwide."

I walked past her, across the room, looking at the wall. The brass hooks were still there.

"At the very least," I added, "you ought to remove these. Or rather have them removed. Because, of course, you can't reach them, can you?"

I swung around. "Any more than you could have reached that tomahawk that night in September. Not with it hanging there on the wall," I said. "I'm quite a bit bigger than you and I've got long arms, and I don't think I could reach it, sitting in that wheelchair. It's much too high."

"In moments of extreme stress, people do seemingly impossible—"

"No. Give it up." I leaned against the wall. "What's the real story? Did you get it down somehow, earlier on—knock it down with an umbrella or something, I don't know, I'm sure it wouldn't have been hard to dislodge if you had time—and hide it under your shawl, and wait for him to come within range? Or did you bushwhack him from behind while he was watching TV? The medical examiner wasn't—"

Behind me a slightly breathy voice said, "Leave her alone, you son of a bitch."

Paula Jordan stood in the doorway. She had on a pink bathrobe and her long blond hair was wet. She was holding a shiny revolver, and she was pointing it at me. I couldn't tell the make. From where I stood it seemed to consist mostly of a lot of very big holes.

Emily Jordan said sharply, "Paula, where did you get that?"

"It's Daddy's." Paula didn't look at her mother. "One of the many things he left us. Don't do anything stupid, Roper.

Daddy shot two men with this a few years ago, when they tried to rob the bank. Both of them were dead before they hit the ground."

I stood very still.

"You leave my mother alone," she said again. "She didn't kill my father. She never killed anybody."

"Paula, be quiet. Don't say anything more."

I said, "Who did, then? Felicia? Is that why you people had to have her put away?"

"No!" Paula Jordan jerked the pistol forward an inch or so for emphasis. I wished she wouldn't do that. "My sister wasn't even in town when it happened. She had nothing to do with it."

Then, suddenly, Paula's face contorted in a grimace of pain and disgust. "Well, that's not true either," she said in a lower voice. "She had everything in the world to do with it, but she didn't know it. She still doesn't."

Emily Jordan said despairingly. "Don't do this, Paula."

"My father," Paula Jordan said. "Dear sweet Daddy. Member of the church. Pillar of the community. Devoted family man. I remember that picture, Roper. They printed it in their stupid damn paper and Felicia sent me a clipping. I remember all the bullshit, too, that they printed under it. Sorry, Mama."

She made a gesture with her free hand. "This room, here—this is where he groped me for the first time, when I was fourteen. I was standing over there looking out the window and he came up behind me and lifted my skirt and put his hand inside my panties, just like that, without saying a word. Mama was in the hospital," she said. "He didn't stop after she came home, though. Pretty soon he wasn't just feeling me up. By the time I was fifteen he was coming into my room and doing things to me almost every night. Mama never knew."

"Yes I did." Emily Jordan's eyes were closed. "If you're

going to tell the truth, at least tell the whole truth. I knew. I was afraid to do anything about it. He said nobody would believe me. He said he'd have me committed—he had the connections to do it, too, it's dreadfully easy to have a person committed in this state—and then he'd be here alone every night with Paula. Or he'd simply kill me."

She touched the controls and her wheelchair rolled forward until she was between Paula and me. "Put the gun down, Paula," she said gently. "No one else is going to be killed in this house."

To me she said, "As you've guessed, most of my confession was a lie. Rowland very rarely struck me, and the fall that crippled me was in fact an accident. But it is true that I was afraid of him. He had ways to keep me afraid. I used to think that simple physical abuse would be easier to live with."

"I left home as soon as I could," Paula said. She hadn't put the gun down, but she wasn't pointing it at me any more. "By then I was all messed up, drinking, getting in trouble in school. Daddy didn't try to come after me or make me come back, even though I was under age. I was starting to embarrass him."

"He forbade me to have any contact with Paula," Emily Jordan put in. "He studied the telephone bills to make sure I wasn't calling her, and went through the mail for letters from her. Felicia wasn't allowed to have anything to do with her sister, either. We weren't even to mention her name in Rowland's presence."

"We found ways to get together now and then, though," Paula said. "Back in September, Felicia spent a weekend in Muskogee with some friends of the family, and I drove down and she slipped away and we got to spend a couple of hours together."

She looked at her mother and then at me. "That's when I found out," she said. "He'd started on Felicia."

Emily Jordan made a strangled sound in her throat.

"And I said okay, that's it, this is where it stops," Paula went on. Her voice had taken on a high, tight-wound note. "What Mama told everybody to begin with—that was pretty close to the truth. She was upstairs asleep when I showed up. He wasn't very happy to see me, but he did let me in. I asked about Felicia and he said she wasn't home. He said I couldn't see her anyway. He called me a whore."

She glanced at the spot on the wall where the tomahawk had hung. "That wasn't why I did it, though. All I wanted was to stop him from doing it to Felicia, like he had to me. I saw that damn tomahawk and I grabbed it and let him have it. He looked so surprised. . . ."

She stopped. After a few seconds of silence Emily Jordan said, "I did wake up, and I recognized Paula's voice. I called out again and again, and finally she came upstairs, all covered with blood, and told me what she had done. She wanted to turn herself in, but I wouldn't allow it. I made her undress and wash herself, and change into some old clothes that she'd left when she ran away, and then I waited for an hour after she'd left before I reached for the telephone."

I said, "And when you heard that Chris Badwater was being released, you were afraid the truth might come out? So you confessed in her place?"

Emily Jordan shrugged minutely. "Please don't make too much of that, Mr. Roper. It wasn't a question of self-sacrificing mother love. I knew I was in no great danger. For one thing, I knew certain things, from having lived with Rowland Jordan. I could have taken the lid off this county and showed the world what a cesspool it was. The people who give Judge Ryson his orders were aware of that," she said. "And for another, I knew that no Oklahoma jury would ever convict a crippled woman of my social station for defending herself against a brutal bully of a husband.

Even that idiot Stinson wouldn't want to take such a case to court."

"Texas defense," I said.

"I beg your pardon?"

"I think it was F. Lee Bailey who defined the principle," I said. "If all else fails, he said, argue that the son of a bitch needed killing."

"Yes. On the other hand," Emily Jordan said, "Paula would have been in much more serious trouble. She already had a certain reputation in Redbud, even before she left. And women in her occupation are regarded in these parts as—forgive me, Paula—little better than prostitutes."

"Wouldn't have done any good to tell the reasons, either," Paula said. "Nobody would have believed it. Nobody ever believes a story like that, in this town. They don't want to believe they live in a place where that kind of thing goes on."

"And that business about dragging yourself up the stairs on your elbows—"

"I made that up, Mr. Roper." Emily Jordan smiled. "I've got quite an imagination, it would appear. Perhaps I should try my own hand at writing fiction."

Paula said, "You realize you can't do anything about this. It'll be your word against Mama's and she's already a big hero to a lot of people."

"I wasn't planning to take this anywhere," I told her. "It's none of my business. I was curious, that's all."

"A poor reason to create so much distress," Emily Jordan said acidly.

"You better hope nobody else comes up with the same questions. The next guy might hand you quite a bit more distress."

"We won't be here much longer, Mr. Roper. I already have a buyer for the house. After the first of the year, the three of us will be moving to Arkansas, where I have relatives. I don't think any of this will follow us."

"The three of you?"

"Felicia gets out next week," Paula said. "I already quit my job at Foxy Ladies. I'm going to get my high school diploma and then go to college."

Emily Jordan pivoted her wheelchair about. "Give me the gun, Paula." She reached out and took the gun from her daughter's hand. The motor whined and she rotated to face me again. "Mr. Roper, would you do one thing for me, since you're here? Would you please take this . . . *thing* out of my house? Dispose of it as you wish."

I took the revolver and started to thank her, but then I decided that wouldn't be appropriate. She didn't consider she was doing me a favor. Maybe she wasn't.

I said, "Well, I better be on my way."

"Staying overnight in Redbud, Mr. Roper?" Emily Jordan asked politely, still the gracious hostess.

"No. As I say, I've got some business to take care of tonight. Should have plenty of time to drive on home."

"Have a safe trip." If there was any sarcasm in her voice I couldn't identify it. "Paula, please show Mr. Roper out."

Halfway through the hall doorway, I stopped and looked back. "You came forward rather than let Paula face a murder charge," I said. "But both of you were willing to let Chris Badwater take the fall. That didn't bother you?"

Paula looked strangely at me, as if I'd suddenly announced that Jesus Christ was waiting in my car.

"What," she said, "like I'm going to worry about what happens to some damn Indian? Get real."

Emily Jordan's pale cheeks showed the least bit of a flush. But her voice was steady as she said, "That was unfortunate, Mr. Roper. But I had to look out for my own blood."

Out in the car, I switched on the dome light and had a look at my newest acquisition. A stainless-steel Smith & Wesson .357 Magnum with a three-inch barrel, the regular Military and Police model rather than the fancy Combat Magnum; I guessed it had been Rowland Jordan's off-duty weapon.

I snapped the cylinder open. It was loaded, all right, with half a dozen evil-looking hollow-point rounds. I thought of Paula Jordan's angry finger on the trigger and my stomach did a slow roll. No harmonica was going to stop one of these boys; they'd go through a grand piano and a couple of tubas without slowing down.

And so here I was, heeled again, despite my good intentions. Well, I'd tried.

I put the Magnum in the glove compartment and started the Camaro and drove off to take care of business.

24

••••••••••

 ECEMBER BEGAN RUNNING OUT of days and
I began running out of money. It was a close race but I had a
solid lead. The advance from Swallow Street Press had looked
like the riches of Xanadu, but . . . There is an ancient
wedding-night joke, the punch line of which is: "I liked it so
much and we've already used up so much of it!" And so, as
Linda Ellerbee used to say, it goes; and so it went.

Of course the obligations of the Christmas season didn't
help. I went to pick up a little something for Rita and nearly
had a heart attack; at Victoria's Secret, less was definitely
more. Considering the skimpiness of the merchandise and the
heftiness of the prices, I figured I was in the wrong business; I
needed to go prospecting for a lingerie mine.

Things were getting pretty tight when I got a call from a guy
I knew in Tulsa.

His name was Shelby and he ran a nightclub I couldn't rec-
ommend. He was calling for a friend of his, a businessman—
nature of business unspecified—who had recently fired a
clerical employee. Said employee had taken with him certain
records, for the return of which he was now asking a generous
reward.

Since the records in question would have been of intense
and calamitous interest to the Internal Revenue Service,
Shelby's friend was inclined to deal. Would I be interested in
handling the negotiations and making the exchange? There
would be a suitable fee in it for me.

So there I went again. What can you say?

The weather warmed up through the last bit of December; Christmas was practically a shirtsleeve day, much to the disappointment of a lot of silly bastards who kept pissing and moaning about the lack of snow. I didn't hear any complaints from cops or ambulance drivers, though, or homeless street people.

A couple of weeks into the new year we finally did get some snow; nothing all that heavy, just a few inches of light powder, but enough to throw the whole metropolitan area into hopeless, sliding, fender-crumpling chaos. I used to think Tulsans couldn't drive in snow because they didn't get enough practice at it. Lately, though, I've come to believe that they simply can't drive worth a damn even under ideal conditions, and a little snow on the street is enough to take them clear out of the envelope.

I was looking out my living room window at the white stuff coming down when the phone rang. It was Lester Bucktail.

"News just came in," he said. "I thought you might like to know. Hardesty Industries is shutting down the Echota Creek plant."

"The government finally came down on them?"

"Hell, no. Oh, they're trying to blame the environmentalists—according to their official statement, the restrictions and requirements became impossible to comply with—but that's a lot of face-saving crap. They don't want to admit it," Lester Bucktail said, "but they never did succeed in getting a profit out of that operation. Been a dead loss all the way. Looks like corporate incompetence did what enlightened protest couldn't."

He laughed. "Of course, Bianca and her pals are giving themselves bursitis patting themselves on the back for having killed the big bad wolf. All of a sudden they're taking a

Hardesty Industries press release as absolute gospel. I haven't had the heart to point out the contradiction."

"They've earned the right to a little fun."

"Agreed. Hey, I've got a buddy of yours working for me now. Chris Badwater's back in town, going to start school next term. He came around wanting a part-time job and I tried him out. Turns out he's a pretty decent photographer."

"What happened to Billy Greenstick?"

"Left me and went to work for this new computer shop that just opened here. Well, he did need the money," Lester said. "He and Judy Littlebear are engaged."

"Christ!"

"Stands your hair on end, doesn't it?"

I laughed. So did Lester Bucktail. "Say," he said, "I heard another funny one. Remember Deputy Tovin? Little prick who used to work with Pace?"

"Uh huh."

"Then maybe you know about his pickup truck. Big fancy high-priced four-wheel-drive job, spent all his money on it like some old guy with a twenty-year-old showgirl."

"I've seen it."

"Right, well, one night back in December somebody torched it. Very professional job, I understand, blasting cap in the gas tank, set off with some kind of timer. Burned that truck down to scrap metal right in front of Tovin's house. They say he was running around the yard screaming, all the time it was burning, no shoes or shirt and the temperature close to freezing."

"Wonder who could have done it."

"I wonder too," Lester Bucktail said.

There was something a little odd in his voice, but maybe we had a bad connection.

"Working on anything now?" he wanted to know.

"Not really. I've got an idea for another novel I want to write, but I'm still at the staring-out-windows stage. Haven't even made any notes yet."

"Good luck, then."

"Thanks."

"Emily Jordan sold the house," he said after a moment. "Took both the girls and moved away."

"Yes," I said. "I heard."

After he had hung up I went back to the window and stood for a long time watching the snow lay its blanket over the red Oklahoma earth.